Just The Pits
by
Jinx Schwartz

Just The Pits
Published by Jinx Schwartz
Copyright 2013
Book 5: Hetta Coffey series
All rights reserved.

ACKNOWLEDGEMENTS

As always, my first reader and hubby, Robert "Mad Dog" Schwartz, is my rock. His patient tackling of techie stuff that makes me scream at my computer is priceless. Maybe I should give him a raise?

Holly Whitman has been the editor of every one of my books, and she keeps me out of the ditch when my story heads there. Thanks, Holly, once again for your wise input.

And, I have beta readers! Thanks so much to Mary Jordan and Clay Rex Chambers, both sharp-eyed and invaluable.

Chapter 1

ALL AT SEA (Nautical term): Lost because of lack of knowledge of one's position: confused.

Alarm clocks top plague and pestilence on my SCOURGES UPON THE PLANET list.

I'd ceremonially tossed my old alarm nag, along with my wrist watch—the cheap one, not my Rolex of course—overboard when I steered *Raymond Johnson* under the Golden Gate Bridge, turned left and headed for Mexico over a year ago.

Now I had this new annoyingly alarming device.

I'd discovered her on a back shelf at a crammed-to-the-ceiling Mexican *tienda* selling everything from squeegees to chicken feed. Ever the optimist, I figured this particular clock, being an analog wind-up job, stood at least half a chance of waking me for the next few months in a place where the power grid goes tits-up on a regular basis, and battery operated devices have the lifespan of a gnat.

My boat is where batteries go to die. A flashlight in my care is simply a repository for expired D-cells, my toothbrush runs through AA's like, well, toothpaste, and my engine room is a shrine to where large, very expensive 8-Ds commit suicide. A windup clock is therefore the best choice, but only if there isn't an operator malfunction resulting in a windup oversight. And this operator malfunctions on a regular basis.

But even with a good chance I'd eventually forget to wind her, who could resist a clock set in a curvy *senorita's* navel with the winding key up her butt? You just gotta give good design its due.

When the *señorita's* belly let loose a raucous clamor at five that first morning, I reached for my gun and then remembered I can't have one in Mexico, the one place where you really, really, could use a little firepower. Despite the fact that one lousy little *pistola* can earn you five years in a Mexican hoosegow, I'd been shot at enough times since arriving south of the border to know that not everyone is on board with this no weapons thing. I cursed, ruing the fact that for once in my almost, uh, thirty-something years, I'd stupidly obeyed a law.

Cramming a pillow over my head did little to mute the wretched wench, so I pushed myself out of bed, stumbled across my cabin—I'd known better than to leave her within grabbing and heaving distance—whammed down the shutoff button, and slogged to my galley for a twenty-ounce mug of Nescafé Classico.

Fortified by caffeine heavily laced with sugar and *crema*, I jumpstarted my day by checking email, then calling Mom and Dad back home in Texas to assure them that I was safely at a dock and gainfully employed, the latter of which my mother accredited to the fact that I had yet to show up for my first day on the job.

Familial duty done, I brushed my teeth—taking note of the low battery alert light on my toothbrush—gave my red pixie cut a brush slap, shimmied and shook my way into a pair of well-worn, suspiciously snug, Ralph Lauren jeans from BB. BB stands for Before Boat, back when I thought nothing of shelling out three hundred bucks for a couple of yards of denim instead of a new bilge pump.

A glance in the mirror reminded me that makeup might come in handy, so I glommed on a goodly amount of mascara, blush and lipstick. In my former life when I'd worked a regular day job, I'd discovered that a good way to get a day off was to show up without makeup; male bosses take one look at a pallid female and send them home to recover. Who knows when a little wanness might come in handy?

Throwing on an oversized long-sleeved tee to camouflage an annoying tortilla-induced roll pouching over my waistband, I grabbed a windbreaker and hat, jammed money, SPF 30 lip-gloss and SPF 50 sunscreen into a pocket, picked up a backpack I'd loaded the night before and walked out on deck.

Gulls wheeled and scolded, pelicans dove for breakfast, a couple of egrets eyed me with suspicion, but only wild life stirred. Not that I expected any sign of humans, as mine was the only occupied boat at the marina. Rumor had it that just before I arrived someone in Mexico City decided to double the slip rates and the place emptied faster than you can say cheap cruiser. The other marina in town, much less expensive, was where I'd stayed before, but it was chock full of said penurious cruisers, so I had the luxury model all to myself. A few boats wandered into my marina for a night or two from time to time, but real cruisers being what they are—low-budget— they quickly left. I was the only liveaboard, and certainly the only one with a J-O-B, which was the very reason for my Monday morning petulance.

For the first time in years I was actually expected to punch a time clock, like, Monday through Friday. Not literally punch in, of course, but I was expected to show up near a certain hour and stay there *all day*. Other people's schedules tend to grate on my already ticklish nerve endings, which is one of two reasons I founded Hetta Coffey, SI LLC in the first place: so I can call my own shots. The other reason was that no one else will put me on their payroll.

I am Hetta Coffey, SI (my little phonetic joke for Civil Engineer), Chief Executive Officer, Chief Financial Officer, and sole employee of my consulting firm specializing in Materials Management for offbeat—some might even say shady—projects.

The only saving factor on this otherwise annoying Monday morning was that I knew this was only a three-month commitment, max. Three whole months, however, of that galling gal's clangorous gut seemed untenable on the first day, but hey, I've been on projects in much less desirable locations than Baja California Sur. At least I can brush my teeth with the tap water. The downside to that is brushing one's pearly whites with local water in many places promotes better fitting jeans.

My new home, Santa Rosalia, is an old mining village with the moldering charm of another era. Because of her French founders, the town looks less Mexican than just about any place I've seen south of the border.

Since the settlement was actually built to plan, the streets are wider than most Mexican village roads, but are now one-way to accommodate parking, wider vehicles and recently, cruisers. Not boat people, but a social event reminiscent of a 1960's movie. With new money in town due to the mine reopening, *everybody* has a car and the young people cruise the circuit, bumper-to-bumper, blasting music and flirting with each other.

The town's wooden houses, each with a porch and many with a tiny balcony on the second floor, were built to the planner's design in a Victorian age and have that look. They are gaily painted, if somewhat peeling, and are festooned with bougainvillea and other flowers, making for a colorful and charming village. Wooden houses in a place where there are few trees? Yep, the unrefined copper was shipped to Washington State for smelting and the ships returned loaded with lumber.

The French are long gone, but unfortunately for my waistline the El Boleo bakery is still cranking out the best *bolillos* on the entire planet.

The main church, designed by Carl Gustav Eiffel, is rumored to have been displayed along with his famed tower at the Paris Expo in 1889, then disassembled and shipped (some say by mistake) to Santa Rosalia and reassembled when the town was still in her mining glory.

History has a way of repeating itself and now that the El Boleo mine just north of town is back in business (this time funded in part by South Koreans) Santa Rosalia is flourishing. The *puebla* is in full boom mode, importing goods and people from everywhere. Costco labels and kimchi abound on the sagging shelves of rickety *tiendas*, living space is at a premium, and now they have their latest import: Hetta Coffey, *ingeniera civil*.

Unfortunately, my new project was neither as well-funded nor as far advanced as El Boleo, for that would be way too easy. Nope, my mine was farther northwest and inland, thereby guaranteeing freezing winter and sizzling summer temps. God forbid I should land work in a place with a water view or some such. Why can't they build copper mines in places like, say, Paris?

As I always do when going onto a new construction site the first day, I squirreled away a couple of just-in-case cheese sandwiches, a bag of chips and some bottled water in my backpack. I'd been told I could eat at the "Man Camp"—welcome to Mexico, land of the less than progressive work place—where I'd break tortillas with a bunch of workers I wasn't welcome to live with. Fine with me. Sharing quarters with a passel of smelly men I didn't know wasn't way up on my warm and fuzzy list, especially when I had my own snazzy yacht to live on.

I'd received an email instructing me to meet my ride in the marina parking lot. Right on time, according to my unearthed Rolex, a shuttle van aimed for me and screeched to a halt close enough to make me scoot back a step. My heel hit a rock and I almost went down, but regained my balance and grabbed the rock. I had a healthy grip on the potential windshield-bashing device when a young man jumped out of the driver's seat, said his name was Pedro, shoved me into the van and slammed the slider just shy of my butt. I did manage to drop the rock on his toe, but unfortunately he was wearing industry standard steel-toed safety boots. So just when did the OSHA rules and regs sneak across the border into Mexico?

A little breathless, I snapped on my seatbelt and turned to my fellow passengers, a handful of sleepy looking guys, all foreigners like me who'd come to work on the mining project. Turns out they were temporarily living in Las Casitas, a small hotel up the hill, where they had individual cabins with an ocean view. I'd been told doublewides were on the way for us management types, but for now, they were busing us in. I'd already decided to remain trawler trash rather than join the trailer trash.

Being the only female, and thereby the most inquisitive person in the van, I quickly ascertained for whom they worked, where they hailed from and more importantly, their marital status. Being men, they asked me how big my boat is (45 feet), what make it is (Californian), and what kind of engines she sports (twin 375hp Caterpillar 3208 TA Diesels).

All of the men were single.

I am technically single.

Hmmm, this job might not be so bad, after all.

Now all I had to find out was what in the *hey-all* I was doing here.

Chapter 2

GIVE A WIDE BERTH (Nautical term):
Provide sufficient space when anchoring or docking
to avoid other ships (keep at a distance).
Something Pedro could learn.

The question, *What in the* hey-all *am I doing
here?* was not a rhetorical one.

I've heard it told that some people, before
they take a job, actually check out a few things, like
what the job *is*. That is not how I operate.

I require a satisfactory answer to the
following: What does it pay?

The larger the amount, the less inclined I am
to delve into petty details, such as, is it legal? Give
me a location, a date, and a willingness to pay in US

dollars, a reasonable escape plan in case things go south, and I'm your gal.

So, on that Monday morning I was the only one on the bus who didn't know why they were there unless you counted the driver, who seemed dead set on doing everything except driving.

Even the delicious-smelling smoke of a taco stand we roared past, normally a beacon for my attention, couldn't draw my horrified eyes from the man who held my life in such an inattentive manner.

Cigarette in one hand, coffee cup in the other, cell phone balanced ear-to-shoulder, Pedro jabbered incessantly except when drawing a puff and taking a sip. What with all the traffic on narrow Mexican Highway Number One (referred to in Mexico as Mex 1) skirting Santa Rosalia, it was a miracle he only grazed a couple of pedestrians. Even more disconcerting was when he stopped talking and smoking, because he appeared to fall asleep. A joke by fellow Texan and humorist Jack Handey sprang to mind: *When I die, I want to go peacefully like my grandfather did—in his sleep. Not yelling and screaming like the passengers in his car.*

Somehow old Jack's humor wasn't quite so amusing on this particular morning. And if I thought the first few minutes were bad, about ten miles out of town we began our ascent of—or more correctly, our assault upon—*La Cuesta del Infierno.*

This lovely little two-lane stretch of Mex 1, charmingly known as the Hill of Hell, snakes over two miles of treacherous hairpin turns, switchbacks, and blind curves, all without benefit of guardrails, shoulders or turnouts. Mere inches from the tires, the maw of an abyss lurked, just waiting for us to slip, plunge and crash. I made the mistake of looking down and saw the scattered remains of almost unidentifiable pieces of twisted metal, broken glass and rotting tires.

Obviously undaunted in the face of cockamamie possibilities like oncoming traffic, Pedro floored the van whenever impeded by a crawling transport truck in our lane. Shaving a thin layer of chrome off the creeping truck's front bumper, we narrowly escaped several head-ons. Only when the road straightened and smoothed did my hair follow suit.

My clawed fingers lost all feeling after the first quarter-mile as I clung to anything within reach, and my right foot was numb from stomping an imaginary brake pedal. The poor guy next to me pried my fingernails from his perforated flesh and tried reassuring me. "It's okay," said he, "Pedro does this every day."

Not with me on board he doesn't. I vowed, on the off chance that I survived this trip, to get a vehicle of my own. Problem is, every car rental agency within two hundred miles evidently has my name flagged with a tag that says, "Don't even *think* of renting a car to this nut job," for a minor incident last year. Okay, maybe not so minor, but it wasn't my fault the car was destroyed by a crazed druggie in a muscle truck. Besides, I'm sure the insurance covered the explosion.

I'd have to go get my pickup out of storage in San Carlos, Sonora, seventy-some-odd miles across the Sea of Cortez. Although I didn't look forward to a return overnight car-ferry ride, it paled in the face of subjecting my precious self to Pedro's daily Passage of Peril.

We swerved—some drivers might turn, but Pedro swerves—off the main highway onto an unpaved but surprisingly smooth road, then up a hill past a large sign reading MINERA LUCIFER.

Before we'd ascended the Hill of Hell, I'd spotted what looked like a smoking volcano much closer than I'd like, but fellow passengers assured me it was dormant and the plume was only a cloud formation. "Heck," one guy told me, "it's been over a hundred years since she blew."

Hello? For a volcano a hundred years is a nanosecond. I hope someone's told it it's dead. And hadn't I read somewhere that the San Andreas Fault runs right smack dab down the center of the Sea of Cortez? Just a few miles east of Santa Rosalia? I'd been in Conception Bay just a few miles south of Santa Rosalia with Jenks, my significant whatever, before he left for Kuwait. We'd anchored off a beach with a rock pool, a soaking tub of sorts. These hot springs simmer up from the fiery bowels of the earth, the water so hot that you can only sit in the pool at high tide when seawater mixes in to cool it to a tolerable level.

And, according to my fellow workers, just a few miles north of the jobsite they were testing for the possibility of a geothermal energy plant.

Was I the only one detecting a pattern here? Hill of Hell, Lucifer's Mine, a smoking volcano, a geothermal field, an unstable fault line *and* hot water boiling up from some seething cauldron under the sea?

I'd have to have a little tête-à-tête with that devil, Wontrobski, about my fee and maybe add a penalty clause to my contract about duty in unstable areas. Oh, wait, that's why they pay me the big bucks; he probably figures I'm more unstable than those I'm sent to mess with.

My *numero uno* job-giver-outer (technical term) back in California, Fidel Wontrobski—his father was a Polish Communist, thus the name—is the one who hires me, or rather my company, on contract. His employers, the brothers Baxter, have made clear I should never again darken their payroll department after a little dust up in Tokyo when I ratted them out for gouging a customer, but somehow they didn't seem to mind when the Trob found me useful for their purposes. In fact, they don't much mess with the Trob in anything he does.

A little younger than me, Fidel is skinny and would top six-five if he'd unfold his horrible posture. With a hooked nose, a black scruffy topknot of frizzy hair, and an entire wardrobe of baggy black clothing, he resembles a giant bird of prey. A buzzard. A buzzard savant.

An engineering genius, Wontrobski is a one-man think tank on the exclusive top floor of the Baxter Building Engineering and Construction in San Francisco. Only the elite, such as the brothers Baxter and a couple of former high-ranking politicos, share his aerie. Which is amazing, in light of the fact that Fidel possesses not a single shred of social or political skill. But corporate heads, former

Secretaries of State and their minions all defer to The Trob's brilliance.

Of course, they highly discourage any Trob interaction with other employees, and certainly never let him talk to clients. When we met many years before, lunch was delivered to his loft and, most nights, dinner. He lived in a nearby hotel, slept only four hours a night—midnight to four—and was the first one in the Baxter employee cafeteria for breakfast each morning. When I worked there, I was usually second.

For weeks after I first joined the firm, the Trob and I sat at opposite ends of the mostly empty cafeteria, studiously ignoring one another. Then one morning as I was passing his table we experienced a power failure. Hearing a frightened whimper, I reached in my purse, whipped out a flashlight, and sat with him until an emergency generator kicked the lights back on. We ate breakfast together that day and every workday until I was shipped off to Japan, where I managed to piss off the brothers Baxter by questioning their shaky ethics. One might argue that I was hardly one to be arguing ethics with anyone else, but if you're going to gouge the client wouldn't you think it wise to at least tell your own project engineer so she won't tip your hand?

Fidel was a prisoner of his superior intelligence, a wunderkind trapped in his own safety zone, until I introduced him to Allison Cuthbert, all five-feet plus a smidgen of her. A product of Houston's fifth ward and the daughter of a black, second generation welfare mom, Ms. Cuthbert came up hard, as we say back home in Texas. Now a prosecutor with political ambitions, she possesses the body of a gymnast, the beauty of a model, the professional scrappiness of an alley cat, and a politician's savvy. How in the hell she and the Trob fell in love is beyond me, but now they are not only married, but expecting a baby any second, the physical attributes of which scares the crap out of me. At least the kid will be smart.

Thanks to the Trob my past three projects, all in Mexico and Baxter Brothers related, have proven profitable if a little on the dodgy side. Since I wasn't too keen on a repeat performance involving running afoul of drug cartels, Jihadist radicals (is that an oxymoron?), suicide bombers or human smugglers, a simple day job at a mine in Baja seemed just the ticket.

Besides, I had time to kill while waiting for my sig-other, Jenks Jenkins, also on contract to Baxter Brothers, to finish up in Dubai. Highly pissed with the present administration in Washington and tired of being used as a punching bag in the mainstream press, the Baxter Brothers were relocating their substantial headquarters to Dubai, as did Halliburton a few years back, and they'd hired Jenks to front for them. When Jenks's Dubai gig is done, our plan is to take *Raymond Johnson* back to the San Francisco Bay Area.

If I lived through Pedro's lousy chauffeuring and a possible violent discharge of steam and molten rock of some sort.

Pedro played chicken with a huge earthmover and won, leaving the driver in a shallow ditch. To take my mind from what was surely my last day on earth, I closed my eyes, decided to think positive and began a mental list of stuff I needed onboard in preparation for a voyage north up the Pacific Coast: six cases of wine, ten bottles of bourbon and a bunch of rum….

The van slewed to a dusty stop in front of a group of doublewides marked:

Gerencia/Administration.

Pedro, still chattering into his cell phone and puffing away, jumped out and opened the slider next to my seat. Once out of the van, my fellow passengers took off walking with purpose toward various buildings, the van left, and I stood alone in the road like a duck looking for thunder. Hearing my name called, I pivoted and spotted a guy waving from a pickup. He climbed out and sauntered toward me.

Six or so inches taller than my five-four, he had that lanky, but muscular, Marlboro Man build that reminded me a bit of Jenks. Longish red hair curled out from under a gold hardhat plastered with stickers like MINERS DO IT IN THE DARK and MINERS DO IT DEEPER. He wore a bright orange vest that almost matched his hair color, and his face was dotted with more freckles than a turkey egg. He had those rugged good looks that always snag my attention, and according to his hat his name was Joe "Safety" Francis. He removed his sunglasses and squinted at me with bright blue, Robert Redford eyes. As he opened his mouth to speak, I beat him to the draw. "Let me take a wild guess here, Joe. You're a miner?"

He grinned and stuck out his hand. "Everyone calls me Safety. He said you were a fast study."

"And *he* be who?"

"Your boss."

"Right answer." I offered my hand, we shook and I trailed him to his truck, a big old diesel dually.

On the passenger seat was a white hard hat, no clever stickers, just my name. I tried it on for fit, adjusted the strap to my head size. "Thanks. How come my hat is white and yours is gold?" I asked, even though I knew the answer: Gold hardhats are for honchos.

"Because I'm a guy?"

"Wrong answer."

"Your *jefe* also said you could be a pain in the ass."

"The Trob is always right."

He grinned, put the dually in gear and took off down the road. "Anything I can fill you in on before we get to your office? Like, what we've hired you to do?"

"Not really, " I lied. "Besides you didn't hire me."

"Point taken. Your official title is Liaison Materials Engineer."

Like I didn't already know that. "I don't liaise well with others, but Materials Management is my game."

"So we've—" He braked to avoid an out of control dirt hauler the size of a locomotive. The big machine rocked to a stop as well and a diminutive

Mexican woman waved, then gave us a "sorry" shrug.

Safety cursed under his breath and said, "Trainee. We're so hard up for people that we started a driver's training program for local Mexican women. Unfortunately we've had one fatality and almost had to dump the program, but the Mexicans wouldn't hear of it. After all, while learning the women get a hundred a week, US, and after that, it doubles. They'd probably faint if they knew what *you* make."

"How do you know what I make?"

"I don't, exactly, but I can guess. People like you don't come cheap."

"Yeah, well, for your information, I can be very cheap."

"Heard that, too."

We shared a chuckle and I decided Joe could be my new best friend. I also noticed his speckled finger didn't sport a wedding ring, and that's a good thing. I've found that male new best friends are better when there's no wife involved.

"Okay, Joe, I lied. I do want to know why I'm here."

"Like I said, you're the project manager's eyes and ears regarding material and equipment purchases and movement. You know, keep a sharp lookout for, uh, inconsistencies."

"So the Trob also told you I'm overly nosy?"

"Not really."

"Well, I am. Who all knows about me?" As soon as I said this I winced. I have tried, honest, to lose my Texas accent when speaking with other professionals, but once in a while something like *who all* slips out. At least I rarely say things like, "Nice meetin' all y'all, y'all," anymore.

"Who all? Well, hell, everybody. Not often we get a female engineer on one of these godforsaken projects."

I wondered if he was bulling me or whether he really thought I was just a material tracker. Time would tell. I wish Time would tell me what I was *really* looking for. Any mid-level grunt can track and expedite materials and equipment.

"How about the Mexicans?" I asked. "What do they think about me being here?"

"You got a problem with Mexicans?"

"Nope. I have a problem with the way their politics work and I've found it pays to expect hanky panky out of Mexico City, not to mention payoffs locally to keep things moving."

"Maybe that's why they want you here."

"To figure out who's on the take?"

"Exactly."

"Then they're wasting their dough. I can figure out who they are, but you can't mess with City Hall, as they say. It's what they do in Mexico. Price of doing bidness."

"Oh, we don't want to *stop* them, we just want to pay off the right people and get it done with. We keep getting hung up on permits and quite frankly we can't figure out who to bribe. Damnedest project I've ever been on. Not that the Canadians especially want to know about any payoffs, but one of my jobs is to grease the skids and I keep running into bureaucratic stonewalling. I don't dare offer any *mordida* for fear we'll insult the wrong guy. And so far, no one has even hinted at being willing to take a gift or two to get the job done. It just ain't natural."

I laughed. "So, the Trob also told you I'm good at ferreting out the bad boys?"

"I heard you're one of the best."

"Did you also hear I *like* bad boys?"

Chapter 3

KNOW THE ROPES (Nautical term):
Understanding knots, ropes and rigging. Or in my
case, getting the lowdown.

On the way to my new office Safety gave me
a quick jobsite tour, pointing out various areas under
construction, laying out schedules for completion,
and explaining which subcontractor did what to
whom. As soon as I settled in, I'd get a plot plan and
an organization chart to put names and companies to
the various phases of the project. He said mining
was being done at some old pits, but most areas were
still under construction.

We parked in a slot with his name on it near
the front door of a doublewide with a hand painted
sign: *Gerente*. Management.

"Hey, Safety, you ever read a book called *Up The Organization*?"

"Naw."

"It was written eons ago and one of the things I remembered from it was about assigned parking. This guy took over a company and the first thing he did was get rid of honcho spots near the door. He reasoned that if management was so damned important, they should get there first."

As expected, the office facilities were hardly plush. This was, after all, a temporary construction site office set up in connected doublewides. I saw only two private offices, a smattering of cubicles and one fairly large room designated as a Conference Room that would seat maybe ten. I'd already seen training class notices posted at my marina's meeting rooms back in Santa Rosalia, so figured onsite buildings were already overcrowded.

Safety guided me to a small cubicle with his name and position printed on a little slide-in plaque beside the door opening.

"You know, I don't always see eye-to-eye with the Safety department," I told him.

He looked toward Heaven as if asking for help, but gave me a wink, showing he'd heard it before. The Safety Engineer's job on any project is one of the most difficult and confrontational. Personality issues can be paramount. These engineers have to be both pleasant and ruthless. They can be the messengers of bad news to a project management concerned with expense and time overruns due to software, chemical, electrical, mechanical, procedural, and training problems. Safety had his job cut out for him in Mexico, what with their tendencies towards mediocre management systems and questionable, to Gringos, business ethics.

"I know what to expect down here," he told me. "My old man was Safety on projects all over the world. We kids were dragged from town-to-town, country-to-country."

"Tell me about it." We chatted a few minutes about our childhoods in construction camps and figured out we almost met a time or two. He was in the middle of recounting a story in India when he was a teen when his pager squawked and we were summoned to the Project Manager's office.

"Am I gonna like him?" I whispered as my new BFF led me through the office building.

"Probably. Most do."

"Good enough for me."

I could sense right off why Safety said most people cottoned to the project manager. Bert Melton had that baby face that makes men appealing to women, and a great head of graying hair envied by men. He exuded a gentle nature with a soft voice and kind demeanor, which made me wonder how in hell he ever achieved project manager status, even though I knew from the corporate literature that the fifty-five year old held a BS in Geology and Mechanical Engineering, as well as an MBA, making him, on paper, more than qualified.

However, in the construction/engineering game most top brass are usually tough SOBs, because brains alone don't count when juggling the politics, budgets, funding, schedules and personnel issues on a project of this caliber. Then I remembered where we were; most companies would deem this a hardship post.

After introductions Safety left, closing the door behind him. Before Bert could say anything, I asked, "So, who did you piss off to get sent down" here?"

He looked startled, then laughed and shook his head. "I know that's what some people might think, but actually I asked for this one. I figure this will be my last assignment, if I can ride it out until I retire. I like to fish, I love Mexico and," he waved his hand toward the coast, "the Sea of Cortez is right out there."

"Do you live in Santa Rosalia?"

"Yep. I've been here almost five years already. I was with the first group of scientists sent to test the waters, so to speak. See if mining again was feasible. I bought an old miner's house near the hospital and spent, or rather the wife did, almost a year renovating it."

As he said this his jaws tightened, which I understand completely. "Been there, done that. I rehabbed a hundred-year-old home in Oakland once and at times wanted to throw a bomb into it. Rewarding, but a lot of work and money. Well, good for you. I love staying in town, but sure don't look forward to the commute."

He smiled knowingly. "I'll get Safety to have another talk with Pedro."

"Don't do it on my account. I'm gonna have my own wheels after this weekend."

"Probably a wise move. I have a company truck, but the downside to that is we can't drive anywhere off site between dusk and dawn."

"Kinda puts a kink in your social life."

He looked uncomfortable for a moment, making my nosy meter twitch, but then he smiled. "Not really. I can walk everywhere in town and if I don't feel like hoofing it back up the hill to the house, there are taxis. I hear you're living on your boat."

Hmmm. There were a lot of I's there for someone whose resume said he was married.

"I love living on a boat, but when we get those trailers up here I might stay over a few nights a week to avoid that death-defying drive twice a day, if that's okay by you. Say, I saw a boat in the marina named *Lucifer*. Is that yours?"

"It's the company boat, but I can use it when I want. Nice little Whaler. Some of us go out any Sunday we can."

Nice little expensive Whaler and perk for a project that was hemorrhaging money, I thought, but kept that comment to myself. "By the way, if you want to hang on to your fishing poles, you'd better take them off of *Lucifer*, or at least put 'em inside the cabin. I thought about snagging one for myself."

"I'll tell the guys. No one has felt much like going down there since the accident."

"What accident?"

"Safety didn't tell you? We still don't know what happened. All we know is one of the guys in

Purchasing, a Mexican national, must have taken *Lucifer* out by himself. Some *pangueros* found the boat beached near their fish camp at San Lucas cove, south of here a few miles. Funny thing is, Rosario wasn't authorized to use the boat and everyone here swears he would never take it out without permission. He was doing us a favor by repairing the radio. He's good with things like that. A nice young man, kind of quiet and, as the kids say these days, nerdy, but a college grad and a big help around here. I miss him."

"You had to fire him?"

"No. He never came back to work. Some say he's too embarrassed that he took the boat out and ran aground or something. But most say there is no way the kid would do anything like that. Who knows?"

"Didn't the guard see him, or the boat, leave the marina?"

"No, it was cold and the night guard was holed up trying to stay warm. Wind was howling. Certainly no night to be out on a boat, that's for sure."

"Well, at least it wasn't an OTJ."

Melton looked surprised, then grinned. "Yeah, I guess. On the job accidents are bad for any project manager's career."

"Never seemed quite fair to me, blaming the head guy for an accident, but it works for the military. Anyhow, how long ago did this guy disappear?"

"Over a week now, so it doesn't look good, even if he—" a whistle blew. "You hungry?" he asked. "The mess hall has pretty good food and we can make the first serving."

"I brought a sandwich, but if you're buying, I could eat."

Biftek Milanesa is breaded cube steak, Mexican-style, served with a side of the ubiquitous refried beans, rice, and tortillas. There was also a salad, and flan for dessert. If that roll above my waistband wasn't gonna balloon, I'd have to bring my own lunch for sure.

During our meal, I grilled Bert like a Texas T-bone, garnering as much info as I could absorb about who did what to whom, project-wise. When we returned to the offices he turned me over to a sweet-faced, middle-aged secretary named Laura. She led me to a desk in a tiny room.

"So Laura, where do you keep the mops and brooms now?"

She looked puzzled. I know better than to use sarcasm on other nationalities. I spent ten minutes explaining my lame joke.

Finally she got it, smiled and then blushed. "I am sorry, Miss Coffey. I am told there will be a trailer brought in for you soon. For now, if you prefer, you can use my desk, but we will have to share the telephone until we can get you one of your own."

Safety stuck his head in the door. "How was lunch?"

"Great. I'd invite you in, but I left my can opener back on the boat."

He found this hilarious and went off to save lives or whatever it is he does.

I settled in at my desk with a plot plan of the site, a long-term construction and operations schedule, a sheaf of organizational charts starting with the big picture. I was penciled in under the Project Manager as: Project Materials Engineer: Temp/Consulting/Liaison.

The organization chart was in its tenth revision in nine months, never a good omen. Personnel instability is the bane of all projects, and turnover makes it harder for me to snoop. My eyes were drawn to the little box still existing for Rosario Pardo. His was a minor position, but still only one rung down from the Purchasing Manager.

I found myself thinking about him taking the Whaler out on a stormy night and wondered whatever possessed him. What a nightmare, falling overboard into an angry sea; it was a fear that plagued me on occasion, making me wake with a dry mouth. In which case, one might think I'd consider living somewhere besides a boat?

I headed for our little break room for a bottle of water and when I returned, there was a guy painting my name on a board. He had sanded it down, but I could see the faint remains of a name: Rosario Pardo. Gone for a little over a week and already being erased. A shiver ran down my spine. I don't really believe in ghosts, but sitting in a guy's chair who was missing and presumed drowned gave me the creeps, and had me asking myself, *If he's dead, was it really an accident?*

I vowed to learn much more about *Señor* Rosario Pardo.

Chapter 4

FALL FOUL OF (Nautical term): Collide
with or become entangled in conflict.
It had to happen.

While my mess hall lunch settled I fired up
my surprisingly new office desktop.

Much to my delight the twenty-inch monitor
showed I had an Internet connection. Logging into
Yahoo, I checked my email, then Googled that
troublesome-looking volcano I'd seen on the way to
work. I wasn't convinced those were just clouds
hovering on the peak.

La Virgen was my smoker, but there were
two more, *El Viejo* and *El Azufre*. Basically meaning
the old one and the sulfurous one. The chain is called
Las Tres Virgenes. According to the site I found,

they line up from the northeast to southwest, and *La Vírgen, the youngest, is an andesitic stratovolcano with numerous dacitic lava domes and lava flows on its flanks. A major plinian explosive eruption from a SW-flank vent was radiocarbon dated at about 6500 years ago, but Helium exposure and Uranium-series dates give a late-Pleistocene age for this event. An ash plume was reported from Tres Vírgenes volcano by a Spanish Jesuit priest while navigating the Sea of Cortez in 1746. No tephra deposits from such a young eruption have been found, but young undated andesitic lava flows at the summit could potentially be related to this event.*

I translated this vulcanologist gobbledygook as, "She ain't gonna blow any time soon, but just in case she does, I'll cover my scientific ass with that last sentence."

Say what they will, those three virgins still spooked me, as if sitting in a potentially dead man's chair hadn't already done the job.

I checked out the Sea of Cortez, geologically, and learned it was only five million years old, making it the youngest sea in the world. I'm not so sure that's such a good thing, for in my uneducated opinion it hasn't had time to cool off. Kinda like a teenager's hormones.

Hormonal thoughts brought Jenks to mind, a diversion from imagining the earth blowing up under my feet. I wanted to email him, maybe catch him live for a chat, but it was still only two **PM in Santa Rosalia** and that meant two in the morning in Dubai. Rats. Jenks is an early riser, but not *that* early.

Instead, I emailed my BFF list: Jan, Craig and Allison. We are all friends from back in the San Francisco Bay Area, and some from Houston before that, but Allison, now married to The Trob, is the only one left in San Francisco.

Jan lives over the mountains from Santa Rosalia, on Baja's Pacific coast, and Craig runs a large animal veterinary clinic in Bisbee, Arizona. I let everyone know I was in Santa Rosalia and had started the new job. After that I did a little mindless online surfing, posted to Facebook and looked at other friends' posts. Ah, the black hole of social media. I soon grew weary of cute kids, dogs and cats and set about arranging my new office.

A raid on the supply room garnered pens, pencils, Post-its—in my opinion the single greatest invention since chocolate—then dug framed pictures of my boat, parents, sister, my dog RJ, and Jenks and me from my knapsack.

Jenks, tall, lean and tanned, looks much like I envision his Viking ancestors. Jan had snapped the photo of us on *Raymond Johnson's* deck, with the Golden Gate Bridge in the background. We wore matching windbreakers, reminding me that even though it can be cool in the Baja this time of year, San Francisco is cold all the time. Jenks had a long arm slung over my shoulder and we looked like Mutt and Jeff, those cartoon characters from my childhood. I sighed, wishing him teleported to my side, right now. I so missed my whatever he is.

I was tacking an overall jobsite plot plan to the wall when my computer dinged and I saw Jenks was awake and online.

He'd been on the go for days, ever since we'd crossed the Sea of Cortez from San Carlos on the Mexican mainland. He took a day to help me settle my boat, *Raymond Johnson*, into a slip at the marina, and then he took off.

About my boat's name, one might think *Raymond Johnson* a little odd, but my dearly departed dog would have liked it just fine. He was given that name by Jan, my bestest friend, after I'd been calling my new pound hound Dawg for a several weeks. Jan felt that maybe if I showed the pooch a little more respect, gave him a real name, he might act better.

She had loved the *Redd Foxx Show* and we both watched reruns of *Sandford and Son* sitcoms whenever we got the chance. Both had this character, Raymond J. Johnson, who did a schtick: "My name is Raymond J. Johnson, Jr. Now you can call me Ray, or you can call me J, or you can call me Johnny, or you can call me Sonny, or you can call me Junie, or you can call me Junior; now you can call me Ray J, or you can call me RJ, or you can call me RJJ, or you can call me RJJ Jr., but you doesn't hasta call me Johnson!" Anyhow, Raymond Johnson it was, and we called him RJ. Naming him did nothing to improve his incorrigible nature, which Jan said was because he took after me. Maybe that's why there was still a hole in my heart he used to fill.

In his photo on my new desk, RJ sported one of those goofy yellow lab grin-shots, stick in mouth, dripping wet. A placid Russian River lazed in the background. I snapped the picture, a canoe floated into sight, the people calling, "Oh, look at that cute dog."

RJ still answered to Dawg.

He perked, turned and rushed back into the river while I yelled warnings neither he nor the canoeists heeded. A strong swimmer, he was on them in seconds. Launching his sixty-pound heft from the water, he hooked his paws over a gunwale. Screams, woofs and curses ensued as people and coolers hit the chilly drink. By the time they righted the boat and climbed back in, they were quite a bit downstream, and had given him a few new names, none of which were, *cute*.

It was losing RJ that launched me into the boating world. I'd been looking around to change my life, and when he died my need for a house no longer existed. I sold my lovingly renovated three-story, hundred-year-old Bay Area home and moved aboard *Raymond Johnson*. Well, at the time it was named *Sea Cock*, but that name had to go.

A forty-five foot Californian motor yacht, she is basically a three-level, two-bedroom floating condo. Carpeted throughout in a rich marine blue, the furniture—real furniture, not built-ins like I'd seen on so many boats—was upholstered in ivory. Had anyone told me back when I was in my snobby decorator mode at my home in Oakland—where almost anything worth covering was done up in buttery soft leather—that I would learn to love pleather, I would've un-friended them on Facebook. On a boat, however, it is ever so practical.

My large aft master suite has a queen-sized bed, tons of closet (locker) and storage (locker again) space, and an en suite head, or bathroom. In the bow there is a two-bunk guest room with its own shower and toilet. Jan's quarters, for the most part.

There is a well-equipped galley with a full-sized AC/DC stainless refrigerator, three-burner stove, oven, microwave, and built-in banquette for informal dining.

In the main cabin, or saloon (pronounced salon, as in beauty shop, not a shoot-em-up western bar), there's a small office area and upholstered sofas and chairs, plus a navigation station for driving from inside the boat. This comes in handy when the flying bridge is being inundated by rain and wind, or in my case, when bad guys are shooting at you.

She (all boats are she, no matter the name) even sports a covered verandah, or sundeck as it is properly called, furnished in slightly faded Brown Jordan fake rattan with blue-and-white striped cushions. There's an ice maker, a rack of blue and white plastic stemware and a wet bar, and the whole thing can be zipped up against crappy weather. Three steps up is the flying bridge, my preferred place for driving the boat and watching for marine life in daylight hours.

Raymond Johnson is my home, which I share on and off with Jenks Jenkins, my whatever he is. He left for Dubai after a little growling and warning of "consequences" if I even *thought* of moving the boat from her slip before he returned. He'd hopped a bus to Loreto, then a plane to San Francisco, where he boarded a Baxter Brothers company jet for Dubai.

I couldn't prove it, but I suspected he and the Trob finagled this job for me so I'd stay out of trouble for the next few months while he finished up in Dubai. Whatever, I never look a gift job in the mouth.

Jenks telling me what to do with my boat or life, and me actually doing it stood a pig's flight chance in Hell, but since we both knew that, I refrained from getting into a dust up with him before he left. Consequences? What was he gonna do, take away my birthday? *That* I can live with.

Or, he could dump me, which I didn't think I could live with, so maybe I *would* leave the boat in her slip and take road trips. Besides, I was probably going to be so busy at my new job, whatever *that* was, I might not have time to take the boat anywhere anyhow.

Seeing he was online, I typed: *Wanna get nekkid with me?*

Sure! Who is this?

Very funny, Jenks.

How's my girl?

Lonely.

You made a typo. Didn't you mean looney?

Aren't you the clever one so early in the day?

Early to bed, early to rise. How's the new job?

Don't know yet. Had lunch and got a desk. That's it so far.

I gotta go. Getting ready for a big meeting. Looks like I might have found land for you-know-who. I'll call you tonight.

I have a date.

Ha! Love you.

You too.

The you-know-who is Baxter Brothers, and Jenks was flying under the radar in Dubai, trying to get stuff done before the world hears the stunning announcement that one of the biggest construction/engineering companies in the world was moving out of San Francisco, lock, stock and barrel. Talk about your brain and economic drain. Too bad Baxters is privately owned; I could make a killing with this kind of insider info.

At four that afternoon I met my problem.

There is one on every project and I instinctively sensed the minute I laid eyes on him sitting behind his desk that he was IT. For starters, he was reading a sheaf of documents when Laura showed me into his office. Unless he was deaf, I'm sure he heard her say, "Señor Sanchez, this is Miss Coffey."

He didn't look up or acknowledge our presence in any way. Laura was obviously embarrassed, but I waved her out of the office with a smile and turned my attention back to my target. The little fart didn't know it yet, but his life was about to take a turn for the worse.

I gave him to a count of five.

"Five! Here, let me help you with that." I whipped a pair of cheaters from my windbreaker pocket and shoved them between him and those important documents. His head snapped up. "I have the same problem. Must be middle age or somethin'. Well, for you anyway. Man your age probably should have those ears checked, as well, 'cause you didn't hear Laura introduce me. Oh, never, mind," I stuck out my hand, thereby knocking a cascade of papers into his lap. "Oopsy-daisy about that. Hetta Coffey here. You can call me *Café* if you like, many of you Mexicans do, because Hetta is so hard to pronounce. Comes out sounding something like, 'I ate ya.' You wanted to see me about something?"

I gave him the full benefit of my latest bleaching session with the dentist and he finally, but reluctantly, took my hand. He gave it a limp shake. I refrained from totally breaking his fingers.

He grimaced, flexed his fingers and growled, "My eyes and ears are perfectly fine, *Hetta*." He was heavy on the H and T to let me know he had no problem pronouncing my name properly.

"Oh. Well, then you were just being rude and self-important? Sorry."

Now I had his full attention. He stood to his full five-six, topping me by a whole two inches. I had to remember to dig out my high-heeled boots. As soon as he stood, I sat. "Please, Osvaldo. Say, was your mother a Wizard of Oz fan? Can I call you Ozzie? Anyhow, go back to what you were doing. I'll sit here until, well, quitting time. When is that, by the way?"

"Three-thirty."

"Oh, goody, I'm on overtime, which I normally don't charge for unless I am being subjected to really annoying people. So, what do you do around here?" As if I didn't know. The guy was head of Purchasing, already a bad thing in my book. My history with purchasing managers was less than sterling. I'd already snooped his resume in the company files: Chicano (US born of Mexican parents), raised in Bakersfield, Business degree from California State University there, then worked in procurement for an oil company in the San Joaquin Valley for ten years before landing this job. Probably by virtue of the fact that he was bilingual, because nothing I saw in his resume qualified him as a Purchasing Manager for a construction project as big as this one. Maybe he has connections?

"I am the Purchasing Manager, as my office indicates."

He meant the sign on the door, but I was on a roll. "Gee, in that case, I must be the Mop Manager. You pick that office out for me?"

"It is all we have for the moment. Arrangements are being made. I did not know you existed until last week."

"Some people would like it to stay that way. Well, it was nice having this little chat. Let me know if you need anything more." I rose to leave.

"Miss Coffey, I have been told you will be working for me."

"Actually, Ozzie, I will be working *with* you. I answer to Bert," I said, using the project manager's first name to further annoy the prick. "Tell you what I'll do. Tomorrow I'll send you a list of what I need, document-wise, and you can have your people send them to my people. Oh, wait, I don't have any people. Well, never mind. I'm sure I'll have a few questions, so I can ask...just who are *your* people, anyhow?"

"Perhaps your requests should come through *Bert*?"

Yep, I'd definitely gotten under his skin. Good. "Sure, if you insist. *Hasta mañana*." I waved and left.

Safety sidled into my office, a smirk on his face. He whispered, "Nice work, Coffey. You're already the office hero."

"I aim to please."

"While we all enjoyed that little show, I'd watch it if I were you. The little Spic could throw a monkey wrench into your works. Nothing overt, just passive aggressive bull. Like that trailer with your name on it might fall off a truck on the way here."

Safety using the word Spic didn't set well with me, even though I'm hardly a poster child for the politically correct, but I let it slide; I needed all the new friends I could get. "Message received, loud and clear, but if he dumps my trailer, that's okay. This closet is growing on me. It's cozy. Uh, this was Pardo's office, wasn't it?"

"You heard about that, huh? Damned shame. Funny little dude. Nice, quiet, and spoke English with hardly any accent. He had a cubicle next to me at first, but he actually requested this closet. Sure wish I knew what happened to him." He shrugged, then asked, "Want a ride back to your boat?"

"Oh, yes. Anything to avoid Pedro Knievel. Uh, does everyone here know where I live?"

"Yep."

I didn't like the sound of that. Judging by what I'd seen and heard on my first day on the job, Lucifer Land might live up to its moniker.

Chapter 5

WHEN ONE'S SHIP COMES HOME
(Nautical Term): The successful arrival of a cargo
ship—achievement.

Early Saturday morning twelve large miners and I crammed ourselves into the tiny seats of Aero Calafia's single-engine Cessna 208 Grand Caravan for the thirty-five minute flight to Guaymas. From there I grabbed a cab to San Carlos and bailed my little red Ford Ranger out of the storage facility. The return ferry didn't start boarding until late afternoon, so I killed time at Barracuda Bob's, my favorite hangout in San Carlos, for breakfast, then lunch. I saw a lot of friends early on, but they faded off to do what they had to do, so I fired up my computer and caught up on Facebook friends, then surfed the Net for tempting boat stuff, and finally headed for the ferry when Barracuda closed at two.

A car ferry is far from my favorite mode of transport, especially one that takes overnight. Unfortunately my other option was to drive to Tijuana and then down Baja's two-lane Mex 1, a twelve hundred mile run I didn't have the time nor the inclination to tackle.

Driving onto the top-heavy-looking, overcrowded ferry was a little unsettling, but the fact that it was a night crossing made it worse. I'd seen those disaster film clips from all over the world where ferries rolled over, hit rocks, or just plain sunk. Since I was doing a one-day turnaround, my suitcase contained the following:

Four one-liter bottles of water.

A hand-operated watermaker capable of making a gallon of water an hour.

Two inflatable life preservers, both for me. Every woman for herself!

A plastic bag with chocolate bars, health bars and dried fruit.

Sunblock.

Floating flashlight with strobe and extra batteries.

Wet suit, fins and a mask.

Water-activated strobe-light armband.

Solar/hand-crank-powered light, with radio and cell phone charger

Handheld marine VHF radio with GPS locator.

Cell phone.

Handheld GPS

Waterproof case for all of the above that needed one

I would have carried a survival raft and flare gun, but figured the flare would probably get me arrested at the airport, and the raft would cost a fortune in overweight charges. Hetta Coffey: Survivalista.

When we finally docked early Sunday morning in Santa Rosalia I was frazzled. I was a mere fifty or so yards away from my nice comfy boat as I waited in a line of cars and trucks exiting the ferry, but getting off that damnable ship took what seemed forever.

I'd tried grabbing a few winks on the noisy, smelly ferry, but it was impossible. All the private cabins were booked, so I was relegated to steerage. There were airline type seats for passengers, but with kids running around and crying, drunks singing and then throwing up, and the general chaos of traveling in the cheap seats, I ended up reading my Kindle all night. I considered sneaking back for a snooze in my pickup bed, but the gangway doors were bolted and locked tight.

The only saving factors were calm wind and seas. I'd been in Santa Rosalia before when the wind howled all night and witnessed the ferry bouncing around outside the breakwater, waiting for daylight and a drop in the wind so they could enter the harbor and dock. At least I was spared that nightmare, and now my little red Ford Ranger and I were home, safe and sound.

By the time I crept by a long line of heavily armed marines and a drug-sniffing dog or two, cleared customs—which I thought was ridiculous since I was traveling *from* Mexico *to* Mexico—parked at the marina and boarded the boat, I was dragging butt. At ten in the morning, I was ready for a cold beer, a ham sandwich and a nice warm bed.

I'd noticed, as I trudged down the dock trailing my survival suitcase, that the mine's fishing boat, *Lucifer*, was out of her slip. Since it was a nice calm day, I figured Bert Melton and his cronies were out fishing. If they were lucky, I hoped they'd share.

I popped a cool one and sat out on deck for a few minutes, enjoying the morning sunshine and sea bird ballet. Spotting fresh raccoon tracks on the deck, I checked for *el mapache* damage and found none. I'd read the word for raccoon in Spanish came from an Aztec word meaning the one who takes everything in their hands. They got that right. The cute, but pesky critters, board me almost every night, looking for food and mischief. I learned that the hard way on my first night at the dock, when I'd left a garbage bag on deck, planning to take it to the bin the next morning. Cleaning old coffee grounds, banana peels, and even seriously smelly raccoon crap from a deck—what do they eat besides my relatively good-smelling garbage?—ain't no way for a lady to start her day. Or me, either.

Someone told me to put dog crap on the deck as a deterrent but I didn't consider that a great alternative.

My plan for the rest of my day was to eat something, catch a short nap, then call Jenks later in the afternoon. I was feeling out of sorts, not only tired, and wondered why. Then I recalled past years of what I called the Sunday Blues, when Monday loomed and with it a loss of freedom. Why did I take a damned job? It was already getting old and I'd only been at it a week. Another Monday morning and my alarming *señorita* loomed large.

Rummaging in the fridge, I couldn't find any ham. Shrugging, I decided on super cheesy scrambled eggs and toast, but soon learned I was also missing my precious block of Velveeta and a loaf of Bimbo. Bimbo bread, with a shelf life of plastic bags, I can live without, but Velveeta? It is almost impossible to come by in Mexico.

I'd had a busy week before I left Saturday morning to fetch my pickup, so between the daily commute to the mine and throwing together a sandwich or two every day, I must have run through more stuff than I realized. I quickly checked for peanut butter and jelly, those other staples of the working girl, and found them gone as well. It was looking like the man camp cafeteria for me Monday unless I hit a store or two later.

I was eating my boring eggs when the trash can caught my eye. I had thrown papers into it before I left, but since there was no perishable garbage, I'd decided to dump it when I returned. It was empty, with a nice new plastic liner. Someone had eaten my food and emptied the trash. My stomach fell, because I got that sick feeling one gets when trying to remember if I'd locked my jewelry, some of it literally the family jewels, in my safe. Adrenalin surged as I hurried to my cabin and checked my cash stash and jewelry. All was there, so it looked like only the fridge was robbed, which is disturbing enough. If true. Was I so tired I was imagining things?

I grabbed the phone and called my best bud, Jan. She lives with her latest—and to date, most tenacious—love interest, Doctor Brigado Comacho Yee, a Mexican marine biologist and whale specialist. Chino, as he is called, was a happy whale counter when he fell for Jan. He had lived in a simple thatched roof beach palapa, contented with fish tacos three times a day and salt water baths. Then he met Jan. Now his previously basic camp consists of not one, but two, brand new fifth wheel trailers with slide-outs, satellite television, and a washer/dryer. Gallons of fresh water and gasoline for large generators are trucked in regularly from miles away. All of this to keep Jan from flying the coop, something she's prone to do.

Chino, so nicknamed for his Chinese ancestors, is almost a dozen years younger than Jan, a major source of irritation for her, but now that he has her ensconced in the relative lap of luxury, she seems content. For a while, anyhow.

Camp Chino is just over the peninsula, as the crow flies, from Santa Rosalia, which is one of the reasons I'd taken this job. We can visit on my days off and hopefully that'll help keep me out of mischief while Jenks is gone.

I distinctly remembered telling her I was going to San Carlos this weekend, because I was trying to drag her along for company. She wisely declined, but she has a key to the boat. Maybe she dropped by?

She answered on the second ring and I asked, "Did you eat my ham and Velveeta?"

"And a good Sunday morning to you, too, Hetta. You drunk already? It ain't even noon."

"Let me rephrase that. Did you visit my boat yesterday?"

"Naw, you said you were gonna go get your pickup. Why?"

"Nothing, I guess. I must be losing my marbles."

"Hetta, you lost your last marble long ago. What's wrong?"

"I could have sworn I had a loaf of bread, a block of Velveeta and some ham in the fridge, but it's gone."

"Oh, man, the *Velveeta*? This is serious. You'd better call in the *federales*. Ya know, that kinda thing used to happen at my house, but then I found out it was you."

"They emptied the trash!"

"Well, you certainly never did that."

I sighed. I'd worked late Friday night, then caught a few short winks before getting up at oh-dark-thirty to catch the airport shuttle. Maybe I ate the ham? Oh, and an entire loaf of bread and a half pound of cheese? I think that might be something I'd remember. I mean, we're talking Velveeta here.

"Jan, someone has been in my boat."

"Maybe that raccoon has figured out how to jimmy the lock."

"The little bandit was on here, all right, but only outside. Someone else broke in."

"They steal anything more valuable than cheese?"

"No, not that I can tell."

"Does the marina office have a key?"

"Yes. That must be it. They're closed today, but I'll ask tomorrow. I feel better already. Maybe a guard got hungry."

"Probably. Just in case maybe you should use that deadbolt Jenks installed on your cabin door when you crash tonight. You know how you draw trouble."

"Come on. I've only been here a week."

"What? A whole week and you haven't pissed anyone off? You slippin'?"

"Okay, there is this one guy. He's a Chicano out of California and thinks he's God's gift to the purchasing world."

"I knew it. Will you never learn?"

"Nope." I yawned. "I'm beat. That ferry ride is a booger. I'm hoping to catch a nap before I call Jenks on Skype later."

"Ya gonna tell him about the reefer raid."

"Why worry him? He can't do anything from Dubai."

"Yes he can. He can fire up that fancy schmancy security system he installed on your boat. Promise me you'll ask him."

"I normally never listen to any advice you give, which has worked in my favor for well-nigh the hundreds of years I've known you, but as bad as I hate to say it, you are right."

"You have made my day. My year. My—"
I hung up.

When Jenks and I first met back in the San Francisco Bay area, I had recently bought my boat and was being stalked by an evil Brit. Jenks installed an Internet-based security system on *Raymond Johnson*, but I hadn't been using it in Mexico because it requires either a landline, or really high quality Internet. I'd had neither until now. This marina had amazingly fast and reliable Internet service.

I had to figure out how to get Jenks to reinstate the service without his getting suspicious that, once again, I'd ended up with a can of worms.

"Good morning," I chirped into my Skype headset.

"Hey, you're back. How was the ferry ride?"

"Grueling. But now I have my pickup and can avoid Pedro of Death's charming company each morning. How's life in Dubai? Must be a bitch living like the point zero one percent?" Jenks was the guest of a Saudi Prince we know who has a suite of some kind in the Burj Al Arab hotel, the one that looks like a giant boat under sail. I'd watched a You Tube tour of the Royal Suite and checked prices for a regular room. Minimum was fifteen hundred buckaroos a night. Jenks was staying for free as the prince's guest, so what in the hell was I doing in a dusty little town on the Baja? I'll bet they have lots of Velveeta in Dubai.

Jenks reads my mind on occasion. "You could be here, you know."

"And do what all day? I saw this thing on television about living in Dubai and the women seemed bored silly. They can't do squat without a husband's written approval. I would, however, like a chance at stealing one of those gold-plated toilet paper dispensers I saw on that You Tube tour."

He evidently didn't think I was being sincere. "Your choice." He was a little curt, not his usual state. It was my job to be snarky, not his.

"Everything okay on your end? You sound a little…tired." I would have said bitchy, but if he said that to me I'd eat his brains.

"Oh, the usual crap, dealing with the local bureaucrats. Found a parcel of land, now we have to pay off the right people to get it."

"Jeez, we have the same problem on my project. I guess some things are global. Say, do you think you can fire up that security system again, now that I have good Internet service?"

There was a pause, dead air for a good count of ten. "Hetta, are you in trouble already?"

"Absolutely not, and I resent the insinuation." I thought I sounded properly indignant without starting a verbal battle.

"Sorry, but you know I worry. Actually I should have thought of that. I'll feel better, knowing you have some protection. Problem is, you're on WiFi, not connected directly. I'll talk to my guy in Oakland and see if he can rig something wirelessly. You should get an email from him within the hour. I hope the cameras are still operational. You're a little far away for any of my guys to make a service call. I should have checked the system out while I was there. Too late, but I'm glad you thought of getting things up and running."

"So, what are you wearing?"

"Hetta, we're on Skype, you can see me."

"I know, I thought I'd try that phone sex thing I see in movies."

"In that case, I'm naked."

"Me too. Well except for..."

I think the long distance sex stuff is either overrated, or I'm lousy at it; was Jenks supposed to break out laughing?

The techie for Jenks's side business in home and boat security systems emailed me, as promised, within the hour. We did a camera check from his end and all was a go. I'd have to try activating them remotely myself from the office tomorrow, but there was no reason to doubt they wouldn't be working well. Meanwhile I accessed the system to re-familiarize myself with how it worked and by bedtime my anti-bad-guy device made sure if so much as a mouse moved inside my boat, or tried to open an outside hatch, I'd know it. Unfortunately, due to pesky raccoons and seabirds, the outside sensor had to be left off, but the cameras worked fine in case I heard anything and wanted to take a look.

Unfortunately, if something did happen, I didn't have so much as a cap pistol on board. While in Mexico, some gringos on boats miss television, fast food, and relatives back home. I miss my mom, dad and sister, but I so long for my guns. Go figure: the one place you seriously need fire power and guess who has it?

After the revolution of 1910, the rebels who won figured out real fast that if they hadn't had guns, they would never have defeated the powers that were. So they took the guns away from the people they'd liberated, in case *they* should decide to rebel against the powers that be.

Mexico ain't got no stinkin' Second Amendment, but I guess the founding fathers weren't counting on the United States government arming their cartels.

Chapter 6

TAKE ANOTHER TACK (Nautical term):
Try another approach

I slept like the dead Sunday night, but that Monday morning alarm clock still went off way too early. This work thing was getting old already, but having my own wheels made for a much better, and certainly safer, start to my week. I still might die on the Hill of Hell, but at least it would be me at the wheel for the cliff dive. I'm such a control freak I'd rather drive myself off a cliff?

Settled into my work closet, I gave the photos on my desk a smile, fired up the computer and accessed my boat's security system. The cameras all worked and I sent a silent hallelujah to Jenks in Dubai. 'Course, Dubai being Muslim, I suppose that hallelujah had to break through a few religious barriers, but it's the thought that counts.

Now, if anything larger than a breadbox entered my boat, I'd get a call on my Mexican Telcel phone. Thank you, Carlos Slim, for making it possible to reach out and touch someone for only a dollar a minute. The Mexicans joke that before they put their pants on in the morning, Slim already has his hand in their pockets. And that, folks, is the way you get to be one of the richest people in the world: overcharge the hell out of an already financially depressed population and make sure you have no competition.

Jenks had tweaked the indoor motion detectors because, after all, a boat is constantly moving, especially where fishing pangas streak in and out of the harbor at Mach speed. Yes, the Port Captain posted a 5km per hour sign on both a buoy and the harbor breakwater, but like all speed limits in Mexico, they are merely a suggestion. Like stop signs.

So, what with Santa Rosalia being the bouncingest (nautical term) harbor I'd ever been in, the camera's motion detectors were set on low sensitivity, but a human would set them off. Outside motion detectors were useless due to critters, but if I want to see what's going on, I can manually engage them and even record the action. All in all I was feeling *mucho* better about my ham thief.

According to the marina office manager, no one could have gotten their hands on my boat keys, so whoever broke in was a lock picker.

A hungry, neat, lock picker.

Since I held the title of Materials Manager (Liaison) on the project, I tackled managing materials, which I do well, and liaising, which I do badly.

Not one to take anyone's word for anything, I started at square one: drawings. On a project this size drawings are in the thousands, each one more detailed than the next. Think of building a car. You could start with a rendition of the finished product, all shiny, sitting on the showroom floor, then start taking it apart, piece by piece, down to the last nut and bolt. Once that's done, you rebuild the whole damned shebang, hoping for no leftover parts.

What I do is sort of the same thing, starting with an overall layout of the entire site, broken down into what's done in each area. On a mine there are pits, processing plants and the like. At some point there is a material takeoff list of the area's needs, with every single bolt accounted for, unless a piece of equipment is built off site, somewhat like a radio for that new car. I don't need to know what is in that radio, only that it does what I want to do and that it fits in the hole size allotted on the drawing. My job is not to design the radio, or the hole, but to make sure the radio is delivered on time and fits into the hole so the car can be assembled and I can listen to Michael Savage rave. You gotta love a guy who hates everyone equally.

Since I was walking into a job where some of the areas were already up and running, I had to backtrack, ferreting out who done what to whom, as it were, to see if things went wonky. Luckily, everything was also uploaded into the computer, making life easier, but I still like to look at drawings I can hold in my hands. Like I love my Kindle, but once in awhile, I just gotta hold a book.

I live by the old proverb:
For want of a nail the shoe was lost.
For want of a shoe the horse was lost.
For want of a horse the rider was lost.
For want of a rider the message was lost.
For want of a message the battle was lost.
For want of a battle the kingdom was lost.
And all for the want of a horseshoe nail.

Since a lost nail leads to a lost battle and thus a kingdom, it is my job to ensure the keys to the Kingdom of Lucifer are kept intact. Boy, if that doesn't have an odd ring, I don't know what does. Hetta Coffey in charge of Lucifer? That's rich. Although there's some folks out there who consider me his spawn.

Anyhow, if something stinks in the kingdom, or is missing, it is my job to find out what and why. So far, I figured all was not well in the kingdom of Luciferville, but no one knew why. The Trob doesn't send me in to babysit anything that's going along just fab; he says there's too much risk factor involved.

So far, all I'd been told is there are cost overruns. Gee, really? In Mexico? Where every single stage of anything has someone out front with his hand in your pocket? What a surprise.

When I estimate any job for Mexico (and to be fair, many other countries) I build in a huge percentage for *mordida*—the bite, or bribe—as well as for theft and bad management. If that sounds uncharitable, sue me. It is a way of life south of the border and anyone who thinks it isn't needs to take Doing Bidness in Mexico 101, better known as How to Steal Gringos Blind and Become a Mexican Hero.

But the Trob knows all that. Sooo, if there are overruns worth worrying about on the Lucifer project, they must be effing humongous. I didn't want to call Wontrobski from the office, nor use the office computer for an email to discuss the details. Besides, he sent me to snoop, not ask him about what. I sighed and went back to seeking out invisible dragons to slay, flying blind and hoping not to get my armor singed.

By Wednesday I'd practically forgotten about that little b&e on my boat despite a dearth of Velveeta. And my morning commute was so much better, thank you. Pedro passed me in a flash daily, but I kept a nice large, slow truck in front of me, running interference from the Pedros coming down the hill. I used that same tactic going home, thereby figuring all that metal in front of me was a little insurance. It was seriously slow going, but I left in plenty of time to get into Santa Rosalia before dusk. I do my best to never drive on Mexican highways after dark, and I sure as hell wasn't planning on challenging the Hill of Hell during non-daylight hours.

It was during this daily twenty-miles-per hour commute that I spotted the dog.

In the middle of nowhere, on a two-lane road with no shoulder to speak of, and few turnouts, this dog was somehow surviving. He looked to be some kind of retriever, fairly young, and not your typical Mex mutt of indefinable lineage that I call canardlys because you can hardly tell what they are.

Because I couldn't stop or, for that matter, even watch him for more than a few seconds, I only caught a glimpse, but the picture of him sitting there skinny, filthy and forsaken, was burned into my brain. How he was managing to survive was a mystery, but one thing was evident; if he didn't get hit by a car he'd starve to death. He crept into my thoughts all day at the office, but as I searched for him on the trip back home, he wasn't there. Hopefully someone had picked him up. At least, that is what I wanted to think.

I decided to visit Jan and Chino, my little whale-watching love dovies, over the coming weekend, so I called to make sure they were up for a visitor.

"Are we going to be home? Surely you jest. We never go anywhere that doesn't involve one of these oversized guppies Chino loves so much."

Uh-oh. Sounds like Dr. Yee buying Jan a couple of luxury fifth-wheels trailers for his lonely stretch of beach didn't do much to soothe Miss Jan's restlessness. "Uh, are the mothers and babies still in the lagoon?"

"They're beginning to leave now, but there are still a few. Wanna go out and pet 'em?"

Pet a whale? I'd have to think about that. I petted a snake once, but it tried to bite me. The snake dude said I must have given it bad vibes. Do whales pick up on stuff like that? Nah. "Yes, I do," I said with far more conviction than I felt.

Saturday night at Camp Chino we sat around the fire drinking beer. I'd driven over on Friday afternoon, even though most everyone else at the mine worked a half day on Saturday. I'd put my foot down on that one. Who ever heard of working weekends, for crying out loud? Not that I still indulged in my former Friday night bar-hopping habit, but still and all, Saturday?

Jan put me in my very own trailer, a forty-foot job with all the amenities. Chino, in an effort to keep the Janster from taking off like one of the sea birds surrounding the camp, had eschewed his grass shack on the beach existence and built what I dubbed the Chino Hilton. Not only were there the two brand new trailers, but a huge generator, and a one thousand gallon water tank. Water was trucked in over more than forty miles of bad road, as was propane for water heaters and cooking. Solar panels ensured lots of power for an inverter (who knew when Jan would need to dry her hair?) and a Hughes network system ensured twenty-four hour television, Internet and telephone.

The neatest things were the toilets. Forbidden from installing a septic tank in the eco park (although they'd been squatting in an outhouse before, so go figure) they'd installed composting toilets that required no water, no plumbing. Chino's bank account had taken a heavy hit, but I guess he figured Jan is worth it.

That Saturday night at Camp Chino, I was so stoked not even a third beer calmed me. I was on an adrenaline high almost better'n sex. I think. It had been awhile.

I'd spent most of the day in a twenty-four foot, open skiff, the ubiquitous *panga* found all over Mexico, communing with creatures three or four times the size of our boat. And because I was with Dr. Chino Yee on a research vessel, I was allowed in areas the poor grunts who paid a fortune to go out commercially were not. Chino first took us looking for Sheba, his favorite whale mom.

Sheba had her calf close by her side and when she spotted Chino, made a beeline for us. Gently nudging the baby—if you can call any twenty foot creature a baby—alongside, she allowed us to pet it. Then, and I swear I saw it, she gave Jan the evil eye, dove, and came up under the panga on her back, gently cradling us on her tummy as she would her baby. Well, gently cradling Chino, anyway. Maybe I'm projecting here, but it looked to me that if Sheba had her druthers, she'd have dumped Jan into the drink and smacked her with her tail. I moved to the other end of the boat, away from Jan, and sent what I thought might be good vibes at Sheba, which wasn't hard because I was experiencing a rush like no other I'd ever felt. Sorry, Jenks.

"…and I think I'll go back to school or something, you know, I could be a marine biologist in a few years, then I could—"

Jan blew a strand of blonde from her eyes and cut me off. "Hetta, for God's sake, cool your jets. You're babbling,"

"And you are...ungrateful. Do you have any idea how lucky you are? People all over the world would kill to be here, living like you and Chino. Hell, they fly in, at great cost I might add, to experience once in a lifetime what you get to do every day."

"Seen one whale, seen 'em all. Hugged one whale, hugged 'em all. Petted —"

My turn to cut her off. "No wonder Sheba hates you. When did you get so cynical?"

"Learned it from you."

"Oh."

We burst into giggles, drawing Chino our way. "What's so funny?" Firelight glistened on his tanned, handsome face. I detected a hint of his Yee ancestor, a shipwreck victim who washed up on Baja's shores over four hundred years ago. Jan stood to get another beer or three and he pulled her to him. They made for a stunning pair. He was a couple of inches taller than Jan's five-eleven and his dark looks complimented those of my Meg Ryan look-alike friend.

She squirmed away and headed for the fridge. Chino flopped down next to me and sighed deeply. Oh, dear.

Hoping to lighten his glumness, I said, "You have a truly wonderful place here, Chino. So beautiful. And what a great job you have. No bad guys, only nature. No offices, time clocks, alarm clocks. I love it."

"Were that Jan did." He spoke English with a slight British accent, a result of his UK education. Chino is a genius who, still in his mid-twenties, holds two doctorates in what I call, Animal Stuff. Along with his degrees, his dedication to onsite studies and a passion for marine life have earned him international recognition. His funding, less than generous because he refuses to glad hand and kiss ass, allows him to live in harmony with the whales, but Jan? Not so much. I feel a little guilty that I played a large part in his meeting Jan, because their relationship is plumb doomed for several reasons, not the least of which is the age difference.

It was my turn to sigh. "You know, Chino, sometimes even people who love and respect each other aren't totally compatible. I know that sounds a little odd, but both Jan and I need more…responsibility. We've been single for a long time. Well, forever. We've fought the battle to succeed in our own careers and giving that up ain't all that easy."

"You mean Jan needs a job?"

I grinned. "That would be a start. Making beds and flippin' torillas ain't her style."

He finished his beer. "Maybe I need to spend more time with her. I am getting a new assistant next week, so with another marine biologist on board I might be able to get away, take Jan on trips. She never said—"

Jan grabbed his empty and shoved a full bottle in his hand, "Hey! Am I the *she* of whom you are speaking?"

I barked a laugh. "Dang, Chino, we can't talk about *her* anymore. She's here."

Chapter 7

Old sailors never die, they just smell that
way.

Jan packed a bag and rode out of camp with
me on Monday morning.

Chino waved a little forlornly as we drove
away, even though the plan was for him to pick her
up at my boat in Santa Rosalia on Wednesday, after
he fetched his new assistant from the Santa Rosalia
airport. She'd be gone only a few days, but I think he
feared Jan would hop a plane out of Dodge before he
could retrieve her.

Seeing the worried Chino in the rearview
mirror, I told Jan, "You're gonna have to do
something about this Chino thing. The way you're

messin' with him isn't right, and not good for either of you."

"Hetta Coffey giving advice on relationships?" she scoffed. "That's rich."

I could have scoffed back, setting us up for a little dustup. Over the years we've had our moments, like sisters do, but sometimes no comeback is the best comeback of all. Besides, the washboard road, one of the worst I'd ever been on, didn't lend itself to conversation. I concentrated on keeping us from skittering off the road, and my teeth from cracking each other. My Ford Ranger pickup is built for roads like this, but the tight suspension is hell on the butt and gut. Jan stared out the window for the next hour, while I tried missing the worst ruts. It is no wonder Jan and Chino rarely go into town.

The asphalt, when we hit Mex 1 over an hour later, felt like Red Velvet cake does on the tongue. I decided to lighten the mood and punched on the stereo, finding "All the girls" with Willie Nelson and Julio Iglesias. This is one of my and Jan's favorite duets, and we've memorized all the words. I whanged the Willie parts, she crooned with Julio, then we harmonized. Where they sung about *girls*, we loudly overrode them with *boys*. Someone else's wife became someone else's strife. We just crack ourselves up.

When the song ended Jan punched down the sound. "You're right. I am messin' with Chino and I hate myself for it. What is wrong with me?"

"I don't have time to answer that. It's only another hour to the jobsite."

"Smartass."

"So if you don't know what's wrong in Chinoville, how can you fix it? I mean, other than acting right, which we both know ain't gonna happen so long as you're feeling sorry for yourself." I actually was feeling sorry for Chino. He is an honorable, hardworking man who adores Jan. The cad.

"I think I'm depressed. And since I've never been depressed before, I don't know what it feels like, but if this is it, I don't want it."

"There're pills for that."

"I don't wanna take pills, I want to be happy, not medicated."

"Medicated always works for me. Okay, tell me what's really bugging you."

"Thank you, Doctor Coffey. Here's the deal. I love Chino, but not enough to live in a fish camp the rest of my life. I wish I liked whales and all that marine stuff, but I don't. Hell, I don't even like salt water. I hate to snorkel, much less scuba dive. I'm such a mess the poor guy would be better off with *you*."

"Hey, watch it."

"You know what I mean. You like all that stuff."

"Yes, I do. Look, he's done everything he can to make you comfortable, far as I can see. Those new living quarters of yours are a sight better than many apartments we've lived in. And the setting! Falling asleep at night to the sound of waves that don't even come out of a machine. What's not to like?"

"Hetta, have you ever had to shake sand out of your sheets every night?"

"Uh, no."

"Well, let me tell you, it's hard to get real romantic with grit *every*where. We built an outdoor rinse down shower and that helps some, but sand gets *every*where anyhow. And I do mean *every*where."

"Okay, that's way too much information. Let's talk about something else."

"How about your birthday?"

"How about you walk back home from here?"

My birthday.

It had to happen, of course, considering the alternative.

I read an article about women's fears of aging, and in a nutshell we are terrified of being old, broke and alone.

The old thing? With me, it's not vanity. As a matter of fact, I've always considered not being beautiful a good thing, having witnessed women who are, and what aging does to their egos.

Broke? I'm not the best money manager in the world, but it's not like I'll end up a Walmart greeter. I do have skills.

Alone? Been there most of my life.

So what is it about turning f-f-f...not in my thirties anymore that has me grabbing for the Pepto-Bismol bottle? I do know that anyone who tells you that fort...uh, over thirty, is the new twenty is full of refrieds, but that's certainly nothing to obsess over. My twenties sucked.

While surfing the Internet one evening, I found one of those How Long Will You Live Q & A things. I lied about my alcohol use and weight and found I'd live approximately forty-five more years. I did the quiz again, this time being as truthful as I am capable of, and lost three years. Heck, eating and drinking what I wanted and only losing three years off the end of eighty someodd years didn't sound all that bad. Of course, that same study nailed my age group with a 0.14% chance of dying this year, but the way my life has been going lately that number might be a tad low.

I hoped I'd upped the odds some by no longer riding with Pedro to work.

Gloom settled in my pickup cab as Jan and I headed for Lucifer, wrestling with our own personal devils.

As always happens when Jan makes an appearance, my pickup and office saw a sudden spike of interest from the male population. I took her around for intros, and even the Chicano purchasing manager I'd taken such a dislike to turned on the charm. I sometimes wonder why I hang out with her.

When she handed her my keys so she could continue on to the boat, she said, "Gee, Hetta, that Ozzie isn't nearly so bad as you told me."

"Here, let me wipe his drool off your chest."

"Silly. Okay, what time will you get back to the boat? I'll cook dinner. Anything in the freezer you want?"

"I should be there by five. How about some donkey dick?"

"Perfect.

I caught a ride back to the boat with Safety instead of Pedro. That .014% thing, you know.

While he wound down Hell Hill, I kept an eye peeled for the dog I'd seen stranded up there. What I'd do if I did see the poor thing, I didn't know. There was no place to stop and he'd probably bolt off the cliff if I tried an approach. We never saw him, but his plight haunted me. I sincerely hoped someone had picked him up.

Safety, for the first time, invited himself to my boat for a drink. What a surprise. We were on our second beer when John, a guy I hardly knew from work, showed. Another first. Said he had to check on the company fishing boat, *Lucifer*, on the dock across from me, but he never went over there. Before dinnertime, two more guys stopped by to check on *Lucifer*.

My, my, such a suddenly popular boat, that *Lucifer*.

Finally shooing off Jan's fan club, we grilled a whole Sonora beef filet (affectionately called donkey dicks by the Gringos) she'd stuffed with bacon and mushrooms. She'd also gone into town for fresh greens and ice cream. Maybe *I'll* marry her and put Chino out of his misery.

Sitting out on the covered aft deck, or sunroom as I call it, we finished our wine while watching pangas streak from the harbor in quest of fish and squid, or maybe a little drug running on the side.

Jan, who was unusually quiet, turned to me with tears in her eyes. "At one point I'll be in my seventies and he'll be in his fifties."

"Chino's only twelve years younger than you, how do you figure that?"

Ever the bean counter, she said, "He's actually eleven and a half years younger, but his birthday comes after mine. I'll turn seventy and he'll still be only fifty-nine."

And I thought I had an age obsession thing going. "Which is almost sixty. You're somehow turning a few days into twenty years? I think I'll get a new accountant."

"Hey, you're not the only one worrying about turning for—"

"Stop! This birthday is my crisis, dang it, and don't you horn in on it!"

For some reason we found this hilarious. Or maybe it was the wine.

Which, had we known what the evening held in store, we might have cut back on a smidgen.

Chapter 8

TAKEN ABACK (Nautical term): Stopped
by a sudden shift of wind; surprised by a discovery

Back when Jenks designed my boat's security
system he wanted me to sleep well at night, secure in
the knowledge that if anyone came aboard, I'd know
it. I have two choices for being alerted: a raucous
claxon mounted on the flying bridge and guaranteed
to wake the dead, or a more subtle blinking light in
both the main saloon and my master cabin.

When Jan and I turned in, I set the blinker
system. I am a light sleeper and a flashing light will
usually wake me, even after a bunch of wine.
Besides, if the light didn't do the job in thirty
seconds, a beeper sounded, growing louder every
fifteen seconds.

The light started flashing at two AM,
according to the senorita's belly. At first I thought
my nemesis, *el mapache*, was back, but then

remembered I hadn't set the outside motion sensors. That meant someone was inside the boat. Had Jan needed a glass of water and forgotten to disable the sensor in the main saloon? I grabbed my handy dandy flare gun and headed for my cabin door, which I had not set the deadbolt on because I had company. Crap.

Throwing open the cabin door I went into defense mode. I stepped back so I wouldn't be highlighted by the flashing light behind me and waited. Nothing happened, so I yelled, "Jan, is that you in the saloon?"

Nada.

"Okay, then, whoever you are, I'm armed and I will shoot." Like I'm gonna fire off a flare gun in my boat? Oh, well, it sounded good.

Nada.

I backed into my cabin and hit the remote to turn off the flashing light in my cabin, but left the one on in the main saloon. Once again I waited, but my patience was running low. I was on the verge of rushing out when I heard a loud, "Oof," and a thump. Time was up.

Holding the flare gun as though it were my .9mm Springfield XDM (oh, that it were!) I vaulted up the three steps leading to the main saloon as though storming Normandy.

Catching movement by the settee, I crouched and crept forward.

"Help!" a male voice cried.

Help?

"Got the bastard," Jan yelled. "Where the hell are you, Hetta?"

I flipped on the cabin lights. Jan had someone flat out on his stomach, with his arms pulled behind him at an odd angle. She sat on his butt, her feet planted firmly on his head, and she'd somehow managed to clutch his wrists and was shoving them at what looked like a seriously painful angle using her feet for leverage against his skull. Whoever the poor dude was, I sort of felt sorry for him.

"Whatcha got there, Jan?"

"Ain't no stinkin' raccoon, but he is kinda cute. Ya wanna shoot him?"

"I'd love to, but there's my carpet to consider." I nudged him with the barrel of the flare gun for effect. "Okay guy, who are you and what do you want?"

Our intruder's face was buried in the carpet, so his answer was muffled.

"I can't heeear you."

Jan roughly wrenched his neck to one side with her feet.

"Oowww!"

"You speak English?" Jan asked.

He didn't answer, so she jammed his face back into the carpet. "Shy, I guess."

"Hookay, then, we'll do this the hard way." Unwilling to free him from Jan's power hold, I fetched a piece of line from the back deck, we trussed him up proper-like and rolled him onto his side. He squealed like a stuck hawg.

While our captive gasped for air and spit carpet threads, I gave Jan a pat on the back.

"Where'd you learn that nifty move? You had him good."

"Goat roping in high school. Comes in handy." She poked him in his unprotected gut, eliciting a loud gasp. "You breathing yet, buddy?"

"*Merde*," he gasped.

"*Merde*?" I repeated. "You French?"

"*Oui.*"

"Well then, today's your lucky day, Mon Sewer. Hetta parlays French."

"I. Speak. English."

"Even luckier," I told him, "so do we. Wanna tell us why you broke into my damned boat? And if it was you who ate my Velveeta cheese, I'm gonna turn you in to Larousse Gastronomique. The French will surely revoke your citizenship for such a gastronomical infraction."

Jan and I found this worthy of a giggle. I can be so clever at times.

"Well?" I nudged him with my foot, very near his nuts.

"Please, I didn't mean any harm. I didn't know you had returned. I was hungry."

I looked at the guy a little closer. He spoke English like an American, said he was French? When a tear rolled down his cheek, my anger melted. Well, almost. There *was* that food stealing thing.

"We're gonna untie your feet and get you into a chair. Don't do anything stupid, okay? Oh, wait, you already did."

Jan gave me an appreciative grin. We shuffled him to a chair, tied him in across his chest and legs, then loosened his wrists. He moved his arms slowly forward and held them out for retying, but I waved them down. "That won't be necessary. For now."

"Could I please have some water?" he croaked.

"Water, coming up." Jan went to the fridge for a small plastic bottle of purified water and handed to him. He drank gratefully, brushed a blondish lock of hair from his face and squinted at us. "I lost my glasses."

"That's okay, you don't need to see, you need to talk, so start. I have to work in a few hours and have to decide what to do with you. Jan here would prefer, I'm sure, to truss you up like a hawg again and dump you overboard, but this being a piece of very expensive, high-tensile-strength line I'd just as soon not waste it on some punk."

"You women are amazing," he said with a shake of his head.

"Oh, you have no idea. So you say you came aboard looking for food? How'd you open the cabin door?"

"Your lock is cheap. I opened it with a my fingernail clipper."

"Isn't there food anywhere else in Santa Rosalia, for heaven's sake? Why my boat?"

"I was here on the dock anyway. I thought this boat was still empty."

"*Still*, huh? So it *was* you who snarfed my Velveeta? That alone is a hanging offense in my book."

"It wasn't very good."

"Okay, that's it. Overboard you go, hot shot."

He threw his hands in the air. "It was a joke. I will work for the food, I need a place to stay until...." He shrugged.

"Until what?"

He hung his head. "I am in trouble and I need help. I don't know where to go, or what to do. I have money in my room, but I cannot go there. People are trying to kill me. People," he looked at Jan, "*besides* you."

"You have any ID?"

"No. Lost."

"What's your name?"

"Russell."

"That ain't French."

"My father is American."

"And you're French?"

"I lied. I'm actually Mexican."

"Russell ain't Mexican, either. Get the old line, Jan. He's going overboard."

"No! Okay, my name is Rosario Pardo."

*Oh no, this can*not *be happening.* "Rosario Pardo?"

"Yes, I used to work at Lucifer Mine and they tried to kill me. I came here because I know you were sent to find who was stealing money. I can help you."

Oh, crap. Now I really wanted to toss him in the drink, and maybe this time it would take.

Jenks had ordered me to stay out of trouble and here it was: A dead guy, in living color.

Chapter 9

THREE SHEETS TO THE WIND (Nautical
term): A reference to the sheets (ropes) of a sail
becoming loosened, rendering the sail useless
(drunk)

I was running a tad behind schedule when I
left Jan and the late Rosario Pardo on the boat. It had
been a very long night, I had a lot to think about, and
the drive to the jobsite gave me time to ponder.
What, in the form of a young Mexican man, had
stumbled into my life here?

Rosario's story had a ring of truth, although I
have been lied to so much over the years—and lied
so much myself—maybe I'm not the best judge when
it comes to verisimilitude. However, his sincerity
convinced both Jan and me that he was the real deal.
He seemed genuinely terrified and if his story was
true, with just cause.

Once at my desk, I embarked upon some
serious delving into Rosario's story. While I was

leaning toward believing him, a gal cannot be too careful. Matter of fact, Jan still had him tied to a chair, waiting to hear back from me before releasing him. I told her I'd email or call when I'd checked him out, so until I knew more he would remain her prisoner. Not that he seemed to mind. Jan's captives never do.

Rosario had given me all the information I needed to hack into the company personnel files so I could check on his identity and that alone gave him major Brownie points in my book. We snoops appreciate one another.

Within minutes I'd read his file and seen the photo they'd taken for his company ID. His thick light-brown hair had that sharp barbered look favored by Mexican businessmen and serious hazel eyes stared into the camera from behind nerdy thick-rimmed glasses. I knew he was at least six-one which, along with his coloring set him apart from the average Mexican office workers I'd met. There was also no hint of the macho smirk most of them seemed to have been born with. The man in the photo and Rosario were one and the same.

I fired a short cryptic email off to Jan: Subject: Him. Okay to let go.

We'd decided that, for now, we'd let Rosario hide out on *Raymond Johnson* until we figured out what to do with him, and she was charged with documenting his story for us. Once she'd sent it to me, I'd know where to start digging without raising suspicion. *Whose* suspicion remained a big question.

One thing was certain; Rosario thought he was safely putting his life in my hands. Silly bugger.

Safety dropped by with a cup of coffee in hand, thanked me for the beers the night before and invited me to dinner. *Us* to dinner. I told him *us* had other plans. He took it fairly well, but I knew as long as Jan was around, he'd be as well. She draws men like I do trouble. Together we constitute a veritable man-trouble sisterhood.

Antsy while waiting to hear from Jan, it was all but impossible to concentrate on anything work related. I spent time emailing almost everyone I knew, telling them about Chino's whale camp, what Jan was up to, how my job was going and everything except the fact that I was harboring an attempted murder victim on my boat. Not that anyone would be surprised.

If Rosario was telling the truth, what he'd told us so far painted an ugly scenario and if someone, or several someones, tried to kill him, they worked right here on site. He was a little foggy on details after we nailed him, so I hoped when not under threat of being keel hauled he could get his story straight.

Jan's email, when it finally arrived, had a document attached and when I opened it it was apparent that Jan had taken my instruction to begin at the beginning a little too literally. Jan has aspirations of one day becoming a *novelista,* which made her report read much more like the prologue to a romance novel than the interrogation I wanted.

Rosario's Life
by Jan Sims.

I groaned.

Rosario wants to be, no *longs* to be, a nerd. A geek.

Or, as they say in East LA, a beanerd.

Not a *nerdo*, *teto*, *tetaso*, or *raton de biblioteca*—although being called a library rat wasn't all that offensive to him, as it was true—as they taunted in Mexico, but an American nerd like Bill Gates or Steve Jobs, his heroes. Like the gamers he met on the Internet. Nerds who were respected for their skills, not mocked.

To fulfill his dream, he knew he had to cross the United States border. Not slink across in the night, although it might come to that, but hopefully get there legally. No easy task for an underpaid office worker, but he'd hit what he thought was pay dirt, his big chance to make a giant step in the right direction. Lady Luck had landed in his lap, or more correctly, his lap*top*.

When, after working at low-level jobs in Mexico City he'd landed the entry-level clerical position at Mina Lucifer he was elated, for even though this was less than a promotion, he knew it was his shot to shine. He was also aware he had to be careful to conceal his dreams, and special skills, from his fellow Mexican workers. It was the American and Canadian supervisors he wanted to make an impression on, for it was with them he might get that all important passport to nerd-dom.

Finally, after months of stultifying drudgery—

I rolled my eyes, then gave them a rub. Stultifying drudgery? How about stultifying prose? I forced myself to continue reading.

—crap work any idiot could handle, had paid off. Not, of course, his forty-five hour a week for minimum payday job, but the titillating unpaid hours he volunteered for. Little by little, without drawing undue attention to himself, the office grunt had endeared himself by taking on others' workloads, learning every aspect of everyone else's job. Not that he couldn't handle those mundane tasks with his eyes closed, but he tried not to make that fact too obvious.

His fellow workers had no problem dumping their work on Rosario, because, after all, they knew he had no life. What they didn't know was that having full access to fast computers and unlimited Internet in the evening hours was a hacker's dream and a gamer's paradise. He was an expert at both, and they were his ticket to America. So while others snoozed at the man camp, Rosario burned the midnight ether.

Of course, no one had asked him to cyberpunk his way into the company systems, because no one knew he could. It was overhearing concerns of financial problems that set him on a personal mission to discover why unexplained costs were threatening layoffs and he was afraid he would be first on the list. This was *his* project. His ticket out of Mexico.

His cyber sleuthing had paid off. He was sure he was on his way! He experienced a moment of sadness that threatened his joy of accomplishment, for he yearned to share his news with someone, anyone. His mother had died months before he got this coveted position, one he knew would make her proud and reward her years of hard struggles to get him through college. His only other known relative, an uncle who'd sneaked across the border years before, also died, but not before sending monthly checks back to his only sister so Rosario could attend private schools. It was to his mother and uncle's credit that he wasn't doomed to a dismal future in Mexico.

He only wished they had shared their secret with him before they both passed on.

Finding that stack of letters when he cleaned out his mother's small house sent him into shock. The father he was told died, hadn't. Or at least not when he was told he did. Who knew now? Turns out Rosario is the result of the ages-old story, this one set in a steamy Puerto Vallartan summer, with even steamier teenaged hanky panky between a Gringo surfer dude and a beautiful waitress. He'd loaded a faded photo of the lovebirds in front of the beachbum bar onto his screen saver as a daily reminder of his mission.

The letters, reading much like the Telenovellas, those Mexican soap operas his mother was so fond of—

And this tale doesn't? I made a silent vow to revoke Jan's poetic license.

— wove a tale of a disowned daughter and a devoted brother who fled Mexico so he could support her. His uncle's letters at first pleaded with Rosario's mother to reveal the father's name so maybe he could find him, but she refused. Now she was dead, but her son finally knew his father's name: Russell Madadhan. A Google search coughed up the information that Russell in Spanish is Rosario, and Madadhan was an old Celtic name, and quite unusual.

Finding out he was half-Gringo came as a surprise, but it shouldn't have; he had never felt, well, totally Mexican. But when he'd queried his mother about his hazel eyes, light hair color and above average height, she'd blown him off with some cock-and-bull story about his Conquistador ancestors. Thanks to his uncle's generosity, he'd studied Mexican and World History at the American School he attended in Mexico City. During field trips to museums, he'd seen paintings of Spaniards with blue eyes and red or blonde hair, but he'd also studied Biology, and the idea of those genes surfacing four hundred years later was a stretch.

And to his credit, Rosario even had to chuckle at his mother's sense of humor when naming him: Rosario (Russell in English) Hidalgo (son of someone in Spanish) Pardo.

His mother and uncle had spent every bit of money they could scrape together on Rosario's education: Alliance Française for French, and twelve years at American Schools, where his classmates hailed from all over the world. He figured he was the poorest kid there. When his uncle died and even that money disappeared, he had already finished high school and landed a two-year scholarship to the University of Mexico. There he earned an Associate Degree in Business, but after that there simply was no more money for continuing.

His mother fell ill and he needed a job to support her for a change. He worked as a clerk in a local government office by day, gamed and surfed the Net at night, and basically stagnated until two things happened: His mother died, and the mine job presented itself.

Now, on the very brink of achieving the first step towards his dream, Rosario tempered the elation of his cyber sleuthing results with the knowledge that his hacking could either launch his career or get him fired, depending on with whom he shared his find. His immediate supervisor was too low on the organization chart, and a Mexican. His boss's boss was a Chicano and everyone knew *they* couldn't be trusted.

So he'd waited, gathering even more information, making flow charts with arrows until his eyes crossed. It was a complicated scheme and one that took more than just one level of conspiracy. He still didn't know who was involved, but he did have suspicions. As the American cop shows say, follow the money, so he did. What he needed though, was someone in his corner he could trust.

Finally, he got the break he'd been waiting for when the VHF radio on the company fishing boat died. Quite naturally it was he, the office geek with no life, called upon to fix it on a Saturday night. He was replacing some corroded wires when a mine supervisor showed up on the boat, someone he knew, liked and trusted, or least he trusted more than most.

Nerves a-jangle—

My nerves were a-jangle by now. Jan, get on with the story!

—Rosario oh, so casually broached the subject of cost overruns and layoffs. He didn't look up, but concentrated on twisting a wire on the radio connector. The supervisor said nothing at first, so Rosario assumed he was surprised that an office grunt knew anything at all about the subject, or maybe figured it inappropriate to talk of such things with such a lowly employee, but a minute later he heard a pop, and the man shoved a Tecate in his hand.

"Take a break. Let's have a beer."

Rosario thought he'd melt into a puddle of relief right on the spot.

I was considering a puddle of my own about now.

He turned, smiled, and raised his bottle as if drinking beer with one of the bosses was all in a day's work. "*Salud.*"

"Here's mud in your eye."

Rosario had no idea what that meant, but he'd seen it in movies and took it as a good sign. He timidly sipped the first beer he'd had in his entire life. It tasted bitter, but he held the smile.

The supervisor waved him to a tiny dinette and sat across the table from him. He complimented Rosario on his excellent English, began asking questions like, where he came from, where he went to school, and things no one else seemed to care about. Aglow with beer and gratitude, he told the supervisor of his life.

I hope, for the supervisor's sake, he'd done it with less mush and pulp than Miss Jan's version.

Many beers later they were best buds and the conversation turned to work. Little by little he revealed his findings about funds gone missing, but even verging on drunk he kept his hacking skills to himself, preferring to let the man think he'd done his grunt work by perusing paper files. Why, he didn't know, but somewhere in his Tecate-soaked brain a faint alarm sounded a warning to keep something back.

Rosario was taking a gulp of beer when his nose went numb. Seconds later he was suddenly stuporous—

Someone, please, just shoot me. Better yet, shoot Jan lest she be unleashed upon an unsuspecting reading public someday.

—unable to talk, much less walk. He curled up on the settee and passed out.

The last thing he remembers as he rolled into a fetal position was the smiling supervisor finishing off his own beer and tipping the bottle in his direction.

He now wondered if he hadn't been gazing into the face of pure evil.

The End

The End?

A little shriek escaped my lips.

Okay, I was going to get in my pickup, drive to the boat and strangle my best friend. Right then and there.

Which supervisor? Who sent Rosario to fix the boat radio? I didn't want a friggin' novella, I wanted facts.

Actually, I wanted a cold beer, but a fact or two would suffice.

Chapter 10

LOOSE CANNON (Nautical term): A piece of artillery that is not secure and therefore can cause damage or injury when it rolls on its wheels from the ship's movement or from its recoil after being fired (out of control or unpredictable).
In this case, my life?

"You okay?" Safety asked from behind me.

Yikes! I quickly hit the DELETE key and swiveled my chair to face him, hoping he hadn't caught a glimpse of Jan's budding and annoying novel. "Yeah, I'm fine. Why?"

"You yelled or something."

"Oh, that. I was cussing my computer, which I do a lot. Swearing at inanimate objects can be somewhat cathartic."

"Somewhat like ex-lax?"

I laughed. One thing I appreciate is someone who knows the multiple meanings for words and uses them in humor. "Good one. There's a thought; ex-lax as a cure for operator malfunction."

"Let me know if it works."

"Not."

"You need a ride to work tomorrow? I can pick you up if you want to leave your pickup for Jan."

"That'll work. Chino's picking her up sometime on Wednesday, so I'll drive myself in that day."

"This Chino her boyfriend?"

"Yes. *Doctor* Brigido Yee." I then added, "The world-famous marine biologist." Okay, so I laid it on a little thick there, but nothing bursts a guy's crush-bubble like some seriously potent-sounding competition. "He has to pick up his new assistant at the airport Wednesday morning, then he'll collect Jan and take her home."

"Oh."

Safety's little "Oh," spoke volumes of dejection.

My office needed rearranging if I didn't want *my* bidness to be everyone else's.

The way it was, my back and therefore my computer screen were turned toward the door, making me unable to see people behind me and allowing them to read my screen. Shutting the door was out of the question because there was no room for it to swing. It had to go.

I fetched a small tool chest from my pickup and removed the door. Laura, after watching me almost flattened by the unhinged and unwieldy door, rushed to my aid and helped me drag it outside.

After I changed the desk's direction, I got lucky, for the snake's nest of cords all reached their plugs and connections. The downside was I now only had about one foot of clearance to enter my office. Sucking it all in and holding my breath helped a little, but losing ten pounds would do wonders. However, I could squeeze in and slide into my chair. I'd accomplished my goal of deterring inquisitive eyes, but sincerely hoped I didn't experience any cathartic intestinal emergencies, because exiting my office in a hurry would be just about impossible. That thought, of course, sent me scurrying to the *Mujeres* room as a safety measure.

I rechecked my email for an update from Jan, maybe with some actual facts gleaned from Rosario, but *nada*. Trying to work remained a bust. I was too distracted by this unfortunate twist on what I thought was going to be a relatively mundane job. Waiting for Jan to fill me in was driving me nuts. I sat, glaring at the screen, willing it to *do* something.

Hearing the welcome ding announcing an incoming email made me smile and I was only slightly disappointed to see it was from my veterinarian buddy, Craig, in Bisbee, Arizona.

Doctor Craig Washington and I had been friends back in the Bay Area, when he was a hundred pounds heavier. Craig and I have a lot in common; we both love dogs, struggle with our weight and have a lousy history with men.

One would think, what with Craig being highly successful monetarily as well as tall, black and gay, he'd have been a rock star in the San Francisco Bay Area, but he was also extremely overweight, insecure, and gentle natured, leaving him prey for opportunists who used his bank account and broke his heart. His nickname, Craigosaurus, didn't help out in the self-esteem department. I never called him that. I know about weight.

Finally when one of these little exploitive pieces of ca-ca he dated went too far and demanded Craig buy him a snazzy red Porsche, he dumped both his crappy old van and crappy old boyfriend and kept the sports car for himself. He then hired a personal trainer—the one I had also hired, but refused to mind—did what she told him to (what a concept!) and dumped a hundred pounds. Now divested of both that little French twerp of a boyfriend and sporting a new look, he also decided he worked too hard and needed a change.

While visiting with me at the golf course home I'd rented in Arizona, he'd been attracted to a cowboy who hung out at the clubhouse bar. When I left for Mexico, I still had time on my lease so Craig stayed on while the miner's shack he bought in Historic Bisbee was renovated. He also took up golf.

Now the original house he renovated is rented out, and although still deep in the closet, he and his new pardner own a successful cattle ranch, a fleet of mobile vet clinics, and a large animal practice serving ranches on both sides of the border.

He has traded in the Porsche—the one Frenchie the Freeloader wanted—and bought a diesel dually pickup the size of Texas. His wardrobe now comes from the local Feed, Seed and Fertilizer store. His partner, Roger, is a fourth generation Arizona rancher. Neither man is anxious to openly share their relationship with their very conservative families. They still do not share quarters, per se, but instead have two separate houses on the same bajillion acres. To see them together, few would guess they were anything other than good old boys—albeit one of them being a *black* good old boy—sharing a business partnership and, on occasion, a beer or two at the golf club.

Craig and I also share an address, as I established a residency in Arizona while I was working there. I mean, California made two of my favorite guns illegal, for crying out loud. I should have sued for alienation of affection.

My car is registered at Craig's house and my snail mail goes to his post office box. Jan is also a paper resident, so for all practical purposes, Craig and Hetta and Roger and Jan all live happily on the ranch together.

Craig's email read: Need to talk, ASAP. SKYPE ME!

Jeez, I hate emails like that. I couldn't Skype him until after work from the boat. Was I doomed to sit here all day, unable to concentrate on work, waiting for Jan to email another inane missive and obsessing over what Craig, who is not one to use terms like "as soon as possible" loosely had to tell me?

Patience not being one of my strong suits, I let out another little screech and pulled my hair, but this time Safety ignored me.

By noon my nerves were frayed.

I had had one glass of wine too many the night before, hadn't gotten enough sleep, and left Jan with a complete stranger, an admitted cheese thief, alone on my boat. It was all too much to take sitting in my office. I decided to pack it in.

Bert Melton, my big boss, was out of the office for the day so I figured I'd let Ozzie, the Chicano purchasing prick, know I was going AWOL. Not that I really needed anyone's leave to leave, but it seemed the right thing to do. Unwilling to take a chance on Ozzie pissing me off, since I was already in a evil mood, I decided to save his life and send him an email.

Before I headed out, I raided the fridge in the break room, found a couple of sandwiches I hadn't eaten and snitched what looked like some burritos. I unwrapped them all, put them into a paper bag and set it on the passenger seat, just in case I spotted that dog again. The best I could hope for, since there were so few turnouts, was to toss the poor thing some food.

Halfway down Hell Hill, there he was, hugging a small space on the edge of a blind corner, but at least there was no one behind me. I hit the brakes and moved into the oncoming lane. Rolling down my window, I had one hand on the steering wheel and was tossing out the bag when an air horn blast ricocheted off the cliffs. A humongous Kenworth logo loomed in my windshield, but luckily he was moving at a snail's pace uphill so I was able to regain my lane before becoming a splat on his bug screen. In my review mirror I caught a glimpse of the dog demolishing bag and all. Tomorrow, with

Safety driving, maybe I could get water to him, as well.

"Looocy, I'm home," I yelled in my best Ricky Ricardo/Desi Arnaz accent as I climbed aboard *Raymond Johnson*.

"Oh, goodie. You're just in time, we're making lunch,."

Jan had untied Rosario and they stood side by side at my galley counter.

Rosario wore my favorite chenille bathrobe, the one with cowgirls lassoing calves.

"Is there something I need to know here?" I asked, hoping Jan hadn't gone robbing cradles again.

Rosario pulled the robe tighter around his body and gave me a silly grin. "Jan washed my clothes and they are still in the marina dryer."

"Yep," Jan added, "if he's gonna live here he has to smell better."

"We need to talk about that *living here* thing, but right now I have to call Craig. Sounds like something's up."

I fired up Skype and caught Craig in his office. *Who wears a cowboy hat at his desk*? I asked myself, but I had to admit he looked very cowboyerly. His face is a smidge off homely, but his big droopy eyes and a keen resemblance to his redbone hound, Coondoggie, give him an endearing look. All in all, Craig is a large, tall, black, handsome dude and, were he not gay, women would fawn. Actually they fawn anyway, every one of them wanting this big old Teddy bear in their—and their animal's—life.

"Hetta, you're looking well."

"And you are looking...Western. It suits you."

"So, I guess you want to know what I emailed about."

"Yep."

He pulled a piece of paper from his desk drawer and held it up to the camera. I squinted and rummaged in my desk drawer for a pair of cheaters. "Hold still, Craig, I can't read it. What is it?"

"You have been served."

"What? Why? Who?"

"You forgot How."

Jan and Rosario had drifted over to see what I was screeching about.

"Looks legally to me," Jan said.

Craig lowered the paper and nodded. "Exactly."

"Legally? What kind of word is that? What is it?" I wanted to know.

"Right now, all they want is a deposition."

"They? Who, they? Deposition? Isn't that some kind of thing they do before they lock you up or something?"

"It's a questionnaire, of sorts, I guess. Anyhow, my partner, Roger, talked to his cousin the local district attorney and says you can do it over the phone since you are out of the country. For now. You answer the questions. Give your side of the story."

Okay, this was getting annoying and Craig seemed to be enjoying it way too much. "What story?" I practically screamed.

I guess he figured he'd monkeyed around with me enough. "It seems someone is considering filing a suit against you."

"What the hell for?"

Craig grinned way too wide and leaned into the camera. "A hate crime."

Jan guffawed behind me, and Craig finally gave in and laughed out loud. Jan said, "That makes sense, Hetta hates everybody."

"I do not. I don't hate you, but if you keep laughing I'll work on it."

Rosario asked, from over my shoulder, "What is a hate crime?"

Craig squinted. "Who is that behind you, Hetta? I kinda like his get up. Is that chenille?"

"You're taken, remember? Anyhow, don't pay him any attention. He's dead."

Craig shook his head. "If you say so."

I took a long, ragged breath. "Who filed this ridiculous thing?"

"One Muhammed Ali. Ring any bells?"

"The boxer? I never even met him!"

"Oh, not *that* Muhammed Ali. This one's had a name change. Used to be Gustavo Espinosa, a.k.a. 'Flaco'. Now is your bell ringing?"

Jan giggled. "Hetta, isn't that the gangbanger you shot in the nuts with a load of bacon rind?"

Chapter 11

GO BY THE BOARD (Nautical term):
Something lost overboard, or abandoned.

"Let me see if I have this right, Craig. That skanky rat's rump who broke into *my* house and threatened Jan and me with a knife is suing *me*? Yeah, well, you tell him this, will you? That the lock he broke to get into my house? It was on the door for *his* protection, not mine!"

"I'll see he gets the message."

"And what is this hate crime thing? Can he do that?"

"I guess he's trying."

"Well, I do hate him 'cuz he scared us, but what about that Castle Law? They have that in

Arizona. You know, the right to defend your Castle?"

"Yep, but you haven't heard the best part."

"I can hardly wait."

"*Why* he's trying to sue you."

Jan and Rosario leaned into the screen. "Why?" they said in unison. I elbowed both of them, but they didn't move an inch.

Craig grinned from ear to ear. "Because, Hetta, you sent him to jail where he has embraced Allah, but since you defiled his body with embedded pig parts, he cannot achieve heaven."

Jan chewed on her tuna sandwich, desperately trying, without much success, to camouflage her glee behind the bread. A hiccup of laughter escaped, along with a shower of crumbs.

"You know, Miz Jan, if you choke on that sammich I shall not render the Heimlich maneuver upon your sorry ass."

Rosario, who was still wearing my bathrobe, bunched his fists near his rib cage where one would, if one were so inclined, eject a piece of sandwich. "No, not the bottom, but to clear the windpipe. I will do it. I took a safety course when I swam for my high school team."

My guess is he was just itching to get Miz Jan in a Heimlich hug. I gave him the evil eye. "You want to get tied up again?"

He slid down in his chair and clammed up.

"Oh, come on, Hetta," Jan said. "Ya gotta admit this lawsuit thing is a hoot."

"Yeah? So why am I not hooting all to hell?"

"You will. I'll get us some wine."

We settled in for a glass of red and my patience level smoothed somewhat. I listened as Rosario basically retold me the same story as Jan's flowery version. I wanted to hear it in his own words, sans Jan Austen's embellishments. While I was anxious to get to the details, I bided my time until he hit the water, so to speak.

"So you passed out on the company boat and the next thing you know you're floating in the Sea of Cortez?"

"Yes. It was very dark and I was so scared."

"Where was the boat?"

"Gone. I was all alone, the wind blew hard and cold waves knocked me around. I felt I would die. Then I saw a light and swam toward it, praying it was not a boat at sea. It was far away, I learned, but when I was on the swim team I practiced long distance swimming. I was never very fast, but I am stronger than I look."

"Yeah, and my bathrobe isn't helping your macho image."

He grinned. He was a handsome kid, and rather endearing. Oh hell, I just called a twenty-six-year-old guy a *kid?* Is this what happens at for...past thirty-five? Five years ago I'd probably have hit on him and now I want to feed him milk and cookies?

Jan gave Rosario a nod to continue. "I finally made land on a rocky shore, near San Bruno. I still have bruises from those rocks." He pulled up my robe and showed us his black and blue knees.

San Bruno is a village about fifteen miles south of Santa Rosalia. I'd seen houses there when driving by and knew many people who lived there worked at a phosphate mine on San Marcos island, a quick panga commute from shore.

Rosario covered his battered knees. "I was so cold I thought maybe my teeth would break from chattering. They taught my swim team about hypothermia, so I knew I was in danger. I had no shoes, pants—I took them off so they would not weigh me down—or money, but I was afraid to ask for help. While I swam, I realized someone had tried to kill me, probably because of what I told the men on the boat. Or man. I cannot remember now for certain, but it seems more men came to the boat while I was drinking."

"Back up a minute, Rosario. You were working on the radio when a man from the mine came to the boat, then offered you a beer, right?"

"Yes."

I filed that away. No one at the office had mentioned seeing Rosario on the boat the night he disappeared. Hmmm.

"Did he offer you the beer before, or after, you mentioned you might have information about a problem at the mine."

He closed his eyes and wrinkled his forehead. Jan and I waited while he sent himself back to the night he almost died. His eyes popped open. "After. He drank beer himself while I worked on the wiring, but it was only after I hinted I might know something that he offered a beer. Is that important?"

"It might be. Did you give him names?"

"Names?"

"Of people you think might be responsible for problems on the job? Money that someone stole?"

"No, because...money stolen? I was looking for money wasted."

"Stolen, wasted, doesn't matter. I am here to find out what is rotten in Denmark. Looks like you may have done some of the job for me."

Rosario looked confused. "Denmark?"

"Just a phrase."

"So, you really are a spy? There was talk at the office that when you arrived you would find the problem."

Oh, great. I was outed before I even showed up.

Rosario noticed my displeasure and added, "They said you are very good."

"Ha!" Jan scoffed. "Hetta's never been good."

"Good at my job, thank you. So what you're saying is that my reputation proceeded me?"

Jan looked like she wanted to say something about my reputation so I gave her a warning finger stab that stopped short of her cute little nose. "But let's get back to that night. Did you give them names, as far as you can remember?"

"No, I didn't."

"How do you know? You were so drunk you passed out."

"I know, because I do not know the names. I only found suspicious information."

"Dang, and here I thought my work was done for me."

Jan had been watching us talk, her head swiveling back and forth like one of those plastic owl's heads meant to ward off pesky birds. "It sorta is. Rosario, the first man you talked with, the one who gave you the beer. Do you think he called others after you blabbed?"

Rosario nodded slowly, "Perhaps."

"But you don't know who they were?"

"I only remember hearing other voices, but by then I was seeing two of everything. And my head was spinning. Also, it was dark."

We took a break while I rummaged around for a voice-activated recorder I had on board and Jan went to retrieve Rosario's clothes from the dryer. When she returned, she had news.

"There are some guys on that company fishing boat, *Lucifer*."

"Anyone we know?"

"Your new BFF is out there."

"Safety? I'm surprised he isn't over here panting after you."

Jan rolled her eyes. "Jealous?"

"Hardly. Rosario...Rosario, are you all right?"

He had turned a bad color, like some do right before they hurl.

Jan went to his side while I grabbed a plastic garbage can. Normally when someone needs to upchuck on my boat I send them outside to do so over the rail, but with the mine guys out there that was out of the question.

Rosario sat down on the galley floor and cradled the garbage pail. I threatened him with a slow painful death should he get throw-up on my favorite chenille robe, then I hightailed it to the sundeck. I rarely throw up, but if someone else starts it can happen. Luckily Rosario recovered and took a glass of water from Jan.

"Safe to come back, Hetta, he ain't gonna barf."

"Thank God for that. Get me a glass of water too, will you?"

"Sure. Anything else, bwana?"

"I could use a pedicure."

"I ain't touching your bony old toes."

"Good help is so hard to find."

She flipped me the bird and pushed Rosario into his cabin to change into his freshly laundered clothes. I went out on the bow and waved at Safety. He was fiddling with a fishing pole on *Lucifer*, but put it down and sauntered over.

"Going fishing?" I asked.

"Maybe this weekend if the weather holds."

"Supposed to. Carry on, I have work to do since I played hooky this afternoon." I went back into the boat, where Jan waited with crossed arms and a frown.

"What's up, picklepuss? Rosario drop my robe for ya?"

"I wish. Hetta, I asked him what upset him so and he pointed out through the cabin porthole at the men working on *Lucifer*. He told me at least one of them was on the boat that night. Not that I blame the poor dude for being frightened, cuz I would be, too. I mean, this could very well be the guy who tried to off him."

"And?"

"And, it's Safety."

My jaw came unhinged. Safety? An attempted murderer?

Okay, historically I've not always been the best judge of character, but this came out of left field.

I like Safety.

He's my new best work-friend.

How *dare* he be a criminal?

Chapter 12

Between the devil and the deep blue sea

I was still reeling from the shock of learning that Safety might be a wolf in Robert Redford clothing when he banged on the hull of *Raymond Johnson*. "Permission to come aboard, Captain Coffey?"

I gave the cabin a once-over, searching for evidence that Rosario was about, but decided to take no chances. Climbing the stairs to the sundeck, I leaned over the rail. "Come on up, Safety. Jan and I were just going to sit outside and have a lemonade."

He boarded, made his way aft and up the outside ladder and joined me.

"Jan," I yelled back over my shoulder, "guess who's here? Safety!"

I heard the guest cabin door slam shut. Minutes later, Jan, looking a little rattled, joined us. "So, fishing poles all fixed?"

"Yep, I thought I'd stop by before I left and see if you two wanted to go fishing this weekend."

Yeah, sure that's why he stopped by.

I shook my head, "Sorry, got plans. Is the radio on *Lucifer* working okay?"

Jan gave me a warning eye squint.

"Far as I know," Safety said. "Why do you ask?"

"Oh, Ozzie the purchasing manager mentioned that guy, Rosario, was working on it the night he disappeared."

"Yeah, so I heard. Guess he fixed it...before."

"Obviously, since it works. Don't you wonder what happened to him?" I asked, ignoring Jan's now wide-eyed stare and slight head shake.

Safety shrugged. "Who knows? You know how Mexicans are."

My blood pressure spiked and my ears roared. I wanted to deck the bastard, right then and there, but knew I couldn't give away the game. Using every bit of self-control I own, which isn't much, I croaked, "I changed my mind about the lemonade, Jan. How's about you get our guest and us a beer?"

"Yes, bwana."

Safety thought that was sooo cute he didn't notice me eyeing the corkscrew hanging by the wet bar. If I plunged it into his heart, cranked it over hard a time or two and jerked, would that constitute open heart surgery? Or if I stuck it in his—

"Hetta! Your beer!" Jan yelled, shoving it into my clenching fist.

Dazed, I focused on the cold thing in my hand, sadly saw it wasn't a weapon and brought myself back to earth. "Thanks, I really, really needed that."

Safety, enthralled by the beautiful Jan, had no idea he'd had a close call with evisceration by corkscrew.

"I need Valium and I need it now!"

"Now Hetta, you know you are not allowed within ten feet of a Valium. Remember that O.D. tag on your toe? Stomach pump ring any bells? Anyhow, you can get through this without drugs. Safety doesn't suspect you know a thing."

Years ago, I took Valium after drinking a lot of gin, a combo now known to kill folks. Luckily I called Jan before I passed out, because I knew something was awfully wrong. That hospital visit convinced me to stay away from any kind of serious tranquilizers or pain pills, darn it. Jan, bless her little heart, never lets me forget it, either. This is why you should change friends often.

"You think he'll get a clue when I toss his sorry ass off Hell Hill?"

"Ya know, Hetta, you might work on that anger management thing. And yes," she grinned an evil grin, "he might get an inkling during free fall."

Jan, Rosario, and I shared a high five at the idea of Safety plummeting through space without a safety.

"Now, take a deep breath, because he's gonna pick you up any minute. Rosario, you'd better vamoose back to your cabin until they're gone."

"Did you know that word, vamoose, comes from the Spanish, *Ir*, meaning to go, but conjugated into the imperative tense becomes *vayamos* which is the same as go! in English. Some however, think it stems from *vamos*, which is simply he/she/it *goes*?"

"Rosario, did you know that the words, *pompous little prick*, comes from the Texan phrase, *get the hell out of my sight before I shoot you*?"

Rosario paled and turned to leave. Jan patted his back. "It's okay, hon, she gets this way sometimes. Well, a lot of times, but especially when she's worried about something. Just go to your room until she's gone."

"Hon? He's *hon*, and I'm being sent to work with the devil incarnate?"

"See what I mean? What a drama queen. Look, take this bag of food for that poor dog, ask Safety to pull over if he can, then sneak up behind him, and—"

"Ahoy, *Raymond Johnson*. Permission to come aboard."

I ran for the medicine chest and was digging for drugs when Jan cooed, "Oh, you're early. Want a cup of coffee?"

Want a cup of hemlock? Does hemlock come in cups? What is hemlock, anyhow?

The only thing I could find resembling a drug was Nyquil. I stuffed the bottle in my windbreaker pocket, then changed my mind and took a hefty hit. Any port in a storm.

Being civil to Safety on the way to work was a real test of my nerves, but the Nyquil did help. He mentioned I was being uncharacteristically quiet during the ride up the hill, and I blamed it on a hangover. I vowed to take another hit of the lovely elixir before we went back down the mountain after work, lest, even though I still didn't know for certain that Safety had anything to do with Rosario's overboard incident, my mouth overloaded my ass, which happens more often than I'd like to admit.

And, Rosario said, Safety did give him beer, but he vaguely recalled other voices on the boat before he finally passed out for good. In Mexico one is guilty until proven innocent, but I still wanted to give Safety the benefit of the doubt and if I showed my hand, let him know I suspected him, he might throw *me* off the cliff.

On the other hand, I had given Safety ample opportunity to say something like, "Yeah, I saw Rosario that night he disappeared and he was drunk, so I left him to sleep it off on the boat." Nope, instead his response was iffy at best, and in my mind, Safety's own omission threw suspicion in his corner.

No dog languished on the hillside on the way to work, and thereby no opportunity to shove Safety to his just deserts.

By midmorning I was fighting some seriously lazy eyelids, but at least I hadn't harmed anyone.

I was also starving. I'd forgotten to bring lunch and I'd already raided the communal fridge the day before and didn't want to push my luck. Mexicans are very generous, but getting caught heisting their burritos for the second time in two days might test their generosity. I didn't feel like going to the mess hall, where I'd probably do a face-plant in my refrieds anyway. Remembering the bag Jan gave me, I pulled it out of a drawer. It was labeled, Po Thang, and since I was feeling poorly, I figured I qualified.

Inside was a perfectly fine leftover ham and cheese sandwich. I justified eating Po Thang's food by telling myself I could use a little practice at being a bag lady, which, according to Oprah, a large percentage of women evidently fear becoming.

Eating the trash somehow lightened my mood, but working under the influence of Nyquil proved beyond my ability. Even with the calming benefit of Benadryl, I was slightly on edge, waiting to hear more from Jan and Rosario.

The plan for the day was for Jan to pass herself off as Rosario's sister and retrieve his stuff from a room he'd secretly rented in town. Although he officially lived at the mine's man camp, he'd figured early on that he needed a place of his own, with his personal stuff safe from prying eyes. Our Rosario, it seems, is a very clever and secretive dude who did his best to conceal that cleverness from his fellow office workers. Too bad he can't keep his mouth shut after too many beers, but who am I to talk?

The old lady who rented him the room in Santa Rosalia had no idea he worked at the mine. He'd told her he was an American tourist studying Baja's wildlife. Rosario knew his landlady had never entered his room, because he'd installed cameras and motion detectors, which Jan also retrieved. Since he was gone almost all the time anyway, the nice lady certainly had no idea he and a missing Mexican from the mine were one and the same. Especially since his disappearance was only a word of mouth occurrence in a town with no newspaper.

I had a feeling Rosario wasn't sharing all his secrets with us as yet, but who can blame him? I wouldn't trust me, either.

Chapter 13

WHISTLE FOR IT/WHISTLE FOR THE WIND
(Nautical term): From the tradition of superstitiously
whistling to summon the wind (hope for the
impossible). Why didn't I think of that?

"You about ready to head for home, Hetta?" Safety's voice torpedoed me from my flu med torpor.

After I'd raided Po Thang's doggy bag, I'd swiveled my desk chair to the back wall and tried to pose myself as though studying some papers in my lap. I promptly fell asleep. That Nyquil is magnificent stuff.

"Uh, yeah, sure." I swiped drool from my chin before swiveling to face him. Judging from his amused smile, I doubt I'd fooled him with that studying the papers in my lap ploy. Probably because I was snoring? And if you think you are really important at work, take a three-hour nap and see if anyone at all notices.

I excused myself for a trip to the *Mujeres*, where I bolstered myself with even more Nyquil, then gathered my backpack and jacket and shuffled out behind Safety. We were almost out of the office when I spotted a big poster festooned with fake flowers. Several candles were lit in front of it, illuminating Rosario's photo. I stopped dead in my tracks, studying the face I now knew quite well.

Safety turned and shook his head sadly. "I guess they've given up the hunt for him. Too bad, he was a nice kid."

A nice kid you got drunk and tried to murder? I wanted to say, but bit my tongue. I guess I didn't bite it hard enough. "Didn't you say you shared an office with him early on? Before he set up shop in my closet?"

"Yes, I did. Why?"

"I kinda wondered if anyone from here went out looking for him when he went missing. I heard the boat was found unharmed on the beach the next morning."

"Mexican Navy did the search."

"Oh." I climbed into the pickup and sulked into my corner.

A mile or so down the road, Safety broke the silence. "You think we didn't care enough to look for him, don't you?"

I shrugged. I'd already said enough and painting Safety with the brush of disapproval would not work in my favor right now. I was dozing off once again when Safety yelled, "There he is!"

"Rosario?" I said, jerking awake confused and a little dazed.

"No. That dog of yours." He pointed ahead and sure enough, there was the dog we now dubbed Po Thang.

Rats, I'd eaten the dog bait.

Safety glanced at his rearview and side mirrors. "No one behind us and as far as I can tell, no one coming. Wanna try to get him?"

"Sure, but how?"

"I'll stay in the truck, you see if you can get a leash on him. There's a length of rope in the back seat."

Paranoia raised its ugly head. Get out? How did I know he wouldn't drive off and leave me? Or worse, turn around and run both me and the dog down? I only had seconds to make up my mind so I undid my seat belt, snatched the piece of line and jumped out of the truck, which isn't a great idea when your balance is already impaired by a soporific.

As I picked myself up and dusted my butt, Safety yelled through the open window, "If I have to leave, I'll come back for you. Good luck."

Good luck? Holy hell, I guess. Po Thang and I shared less than a six-foot shoulder, a tiny piece of real estate he'd staked out as his own. When I stood, he'd skittered backward, perilously close to the edge of the bajillion-foot drop-off behind him. Less than five feet of trash-strewn roadside separated us.

I knelt down to his level. "Hey, sweetie," I cooed, "I'm not going to hurt you. I'm trying to save you."

He let loose with a low rumble. It wasn't a very convincing growl, but there was a show of teeth.

An air horn sounded behind me and I heard Safety drive off in response. Both trucks disappeared around a sharp curve and there was a sudden hush unlike anything I'd ever experienced. A brisk wind blowing up the cliff gave off an eerie wail, raising goose bumps the size of Kilimanjaro.

Beyond Po Thang's tiny piece of roadside and far, far below, miles of jagged frozen lava wrinkles covered in red dust brought Mars to mind. *Los Tres Virgenes* volcanoes loomed menacingly on the horizon. I cast a longing look at the too distant turquoise water of the Sea of Cortez sparkling in the late afternoon sun like a small beacon of hope. Tears sprang into my eyes for no apparent reason, other than the fact that I was stranded on Hell Hill with a possibly vicious dog.

Another air horn startled me as a truck rounded the curve, the driver no doubt thinking, *What in the hell is that stupid Gringa doing up here?*

Yeah, what *was* this stupid Gringa doing up here? The dog barked, reminding me of my mission, then he glowered and growled again. I think he somehow knew I ate his lunch.

"Okay, big guy," I said in my nice-doggy voice, "let's see if I can lasso your scrawny ass."

That garnered a faint tail wag, so I took a step forward. Once again he backed up. This was not going to work. I didn't come out here to kill Po Thang by running him off a bluff, or worse, into oncoming traffic. I sat down in the dust, cross-legged, and waited. Oh, for a dog biscuit!

Feeling in my pockets, all I came up with was a pack of gum. Slowly unwrapping a stick, making sure the foil made lots of noise, I held it out. He craned his neck toward it, sniffing, but sitting his ground.

Scooting ever so slightly forward on my butt, I inched toward him. He didn't move. I waited. He waited. We waited. He/she/it waited.

Several trucks and cars rumbled by, the people in them probably shocked to see a red-haired Gringa and a reddish golden retriever, both sitting on a tiny sliver of dirt on one of the most forbidding stretches of highway in the Baja. No one stopped, but I can't blame them; stopping on this road is for the insane and they could clearly see that someone had already filled that slot.

I heard a horn beep out, "Shave and a Haircut, Two Bits," and figured it was Safety returning. However, the ditty is also used by Mexicans, but never in the presence of cops because it will earn the driver a ticket. The Mexicans have changed the words to the song to charmingly say *"Chinga tu madre, cabrón"*: Go eff your mother, A-hole. Their insults have a recurring fixation with mothers and sexual acts, as long as it's someone else's mom.

I stood and so did the dog. One of his back legs slid over the edge, sending a cascade of rocks down the precipice and my heart cascading into my stomach. I quickly retreated, lest I send him over the edge. A horn blared and a whoosh of air hit my back close enough to scare the living hell out of me. Or something else.

"Okay, that's it! You listen to me you little turd," I commanded in my best bossy yell, "I've about had it with your lousy attitude. Now you come over here," I stabbed my finger down next to me, "and let's get off this godforsaken mountain before one of us gets killed. And I mean right now!"

Po Thang stood his ground. I hurled down the line in disgust just as Safety rolled to a stop next to me, threw the door open and yelled, "We've got about three minutes before a truck coming up behind me knocks us off this bluff. Let's go!"

In a sudden head rush, the Nyquil hit and almost knocked me off my feet. I swayed and took a step forward, only to feel my legs splay in two different directions. I wondered if I was experiencing an overdose when rocks showered down a steep bluff onto the other side of the highway, and I realized it wasn't cough medicine rocking my world, it was an earthquake.

Catching my balance I sprinted—or as close to a sprint as I could manage on moving earth, or solid dirt, for that matter—for the waiting truck. Bad as I hated leaving Po Thang out there, when it comes to self-preservation its every dog for herself. Maybe that didn't come out quite right. Anyhow, I abandoned my rescue attempt faster than you can say cluck.

Hitching myself onto the bottom step of the dually, I grabbed a handle and launched myself upward, planning to swing into the seat.

An ear-splitting whistle almost made me lose my hold, as did the sudden flurry of paws, fur, and slobber vaulting over me, into the truck's back seat.

Safety reached over, snagged my jacket collar and hauled me in as he stomped the gas and the heavy door slammed, barely avoiding breaking my ankles.

Catching my breath I turned and glared into the back seat.

Po Thang was already asleep, looking for all the world like any other dog happily taking a ride with his people.

"You whistled and he came?" I yowled. I didn't know I could yowl so good, but this seemed like an appropriate time. "I risked my life for the ungrateful little cur and all you had to do was whistle?"

Safety smiled. "Sometimes, Hetta, it's all in the lips."

Chapter 14

If you pick up a starving dog and make him prosperous he will not bite you. This is the principal difference between a dog and man.—Mark Twain

I later learned the quake was only a four pointer and no damage occurred except to my nerve endings.

The epicenter was somewhere out in the Sea, sixty miles away, and the quake was felt as far as San Carlos. I also found out this was a common occurrence, not something I wanted to hear, especially since I survived a couple of years of the pesky temblors while working in Tokyo. A four on the Richter scale barely makes the evening news in Japan, so I was usually the only one who ducked under my desk in our high-rise office building, which, by the way, was built on rollers. After awhile even I became accustomed to the almost daily shakeup and constant swaying of the building.

Before we opened the truck doors, Safety tied a line on Po Thang so he couldn't escape into the marina parking lot. After being personally snubbed by the mutt I'd just as soon he took off, because now that we'd snagged him, I really didn't know what to do with him.

Jan never even felt the quake on the boat, as is usually the case. She took one look at our new fur-faced friend, sniffed and decreed, "Food and soap and water, in that order and lots of all of it."

Po Thang decimated my refrigerator's contents, eating almost everything that wasn't frozen solid and some that were not completely thawed.

Jan was nuking the last of my leftover beef stew when Safety and I tackled the dog with Dawn dishwashing liquid and a garden hose. The water ran red around us, and it took several soapings to rid his matted coat of accumulated desert dust and crud. Po Thang liked the bath and attention, not growling at us even once. I guess he forgave me for stealing his lunch.

His good behavior supported my opinion that he wasn't a total *perro de calle*—street dog—but someone's lost pet. Cleaned up, he looked to be about a year old and maybe even a pedigreed Golden Retriever. Although with all the designer dogs on the market these day, I'm not sure what a pedigree is worth. One thing for certain, this was no plain old Mexican dawg.

Rosario, quiet as a mouse, was imprisoned in the guest cabin while Safety was around, so as soon as we had Po Thang towel dried and basking in what was left of the late afternoon sun, I shooed Safety away. He wasn't all that happy about leaving the presence of the loverly Jan, but I told him since it was Jan's last night on the boat for a while I wanted my friend to myself.

As soon as Safety left, Jan rapped on Rosario's door. "All clear."

He looked out on the deck and smiled. "That is a very handsome dog you have." Po Thang, now practically dry, did look good. With his fluffy reddish-gold coat and contented smile, it was hard to believe that only a couple of hours before he'd been a belligerent mess. The dog gave out a sigh, thumped his tail, and went back to sleep.

"He's all yours, Rosario."

Rosario lost his smile. "Hetta, I have no place to keep a dog. I have no job, no home, no life."

Jan walked over and put her arm around his shoulders. "Don't feel bad, Rosario, Hetta's quite often without those things and look at her."

Rosario's face fell even farther and I gave Jan the look she so richly deserved.

"And anyhow," Jan continued, "we're gonna get this whole thing straightened out for you. Aren't we, Hetta?"

"I hope to hell. But we need some kind of plan. First and foremost, we have to figure out who tried to kill you, Rosario. If they did."

"What do you mean? Of course they did."

I shook my head. "Maybe, maybe not. What if the guys all got drunk, decided to go out fishing or some dumb thing like drunks do? Then you fell overboard, they were too drunk to find you, they panicked and beached the boat at San Lucas and left it. Maybe they didn't want to get in trouble for taking the boat out and decided on a cover up?"

Jan nodded. "Yeah, Hetta, should know. She does lots of dumb stuff when she's drunk."

"I might remind you that you are usually with me, Miz Jan."

"Well, yeah, but the dumb stuff is always your idea."

Rosario had evidently grown tired of our banter. "Ladies, please. Let us get back to the idea of a plan."

Jan and I glared at him and yelled, in unison, "Don't call us ladies!"

Rosario looked confused. "You are not ladies?"

"No," I told him. At his perplexed look, I explained. "Rosario, your English is excellent, but trust me, do not ever call a woman a lady unless she has a British title. It pisses us off."

"What about Lady Gaga?"

"*Her* you can call Lady, even if she ain't one. Just not us."

Rosario's computer held a wealth of project-related information, which he transferred to both our PCs. He'd downloaded purchase orders, change orders, material takeoffs, and about anything else to do with equipment and material for the project. He didn't have all the financials, but it was pretty clear, after Jan and I spent several hours going over what he had, that at least payouts to the subcontractors were pretty straight forward. Not that there couldn't be ripoffs, but at least we could move the subs to our least likely suspect file.

We knew, from the latest report to investors, that there were cost overruns in the hundreds of thousands, so either the original estimates sucked or something more sinister was afoot. Finding the fishy stuff wasn't going to be all that easy. Hell, auditors had spent weeks going over the financial reports and still came up puzzled. No one area raised a red flag as the cause of a budgetary deficit. Maybe, if Rosario *had* stumbled onto something, he'd told what he knew to the wrong men, and they tried to kill him because he was too close to the truth? Problem is, he had no idea what could have tipped him close enough to get him killed for his findings.

Yep, we needed a plan.

Jan had inspected Po Thang for fleas during his bath and found none, so he was deemed suitable for an inside dog. When he was dry enough, I brought him in, but didn't trust him yet with my decor so we kept him tied to a chair leg.

"Hetta, do you make it a habit to tie both people and dogs to chairs?" Rosario asked in what he thought was an attempt at humor.

"Only until we can trust them. Which, by the way, the jury is still out on you, so don't get cocky."

All Po Thang wanted to do was eat and sleep, so didn't balk at being tethered. When I took him for a walk it was evident he'd been leash trained, once again confirming my suspicion that he was someone's pet.

"Maybe he's got a chip," Jan speculated when I reported that he heeled on the leash.

Rosario, who knew all about computer chips, wanted to know what a chip has to do with a dog. Jan explained the implanted chip was to ID lost dogs and Rosario thought that a great, if very un-Mexican idea. I had to keep reminding myself that even though he spoke English with an American accent because of his schooling, he had still never been outside of Mexico. I also didn't know if they chipped dogs in Mexico, but I'd find out.

"My friend, Craig, who is a veterinarian in Arizona has invented a GPS tracking implant for finding animals who have strayed. He uses them on his cattle ranch to track his herd. Saves time and money. Also, if the cattle are stampeding because of a predator, an alarm goes off, alerting him to grab his rifle and take off on his four wheeler to save the day."

Rosario grinned. "A modern day cowboy."

"Oh, you have no idea," I told him, thinking of my friend, the gay caballero.

Talking about Craig reminded me I should call him and see if he'd heard any more about that stupid lawsuit. I'd told the Cochise County authorities my side of the story by phone and Craig had a lawyer working the problem for me so maybe that was the end of if.

Hope springs infernal.

After dinner, which Jan had to fetch from the local Chinese restaurant because Po Thang had eaten us out of boat and home, we sat around the dining table and forged that much-needed plan. I had all the window blinds closed so no one could spot Rosario with us, even though Jan had disguised him pretty well.

He now sported a bleached blonde buzz cut and was growing a beard. In a few days he would be barely recognizable as the mining nerd someone tried to off. I'd unearthed a Hawaiian shirt and shorts from Jenks's locker, along with a pair of wraparound sunglasses. Add sandals and a backpack and he fairly screamed Gringo tourist.

Still though, he could not stay on the boat much longer, what with Safety popping by. No amount of peroxide would keep him from figuring out who Rosario was up close.

Rosario, reunited with his computer, was happy as a tornado in a trailer park. While Jan and I cleaned up the galley after dinner and took our wine outside to the sundeck, he went online with his gaming buddies from around the planet and was soon lost in a world neither Jan nor I knew anything about.

Jan nodded her head toward the main saloon. "He's a nice guy, just really naïve. We really ought to cut him some slack."

I thought back to the couple of times we'd reprimanded him and agreed. "We keep forgetting he's not an American."

"Yeah, but it's more than that. He told me today about how he grew up. The uncle in the States couldn't visit because he was an illegal alien and afraid he'd get caught trying to re-cross the border. His mother basically lived only for her son. Between his mom and uncle they sent him to a whole string of expensive schools, but his social life was nil to none when it came to the other students. He was basically a shut in. Home straight from school every day, he and his computer were best friends."

"Didn't he say he was on a swim team?"

"Yeah, for one year. Mom kept changing his schools, I think in a well-meaning attempt to protect him from being outed as a poor kid. The swim team was the only sport where they provided all his equipment and paid for trips to swim meets. When he attended a school that required a clean uniform each day, he came home, washed and dried and ironed it for the next day. His fellow students didn't know he only had one."

I could relate, in a small way. We moved around so much I barely got to know my classmates before we took off, usually for another country. Still, I did make friends in each place. Didn't keep them over the years, except a couple from my senior year in Texas, but I wasn't a hermit. Hell, I was even a cheerleader one year.

"I know what you're thinking, Hetta, but you have an outgoing, if sometimes annoying, personality. Rosario doesn't. Your privileged childhood went way beyond the classroom. When he left the school each day, he became a lower-class Mexican. He lived a charade. It's a miracle he isn't bitter."

"Yeah. We have to find his father, you know. We have to help him out."

"Agreed. Let's get to it."

Chapter 15

The key for us, number one, has always been hiring very smart people.— Bill Gates

It was a cozy cyber-world-century family scene in the main saloon after a dinner of order-out Chinese.

Rosario gamed on his computer, Jan and I researched on ours. Whatever happened to being perfectly good couch potatoes? Watching mindless sitcoms and game shows? At least then kids talked to each other, even if it was to say something like, "Oh, that Fonz." Even though *Happy Days* went off the air when I was ten, I still wondered if my fascination with The Fonz didn't lead to a later penchant for bad boys.

Jan took the genealogy route via Ancestry.com and I hit the social media. I was tired and wanted nothing more than to crawl into bed, but I am a research junkie. My dad says I'm part bloodhound; point me at a problem and I'll run it to ground.

My search paid off fast. "Bingo," I said fifteen minutes later.

Jan came around to my side of the table. "What?"

I put my finger to my lips. I didn't want Rosario to know we were looking for his dad, just in case we came up cold. Jan squinted at the screen. "Send it to me," she said and returned to her own PC.

A minute later we were only three feet apart, chatting online. And they say the art of conversation is dead.

Jan: Looks like you are onto something. Age is right.

Me: Let's see if we can find him on Facebook.

Jan: Roger that.

Another minute or two went by.

Me: Bingo again.

Jan: For sure. I mean, look at him. Rosario is a dead ringer.

Me: What should we do?

Jan: Let's Friend him.

Me: You Friend him, I'm going fishing on LinkedIn and Pinterest.

Jan: You're afraid you'll land in Facebook jail again for pestering people.

Me: Yeah, well, you ended up in Twitmo more than once.

Jan: That was before I learned how to stay out of trouble with those Twitter cops. Let's both send a Friend request to this dude.

Me: Oh, all right. I hope he doesn't think I'm some kind of stalker like that last guy.

I was pretty sure we had our man.

Forty-two years old, divorced, no kids mentioned, loves surfing (which is why we have little Rosario sitting nearby right now), Software Engineer (of course) in the San Francisco Bay Area. I even snagged his resume off LinkedIn.

Jan: Should we show Rosario?

Me: Not yet. What if this Russell character doesn't care if he has a son?

Jan: Yeah, you're probably right, although I really hate it when that happens.

Me: What with Rosario being so computer literate, and a hacker to boot, wouldn't you think he'd have found this guy himself?

Jan: That is odd. Maybe he has?

Me: Feel him out tomorrow. You know, you and Chino have to take him with you to the whale camp. He can't stay here.

Jan: Right you are.

Me: Uh, why are we sending each other messages on the computer when we could be *talking?*

Jan: B/C TLK2U is a PITA

I hugged Jan, Rosario and Po Thang, before leaving for the mine the next morning. I wasn't sure who I was going to miss the most when I returned to an empty boat later that day. But since it was already Wednesday and I planned on heading for Camp Chino on Friday, I wasn't all that sad to have a couple of days of solitude.

And, of course, there's the Internet. What on earth did we do without it? Oh, now I remember: We read paper books, played cards with actual physical cards, wrote letters in longhand, took walks, and had meaningful conversations with people we actually knew. Or not. I spent a lot of time in bars having meaningful conversations with total strangers.

Well, at least I no longer watched television, and a side bonus is that stuffing one's self with after-dinner snacks is harder when you have your fingers on the keys instead of a channel changer. So why can't I dump that pesky ten pounds? Okay, fifteen.

Safety, by rescuing Po Thang, had redeemed himself in my mind. I found it hard to believe he was a killer after that pooch cottoned to him so, but then again, dogs are not always the best judge of character.

However, I consider myself a brilliant judge of others. Matter of fact, being judgmental is a Texan birthright. Others may find my opinions somewhat harsh at times, but I'm usually pretty good at sniffing out nefariousness. Unfortunately, I have been attracted to some fairly villainous characters in my past, but that didn't mean I didn't know them when I sniffed them out, so to speak.

I was reminded of an old song, "The Snake" by Al Wilson. Like the woman in the song, I knew a snake when I saw one, but sometimes took them in anyhow. I'd gotten a vicious bite or two for my efforts, but until very recently I had still managed to be mesmerized under the s-s-spell of a charming snake or two.

So, if S-S-Safety was involved in Rosario's boating "accident" and an ensuing cover-up, then while not exactly innocent, he was at least not guilty of participating in an intentional attempted murder. On the other hand, maybe there was a vast conspiracy on site and I was gonna have a hell of a time finding the culprits if more than a couple were involved.

My investigation was going to have to start with the first piece of paper ever generated that had anything to do with costs and the idea of starting at the beginning made me groan.

For years before the project ever broke ground, a lengthy feasibility study was made. For starters, a team of Canadian geologists, one of whom was the now project manager, Bert Melton, literally unearthed evidence that the old mine might be profitable using new technology. Copper deposits were left untapped when, using the old techniques, Lucifer's ore plumb petered out.

I'm certain there is some profound life lesson here, but it escapes me.

However, this team of scientists also knew there was a possibility of rich cobalt deposits, and that is a game changer. Cobalt has been, in the western hemisphere, a by-product of copper mining in the past, but demand in high-tech applications and the aircraft industry has made it more important.

Lucifer is primarily a copper mining facility, but it is the cobalt that will make it so valuable. The cobalt supply coming from the Congo is threatened by political unrest and the other sources, namely China and Russia, are also open to shaky politics at times. Canada and the United States are looking to cut back their reliance on overseas sources, and Mexico is not, technically, overseas.

Hopefully I wasn't taking part in another Blackbird mine fiasco, but since there is going to be a cobalt mining facility opening in Idaho near that disaster, maybe history has taught us a lesson.

Blackbird left almost four-million tons of waste rock, a ten-acre open pit and tons of tailings that contaminated the soil before it was shut down in the nineteen eighties.

Anyhow, once cobalt was deemed viable to extract as a new product from Lucifer, the pencil pushers moved in to estimate the financial possibilities, or lack thereof. If what I'd learned was true about extensive cost overruns, then the estimating team was either incompetent or someone had their hand in the till. I suspected the latter, but now I had to prove it.

Rosario had done some of the work for me. Payroll costs appeared consistent with what they should be, as well as the expense of housing and feeding so many workers. Well, until they get *my* bill.

Using a tried and almost true formula or two I'd learned when doing ball park estimates of my own on former projects, the quantity of purchase orders issues seemed slightly high, but not terribly out of line. I couldn't find what I called double-dip vendors; these are phantom purveyors, usually of something like tortillas. In that case, Vendor Jose would actually supply tortillas to the jobsite, and get paid for them. Jose's phantom brother, Vendor Jorge, gets paid off the same Material Receiving Report.

One of the problems of doing business in Mexico is that there are so many *agencias*, which are basically middlemen for products ranging from design services to equipment. I read somewhere that the drug cartels had wormed their way into legitimate business by acquiring agencies for high-end vehicles such as Jaguars, and I sincerely hoped I wasn't headed for another showdown with those guys.

At any rate, the *agencia* middlemen gave much opportunity for kickbacks and the like.

The Trob sent me a program I downloaded that would allow me to enter a key word, like tortilla, and a search would ensue throughout the system for duplicates. None of that showed up.

After a frustrating few hours, I emailed the Trob that I needed help and wanted Jan on the payroll.

His answer came back almost immediately: Whatever.

I love a man of few words. Gives me more time to talk.

Putting Jan to work would solve a couple of problems. First off she wouldn't have time to make poor Chino miserable, and I'd have a cohort since I planned to have her work from the boat. I'd also glean a dog sitter for Po Thang and we could delay sending Rosario away. Although I gave it long and hard thought, I couldn't figure out how to get a dead man back on the mine's payroll, but figured I'd pad my expense account to make up for feeding both him and Po Thang.

I emailed Jan, hoping to catch her before Chino picked her up. She had not been looking forward to returning to Camp Chino so soon and now, when Chino showed up to take her back home to her rivals, the whales, she had a legitimate reason to stay on with me. And if she was busily employed, Chino didn't have to worry about her taking off, as she does on occasion.

I should hire myself out as a problem solver, extraordinaire.

Oh, wait, I already do that.

Less than an hour after the Trob approved the hiring of Jan, one pissed off Chicano stormed my closet waving a sheet of paper. "CPA? CPA? We are in Mexico! What is this all about?"

"A CPA," I said with a smile, "means Certified Public Accountant."

Ozzie's face turned an alarming shade of purple, which isn't all that easy when one is of Hispanic descent. "I am aware of what it means, Miss Coffey. I simply don't understand why on earth we need one on a project in Mexico! And where will we put another person? This office is already over-crowded. I knew you were trouble from the first day, and –"

I cut him off before he imploded. "You do realize this CPA is my friend, the lovely Jan, don't you?"

His anger dissipated as fast as you can say tall hot blonde. "Oh. Well. I, uh, in that case—"

"Yeah, I get that a lot."

Chapter 16

No good deed goes unpunished.

After a frustrating day of unrequited snoopery, and realizing I was in over my head, snoop-wise, I was elated I'd have Jan in my corner to help out in the future. She has a degree in mathematics, an MBA in accounting, is a PeopleSoft (Oracle's whizbang capitol management program) guru, and can ferret out accounting snafus where I wouldn't have a clue to even look. I know the construction/engineering bidness, but can barely balance my checkbook. Okay, I never balance my checkbook.

For engineers, one would think being math savvy is second nature and it sort of is, but I don't like doing it. You would be surprised how many engineers feel the same way. If we are designing something that's one thing, but anything that smacks of simple subtraction and addition? Nah.

I was somewhat surprised by my relief that Jan and Rosario were staying on for awhile. A bit of a loner, I've never really enjoyed being around people a lot, and especially in my living quarters. Given my druthers, I would have had my own house as a child. Next door to the parents, mind you, but separate. Maybe this getting near for...late thirties had something to do with it? Or maybe I just liked coming home to a home cooked meal. *If* I beat Po Thang to it.

As I headed for the boat after securing Jan a place on the payroll, I thought I'd find an elated Jan, as she was back to working at something she loved instead of flipping tortillas at the whale camp. I had another think coming, for the Jan waiting for me was one I had never known: an insecure one.

I barely made it into the main saloon when she began spouting angst and fury, all because of Chino's new assistant.

After ten minutes of listening to her totally unfounded anxiety, I had had enough. "Oh, for crap's sake, Jan, you knew Chino was getting an assistant."

"An assistant marine biologist. A doctor. Not a golderned centerfold."

"I think you must be exaggerating."

Rosario piped up. "Oh, no, she is not. Doctor Diane is one of the most beautiful women I have ever seen. She has the most amazing hair with these gold streaks, sexy eyes, and her figure—"

I cut him off in order to save his life, as I caught sight of Jan reaching for my fish filleting kit. "Okay, Rosario, I think I've got the picture here."

Not heeding my attempt at a warning, he whipped out the cell phone Jan had retrieved from his rental room and shoved it in my face. Jennifer Lopez peered at me from the screen. No, not Jennifer, because the actress doesn't have jade green eyes. And in the photo Rosario snapped early that day, those emerald orbs were trained, laser-like, on Doctor Brigido Chino Comacho Yee, who had a silly grin pasted on his face.

"Well, crap."

"Well crap, indeed Hetta," Jan growled. "I should have never let them drive off without me. What was I thinking? They will be together all day, every day, and half the night and it's *your* fault."

"What? My fault?"

"Well, you hired me and now Chino and that, that, *doctor* will be *way* too together while you have me slaving away over here."

"They'll be counting whales and such," I reminded her. "Something you hate doing."

"Yabbut, they are *my* whales to hate."

"Gosh, why on earth would Chino be interested in someone else when you are so reasonable?"

"You know what I mean."

"I guess. Look, Chino is in love with you, in spite of your lousy attitude. He is a wonderful man, an honorable one, and someone who would never do anything nefarious."

"Wanna bet? He stole your dog."

"What?" I hadn't even had time to notice Po Thang was missing. "The dirty low down sonuvabitch!"

Later, when Jan was taking a shower out of hearing range, I whispered to Rosario, "I'm almost afraid to ask, but just how old is this Doctor Bombshell? She looks fairly young in her photo, I mean for a doctor."

As I said this I had a twinge of my own angst, as I'd heard it told that you know you're getting old when doctors start looking young.

Rosario's answer gave me even more to worry about. "I think she is about twenty-six. My age."

Yikes, no wonder Jan was in such a tizzy, what with her concerns of the age difference between herself and Chino.

"And Hetta, Doctor Yee took your dog so he can check him for worms and any other health problems. He is, after all, a veterinarian as well as a marine biologist. I do not think he wishes to keep Po Thang."

I'd had time to calm down over my missing mutt and when I thought it over, Po Thang was in good hands. "Truth is, I really don't need a dog. I'm gone all day and you and Jan won't be here for long to dogsit. I guess Camp Chino is actually a better place for him in the long run."

"Perhaps." He cut his eyes toward my cabin, where Jan went to shower. "I think Jan is...confused. She says she doesn't want to work with Doctor Yee, but then she doesn't want him to have an assistant."

"Oh, I think it is the *type* of assistant she's worried about. Did you learn anything else about Doctor Powell? Like, is she married or anything?"

"She wore no ring." He blushed. "I sort of noticed."

"Like you sort of noticed she's got more curves than Hell Hill?"

"But she is not so beautiful as Jan," he said loyally.

"You might want to mention that to Jan."

To keep Jan's mind off possible hanky-panky afoot at Camp Chino, I had her download every single accounting number for the project, no matter whose it was. This was no small task, for we had subcontractors galore and they had their own purchase orders. I also wanted to look at any large outstanding invoices, maybe glean an anomaly somewhere.

Luckily the numbering system was such that the string of numbers and letters actually meant something, once you get the hang of it. Or rather, Jan got the hang of it, because my pea brain only saw hieroglyphics. In what looked to me like a meaningless string of alphanumeric nonsense, Jan deciphered information. Under Jan's tutelage I slowly learned to recognize subcontractors, vendors, products, and the like, but it was still a pain.

I was complaining about learning a new language—Accounting—when Rosario stepped in and wrote a translation program for me. Jan was more than impressed with how quickly he grasped not only the concept, but his ability to quickly put it all in plain English for me. He also acted as our project personnel guide, filling us in on who did what for whom. We made a good team, each of us possessing a particular knowledge or skill, and none of us with another damned thing to do.

Things were looking much rosier until my office phone rang.

"Hetta," Rosario whispered.

"Ro—" I looked around to see if anyone was nearby my office. "Uh, hi there. What's up?"

"Someone is on the boat."

"Where's Jan?"

"She went shopping."

"Can you see who it is?"

"No, when I heard someone walking around on the decks, I hid in my cabin. Can you turn on the cameras? Whoever it is is still here."

"Okay, are all the hatches locked?"

"Yes. And so is my cabin door."

"Good. Standby." I pulled up my security system and activated all the cameras on the boat. At first I saw nothing, then a deck camera caught movement and rotated towards it. A man was walking along the starboard side, his back to the camera. It looked as though he was getting ready to leave the boat.

"Rosario, make a noise. I need him to turn around."

"What noise?"

"I don't care. Whistle, yell, bang on the wall. Whatever."

"Okay." Seconds later I heard a loud thud and the man whirled to face the camera.

I almost fainted with fright as I stared into the ugly mug of an old arch enemy, one who had vowed to get even with me if it was the last thing he did.

"Hetta?"

I couldn't speak, I was in such shock.

"Hetta?"

I drew a deep breath. "I'm here. Stay put. No more noise. If he tries to break in, I'll set off the alarm. That should scare him off, pronto."

I watched, a shaky finger on the alarm key, as the creepy lowlife finally shrugged and stepped off the boat.

"I think he's gone. Peek out from the main saloon and see if he's on the dock."

After a few seconds, Rosario let out a sigh of relief. "Yes, he went out the gate and walked toward the parking lot. What do you want me to do?"

"Nothing. Have Jan call me as soon as she gets back. We have more to worry about now than who tried to kill you. Now we have a guy who wants to kill *me*."

Ricardo Lujàn, whom Jan and I had dubbed Dickless Richard after the smarmy *cabrón* told us, upon our making his sleazy acquaintance, that we could call him Richard, or Ricardo, but not to call him Dick.

I've called him many things since then, none of them nice. Lujàn is in real estate. Stealing it, as best I can figure. And he tried doing serious harm to me and Jan the year before, but Jenks rode in on his white horse and saved the day by launching a Molotov cocktail at him and blowing up his boat.

The last I saw of Dickless, we set him afloat in a leaky skiff.

Last I *heard* of him, he still held a grudge.

And now he had found me. Or at least my boat.

Chapter 17

Jealousy is all the fun you think they had.—
Erica Jong

Jan called twenty minutes after my boat's security cameras spied Ricardo Dickless Luján skulking around *Raymond Johnson*.

"Well, hell and damnation, Hetta. Ya know, Chino heard something about Lujàn moving his operations over here somewhere."

"Over here, where? And didn't you think I should know this before I signed up for a job on this side of the peninsula?"

"Oh, come on, Hetta, Baja's a big place. What are the odds? Just relax, we'll find out what he's up to."

"Easy for you to say. It isn't you he wants to kill. And right now I'd like to kill *you* for not telling me that slimeball was in my neighborhood."

Jan called Chino, told him about Lujàn's prowling and Chino said he'd get his cousins to ask around about what he was up to. And maybe why, other than wanting to kill me, he was lurking around my boat.

I reported a prowler to the marina office, along with a copy of Luján's mugshot caught by my security camera. They promised to make sure the guards and all personnel stayed on the lookout for him.

Meanwhile we went into a defense mode, with cameras rolling twenty-four hours a day and all doors locked at all times. It's times like this when I really, really miss my guns.

After a couple of days on high alert, we needed a break.

Poor Rosario couldn't even leave the boat for fear of being recognized, even with his new blonde do.

Jan was obsessing over Chino's possible hanky panky.

And me? I didn't even have a dog to feed and walk to take my mind off Dickless. I considered getting back into an exercise routine, if one can refer to something one never does routinely a routine, but was spooked about being seen on the streets of Santa Rosalia, now that Luján had been spotted in the vicinity. Or maybe I'm too lazy. Frustration had set in because I wasn't getting anywhere in my quest to find out who was stealing from what I now thought of as *my* project, and had probably tried to kill *my* Rosario.

Yep, we all needed a break, so Saturday morning I declared a hiatus to our sleuthing and obsessing and we all took off for Camp Chino.

Before we left I made Jan promise to leave the cutlery on the boat.

Unfortunately Doctor Bombshell/Centerfold a.k.a Doctor Diane Powell lived up to her billing. It was obvious she was taken with Chino and followed him around like a puppy dog, which she did at her peril, since *my* puppy dog seemed determined to cut her off at every turn, even offering up a small growl and lip curl on occasion. He learned that part from Jan.

Needless to say, the weekend was a tad tense what with Po Thang and Jan both snarling at Doc Di.

"Well, at least Po Thang has a sense of loyalty," Jan sniffed. I guess she hadn't noticed that Po Thang, once he greeted Jan, went back to dogging Chino's every step. As for me, my own dog couldn't care less about me unless I had food in my hand, but at least he didn't grumble at me like he did Diane.

"Chino's loyal too," I reminded her. "He's overjoyed that you're here."

"We'll see."

"Jan, I've never seen you jealous before. I kinda like it."

She flipped her hair. "I am not jealous."

"Are too."

"Am not."

"Then what would you call the way you're acting? You're treating Diane as an arch enemy when she's actually pretty darned nice. It isn't becoming, you know."

Jan teared up and I wanted to kick myself. "Sorry. I didn't mean to hurt your feelings. Since when can I do that, anyhow?"

"When you're right, which I hate."

I reached over and patted her hand, which provoked a nose push from Po Thang who had deigned to join us since Chino went off to do some whale thing. "Yeah, yeah, dog. I know you like Jan more than me, but she's my best friend too."

Jan sighed deeply. "Yes, we are best friends. More like sisters," she explained to Po Thang, who cocked his head and ears to her singsong doggy voice. "And that is why I want to warn you, right now. Should you decide to adopt her permanently, she eats all the good stuff."

Po Thang gave me the squinty eye, which set Jan and me off. Chino, back from the sea, sidled up to our campfire chairs and plopped down next to Jan. He looked a little leery, as though our laughter might not be a good thing.

"Mind if I join you?"

Jan smiled and patted his knee. Po Thang nosed her hand away and Jan pushed back. "Watch it, mutt. Remember, you have to spend *all* day with me, *every* day. And Chino," she replaced her hand on his knee, "it's your camp. You don't have to ask if you can join us."

"No, Jan, it is *our* camp and I miss you being here."

"Oh, really? When? Before or after you've spent an entire day and half the night with your new assistant?"

Well, mee-oow!

I stood so fast my chair fell over backward. "Uh, I'll go get us a beer."

Po Thang, since I was headed in the direction of the fridge, followed. "So you don't want to get involved either, you cowardly cur?"

He gave me a woof.

"Gimme five."

Po Thang raised his paw and I shook it. "Well, welcome to the Coward's Club. I am the president."

A raised voice cut through the night and we turned to see Jan and Chino, now standing nose to nose and throwing their arms around.

"Po Thang, your friend Jan is screwing up big time. There is nothing worse than accusing a man of something before he does it, because then he probably will do it. Trust me, I know from experience."

Chino, Diane and Rosario left in a panga early Sunday morning when one of the tour guides told them of a new calf in the lagoon. Jan demurred, still in a snit over the argument from the night before, I guess. I didn't want to leave her alone to stew, so I stayed in camp as well although I really wanted to go see that baby whale. A friend in need is a pest.

I was on Skype, talking with Craig in Arizona about my alleged hate crime when Jan sauntered in with a plate of freshly baked chocolate chip cookies, Po Thang in hot pursuit.

She leaned into camera range and gave Craig a wave. "Hi, big guy. Hetta gonna go to jail?"

Craig grinned. "Not if I can help it. At least not for this particular crime."

"Hey, it's not like I have a list of crimes, you two. Craig, guess what? Jan's got a hot new rival and a little green monster is plaguing her."

Jan harrumphed. "I am *not* jealous. Hetta's just being mean because her dog likes me better."

"Children, children," Craig scolded. "Play nice. Now, tell me everything that's been going on. I know for sure you two can't stay out of hot water."

We took turns telling Craig everything we knew to date about the project, Rosario, and Dickless's poking around the boat. When we were through, he frowned and shook his head. "I don't like it. You may be in over your heads this time. I think you need some more help down there."

"You gonna ride in and save us, cowboy?"

"Nah, way too much going on up here."

"Who, then?"

"How about Topaz Sawyer, that Sheriff's deputy who helped you out when you shot that skank in the balls. She might like a little Baja vacation."

"Can she do that? Cross the border, her being law enforcement and all?"

"I don't see why not. Long as no one down there knows she's a cop and she leaves her gun at home. Want me to call her?"

"Oh, why not? Can't hurt. While you have her on the phone, run that stupid hate crime thing by her, see what she thinks."

"Will do. Anything else you two want to tell me about? Other than harboring a dead guy, looking for his would-be killers, hiding from a villain who has vowed to do serious harm to Hetta, and Jan being jealous of another woman?"

Jan leaned in again. "I am not jealous. Chino's the one who's being pissy."

I pushed her away, "Nah, I guess that's it. Well, except for jailbirds suing me, the usual."

"Oh, good. Now I won't worry. Bye."

I said bye, Jan waved a hand into the screen, I signed off Skype and turned to Jan. "You have a lot of nerve accusing Chino of being pissy. You're the one who picked that fight, if you ask me."

"I didn't ask you, but now that you've maligned me, I have to set the record straight. He had the nerve to say he's unhappy about me being alone on the boat with Rosario while you're gone all day."

"Well, he sure doesn't know *you* very well."

She smiled. "Yeah, that's what *I* thought."

"I mean, me being around has never kept you from cuckolding *any*body."

Chapter 18

"Who knows what evil lurks in the hearts of men? The Shadow knows." The introduction for the radio program.

Jan and I left Camp Chino Monday morning.

Rosario remained at the whale camp, thereby relieving Chino's worries about his proximity to Jan. Po Thang, declared parasite free, joined me and Jan on the return trip to Santa Rosalia via the jobsite.

As we drove on Mex 1, I summarized the situation. "So, let me get this straight. You're thinking that leaving Rosario at the camp will keep Doc Dish and Chino from getting any ideas about each other, and now that Rosario is there, he won't be alone on the boat with you all day, which should make Chino happier. And you didn't want him to worry, even though you were debating leaving Chino because, although you say you love him, you don't like the age difference or living with him in a whale camp. Do I have it right?"

She looked sheepish. "Put that way it sounds like high school stuff."

"Or middle grade, but with an attempted murder thrown in to keep it more grownup."

"Speaking of attempted murder victims, I think Rosario has developed a crush on Doctor Powell. Jeez, what is it with her? What does she have that has all the men panting?"

"You mean instead of you? Welcome to my world. Sounds like the story of my life with Jan."

"Oh, come on. You get plenty of attention. Problem is, they usually want to kill you, but hey, attention is attention."

"I have that effect on people. It's a gift."

"So, whaddya think? Did Safety do it?"

"I'm having my doubts. After all, Po Thang likes him."

Po Thang, on hearing his name, stuck his head over the pickup seat and gave Jan a lick.

She scratched the dog's ears and cooed, "And he doesn't like Doctor Diane, so his judgment must be pretty darned good, huh?"

"So, if we eliminate Safety as the one who tossed Rosario in the drink, we need a new bad guy. Guys. I still say it all gets down to following the money and that's where you come in. When you drop me off at the jobsite this morning, come on into my office, if we can both fit, and let's stir the pot some. See if we can make someone squirm."

"Hetta, you always make guys squirm. And not in a good way, if you know what I mean."

"It's a curse."

"So, Miss Sims," I said loud enough for anyone in the office building to hear, "you think you may have found a serious lead on our cost overrun problem?"

Jan looked startled, and hissed, "Hetta, I said you could make them nervous, not make me a target."

I lowered my voice. "Oh, so now that *you're* a target it's not so much fun, is it? You didn't seem overly worried when Dickless showed up because he doesn't hate you. Besides, you make a great target, what with your size and all."

"Listen, short stuff, I'm not having fun any more. Keep it up and I'll quit."

"Oh, relax. I'm trying to stir that pot we talked about."

"And speaking of pots, maybe you should cut back on the tortillas a tad."

"Yeah, well you could…get shorter, then you'd be fat, too."

This, of course, set us to tittering, which drew Safety to my office.

"What's so funny? Or do I dare ask?"

"Oh, nothing much," I told him then let loose a piggy nose snort that sent Jan into gales of even louder laughter. I took a deep breath to control myself, then added, "Jan was speculating that if someone tried to, uh, *killed* that Rosario fellow, it was probably over some kind of conspiracy and cover-up related to the cost overruns on the job."

Well, that was about the lamest segue I've ever heard.

Jan stopped laughing and shot me a look she meant would freeze my heart. And mouth. Safety turned so pale his freckles popped. Silence ensued, finally broken by an incredulous Safety. "Whoa, are you saying you think someone *killed* Rosario?"

Jan stood there with her mouth working like a guppy out of water. Since she was uncharacteristically speechless, I stepped in on her behalf. "It is a possibility."

Safety shook his head. "Might I remind you there is no body? And the police have practically declared his disappearance a boating accident?"

"Jan is a very suspicious person. She doesn't even trust the police back home, much less down here. Why—"

She cut me off. "Jan is here. Look Safety, don't pay any attention to a word Hetta says. She's been hitting the Nyquil of late, if you know what I mean. It's the stress. The first thirty-nine years of her childhood have been hard on her. Ouch!"

Some times a little pinch goes a long way.

Jan and Po Thang left my office for the boat, once again sticking me with Safety for a ride home. And now that Safety was alerted that Jan and I were on the snoop, hanging out with him could prove dangerous, but certainly less life-threatening than hopping aboard Pedro's Van of Death.

Apparently prompted by our previous conversation, Safety talked about Rosario all the way back to Santa Rosalia: how smart he was, how nice, how educated, and did I really think someone killed him?

"I dunno. Can you think of any reason why someone would off the guy? What with him being so nice and all?"

"Beats me. I mean, what could Rosario know that could put him in that kind of danger?"

"I thought you might know, Safety."

"Nope."

"You do realize the project has been experiencing unexplained cost overruns, don't you?"

"Hell, everyone knows. I figured it was due to dealing with Mexico as usual."

"Mexico *as usual* will run ten, fifteen percent. We're looking more like thirty."

He turned slightly pink in the face, but redheads will do that. "Thirty? That's…uh…that's not right."

"Oh? What is right?"

"Ten percent."

"And you know this how?"

He shrugged. "Common knowledge. You know, the grapevine."

"Does this grapevine define whether that rumored ten percent is over and above the usual twenty percent in Mexico?"

He didn't answer and remained a little surly until we reached the boat and Po Thang licked him back into civility. Po Thang was ecstatic to see him, even though they'd had an ear-rubbing and licking session back at the jobsite that morning. No, Safety did not lick Po Thang's ears.

After Safety left, Jan and I pulled our dinner together. She was whipping up some Louis sauce for our Lobster Louis when she stopped in mid-wisk. "Safety's hiding something. I feel it in my bones."

"Oh, I think he'd seriously enjoy a feel from you. In his bone."

Jan guffawed. "From my point of view he seems to hang around you a lot, as well. Dang, I guess one of us is gonna have to sleep with him. Wanna flip a coin?"

I swatted her on the head. "Let's use our brains instead."

"Why didn't we think of that novel idea years ago?"

We took our salads and wine onto the sundeck, even though I was still edgy about being so exposed after that little visit by Dickless. Several seagulls eyed our dinner with interest and cawed for a handout. We ignored them. If you feed 'em, next thing you know they crap all over you, kind of like a lot of men I've known.

"Chino called today."

"Yeah? Did you two make up?"

"Sort of. He wants me to go to Lopez Mateos next weekend for a visit with the relatives. Wanna take me over there?"

"Might I remind you that yesterday was the official start of Semana Santa?"

"I know, maybe we should play it safe and hunker down here."

"Where's the fun in that?"

Semana Santa, or Holy Week in Mexico is a Catholic tradition that has morphed into a free-for-all beach event in the Baja. Families from the States and all over Mexico converge upon Baja Beaches, and especially Conception Bay, for family reunions to beat all family reunions.

In many cases, several generations meet there, pitch tents, roll out the water toys and spend several days having a grand old time. For the most part it is an orderly (by Mexican standards) if noisy gathering, but the beaches, with tents five to ten deep, go from little pieces of paradise to something resembling Ft. Lauderdale at spring break.

The mine was scheduled to close at noon on Wednesday, allowing everyone to get home before the main influx of traffic reached us from up north. By the time the working stiffs up there left at noon and drove many hours to get to the beaches where the older generations had staked out a claim, most of the drivers had had a few *cervezas*. Quite a few.

I was told the town of Santa Rosalia is unusually quiet during this holiday week, with only restaurants, grocery stores, the ubiquitous *depositos* (beer wholesalers selling as an agency of a particular brand), OXXOs—the Mexican equivalent of 7-Eleven—and gas stations making a killing off the migrating celebrants.

The question was, were Jan and I willing to run the gauntlet of revelers past Conception Bay to get to Lopez Mateos, and Chino's own family reunion?

"I wonder how bad it's going to be on that stretch of beach. How come Chino's not picking you up, by the way?

"He's taking the back road, and he's going on Wednesday or Thursday. I can take the bus if you don't want to join us. If I can get a ticket."

"Are you two gonna fight?"

"No."

"Then I'll stay here."

"Okay, I'll pick a fight."

"Then I wouldn't miss it. We just have to be prepared for a bunch of traffic and tons of people on the way. We're good to go then, but I don't want to leave until Saturday. This boat needs a good cleaning and I figured to get it done on my days off."

"I forgot to tell you. The guy who washes your boat can't do it this week. He's gotta practice lugging a cross up the mountain to the cemetery. He invited us to join in the procession if we're here."

I looked at the dirt path winding up to the cemetery and imagined hiking it at night, by candlelight. "No way. I'd probably end up as a speed bump by the fourth station of the cross. On the other hand, if I did make it to the top it would probably constitute an Easter miracle."

"Saint Hetta? Spare me."

I was a little worried about leaving the boat unattended after that visit from Dickless, and told Jan so. "And even though I know now that Luján is lurking on this side of the peninsula, and that I don't have to worry about going to Lopez Mateos, or

Magdalena Bay, I'd be a lot more secure if I knew exactly where the thievin' jackass is."

"Don't be silly, Hetta. You'll never be secure."

"Thanks, I really needed that."

She smiled. "But anyhow, I'll call Chino, tell him we're coming over and ask if his cousins have heard anything new about Dickless. How's that?"

"It will have to do. Come on, Po Thang, let's take a walk while your Aunt Jan calls your Uncle Chino."

"Woof."

Jan was just hanging up the phone and had a frown on her face when Po Thang and I returned from our potty run. Yes, both of us. I try to use the marine facilities as much as possible to cut down on my black water pump-out fees. Life without sewer lines can get a mite complicated.

"What? Why so glum?"

"You ain't gonna like it. Chino's cousins heard that Dickless has something going down in Conception Bay. Shady real estate deal of some sort, no doubt."

"Conception Bay? I really didn't want to hear that. Makes sense though, with so many disputed properties down there. Lujàn doesn't build or sell anything he doesn't expect to steal later on. Oh well, at least it's safe for us to go visit with Granny Yee in Lopez Mateos. And with the hordes of people at Conception this weekend, what are the odds of running into that dirty rat bastard, Luján?"

I should'a bought a lottery ticket.

While we were making plans for our run over to Lopez Mateos, Jan commented, "Granny Yee likes you. Says if it wasn't for you she'd probably be dead, along with that entire village she lived in. Ya know, though, we never heard one bit of news about that super meth factory you blew up in the Baja."

"Of course not. Bad for tourism. Besides, I didn't blow it up, Nacho did. I only helped to distract the bad guys."

"Wonder where Nacho is now? Hell, I wonder *who* Nacho is now."

Nacho, a.k.a. The Shadow, or Ignacio, is indeed a shadowy character, but handsome in a criminal sort of way, and one of our favorite topics of discussion.

He shows up in my life periodically, usually when I'm up to my ass in alligators, and helps pull me from the swamp. We don't know who he really is, or for whom he works, but I imagined his card should read:

Lamont "Nacho" Cranston
Shady undertakings our specialty
www.nachomuchomacho.com
Se Habla Espanol

After a recent encounter with him on the Arizona border, he gave me his actual card, the one I was supposed to burn, eat, or whatever those undercover guys do. It reads:

L. Cranston Pest Control

1-800-got-bads?
We get what's bugging you.

I didn't burn or eat it, as instructed, for a card like that is way too priceless to destroy. Besides, who knows when I might need him?

Fairly soon if Luján doesn't leave me the hell alone.

Chapter 19

Nobody goes there anymore because it's too
crowded.—Yogi Berra

I looked forward to going with Jan to Lopez
Mateos for the weekend for several reasons, not the
least of which is Chino's large and boisterous family
make really good fish tacos and never run out of
cold beer. As an added bonus, I love delving deeper
into their family history. Proud of my own
genealogical roots, my ancestors were pikers when it
came to adventurous voyaging onto North American
shores.

Doctor Brigido Comacho Yee, better known
as Chino, is a descendant of a couple of men
stranded in Magdalena Bay when their Manila
Galleon sunk there in the late fifteen hundreds.

Comacho was a Filipino businessman who
was moving his business from the Philippines to
Acapulco in *Nueva España*. He and his family

boarded the galleon, taking with them a few slaves, his head jewelry designer—a Chinese man named Yee and *his* family—a fortune in jewelry, silver coins, silks, Chinese porcelain and spices.

According to a written account passed down through the generations, Gómez Pérez Comacho and his family survived the ill-fated voyage of the galleon; a hobbyhorsing, rat-infested vessel dubbed a "flying pig" because of her rotund shape. Comacho thought of her as a *fat* pig. With her round belly engorged with over two tons of cargo, and a forty-foot draft, the ship was a nightmare to navigate. Because she could not sail into the wind their ship, as well as the other galleons in their fleet, first voyaged north and east from the Philippines, striving to stay as near thirty degrees north latitude as possible. On this voyage, however, they had been driven far to the north in their quest for favorable winds.

They were badly off course and schedule before finally sighting land and turning southward. Plodding along the shore, they could only pray for northerlies to push them safely to Acapulco, but the treasure-laden ship sunk, stranding them in the uninhabited area of Magdalena Bay on Baja's Pacific coast, and generations later Chino is still looking for the shipwreck. He was elated when I dredged up an astrolabe—the ancient precursor to the GPS—with my anchor.

The son of a panga fisherman, Chino became fascinated at a young age with the influx of migrating whales each year, and especially their birthing grounds. Hired as a guide and boat driver to a British marine biologist expedition studying the migratory habits of those whales, he astounded the scientists with his knowledge. Chino, who later tested at genius levels, was an autodidact, self-taught in English, French, and German, and had read every book available to him on whales. He knew as much or more about the subject as the scientists who ended up mentoring him because he'd lived with the whales all his life.

His admiring mentors arranged for him to attend special schools in the UK, then on to Imperial College, near Hyde Park in the heart of London, which focuses on science, engineering, and medicine.

After graduating, at sixteen no less, with an education equal to that of a British Royal, he returned to Mexico and was back to running whale tour boats when the University of California Davis School of Veterinary Medicine got wind of him and offered him a full ticket to their doctorate program. It was there that he met Craig, my gay vet friend.

When I hired Chino, on a recommendation from Craig, for a study on the effects of a large water desalination project in Baja's Magdalena Bay, with its large migratory whale population, he fell hard for Jan and the rest, as they say, is history. History with one small twist: It never occurred to Jan her new amour, with two doctorates under his belt (along with, evidently, some other manly stuff left better un-discussed in polite circles) could be so young. When she discovered he was a dozen years her junior, she was dumbfounded. Now this age thing had become a relationship-killing obsession, which ticks me off because this is *my* year to obsess about age.

The matriarch of the Yee clan is Grandmother, or *Abuela*, Yee, who evidently started a familial tradition of early childbearing. She was fourteen when Chino's mom was born, and then Chino's mother was only fifteen when Chino arrived. The fact that Chino's mother is in her early forties sends Ms. Jan into a Texas tailspin.

Not as bad a tailspin as mine at being for...in my late thirties does, but close.

Jan and I left early on Saturday morning, taking my friend Geary's advice that during Semana Santa most of the revelers didn't start stirring until noon.

We planned on eating and visiting our way to Lopez Mateos, seeing old friends and indulging in Mexican cuisine along the way. We love road trips and from the grin on Po Thang's face, so did he. And like most dogs, he insisted on leaning over Jan's shoulder to catch a breeze from an open window and deposit dog drool on the side of my pickup.

Our first stop of the day was at Burro Beach, in Conception Bay, to see Baja Geary. He is one of the few full time residents there and a better man than me, because in the summer even the water temp is in the nineties. With no electricity other than what is provided by solar panels and a generator, he lives without the benefit of what I consider one of the staffs of life: air conditioning.

Geary is on ham radio every morning, giving the Sonrisa Net weather to eagerly awaiting boaters from San Diego to the Gulf of Tehuantepec. If there's gonna be a blow, he lets us know days in advance so we can hunker down in a safe anchorage. He is especially valuable to cruisers during hurricane season and even though Baja hurricanes can be fairly unpredictable, he at least is able to give boaters a heads up.

We timed our arrival at Geary's to coincide with his eight AM ritual of blasting a bagpipe version of "Amazing Grace" from speakers on his front porch. Boaters anchored in his bay come out on deck with their coffee each morning to enjoy such an enlightening start to the day.

Jan and I met Geary years before when we landed on his beach during a blow that neither our kayaks nor we could handle. I'd stopped in to see him again a couple of weeks before, when Jenks and I visited Conception Bay prior to his leaving for Dubai. Today, though, I was on a mission to find out what, if anything, he knew of Dickless Richard's activities at Conception Bay.

I'd spoken with Geary the day before on the Sonrisa Net. After listening to boaters all over the Sea griping about the Semana Santa crowds, I was a little worried we wouldn't even be able to reach his house from the main road.

Cruisers in San Carlos reported the normal ten minute trip from one end of town to the other was taking up to three hours as the population skyrocketed from three thousand to thirty thousand. Most had stocked up and were laying low in well-guarded marinas.

Geary's Playa Burro, however, was indeed crowded, but as he'd told us, there was a clear path to his palapa, which was surrounded by a family he'd known for years.

One thing I've always admired about Geary is his non-judgmental, laissez-faire philosophy about life on the beach, and life in general. Hurricane blows down his Hughes system and washes water up onto his porch? Move upstairs and get the system operational when he can. Neighbors squabble? Let 'em. Hoards of Mexicans, in an old tradition of eating and drinking everything in sight while partying hardy on his beach during *Semana Santa*, or All Saints Week? Go with the flow and enjoy the company. He lives with amazing grace, indeed.

As we picked our way through tents to his front porch, I noted that the only ones stirring were the old and young. Lumps rolled in sleeping bags and blankets accounted for the rest of the population.

Within an hour, however, jet skis began firing up and what looked like ten-year-olds, with two or three younger kids clinging on for dear life behind them, were zipping back and forth in shallow water. Not a life jacket or helmet to be seen.

I started to make some grumpy grownup-sounding comment about it, but then thought better. "Man, when I was a kid I would have loved being turned loose on a jet ski."

"Hetta," Jan said, "when you were a kid jet skis weren't invented yet."

"Smarty pants. Geary, anybody ever get hurt out here on those things?"

"Every year. Even had a couple of deaths. Same as in the States."

"I see all the boats that were anchored here in front of your place have taken a powder."

"Yep. Jet skiers use them for racing pylons, and once in a while, a bumper car. The cruisers are hiding out there." He waved his hand toward several small islands.

"Can't blame them. We gotta get on down the road, but first I have to ask you about somebody. You know pretty much everyone around here, right?"

"If they live on the beach, I probably do."

I recounted the story of our previous run-in with Luján at Mag Bay and asked if he'd heard of him. "He's a low-life real estate scammer and he's reportedly moved his slimy operations to Conception Bay."

Geary shook his head. "Don't know him, but real estate problems are always cropping up. I even thought I might have to move a while back, but it blew over. After the revolution the government granted parcels of land to *ejidos*, or farmer/family groups. Problem is, no one told the grantees, and land grabbers moved in, and some places have been sold and resold for a hundred years. Now, several generations later, educated children of the *ejidatarios* and their lawyers are suing for possession of the land they'd been duped out of."

I nodded, having already made the unpleasant acquaintance of one of these smarmy land thieves: Luján. "Oh, yeah, and people like him have bought their way into the *ejidos'* pockets and practically stolen the property again. No wonder so many Gringos are afraid to buy anything down here. You pay rent for the land you're on, right Geary?"

"Yes, and you never know when things will change and a new so-called owner will decide to burn down everything on the beach. Especially happens in the summer, when most of the Gringos have gone north."

I pointed toward barely visible blackened skeletal remains on an beach where houses used to be. "Like there?"

"Exactly."

Our next stop was scheduled for Café Olé, a small beach settlement at the south end of the bay. Philly, a Mexican national and a member of an *ejido*, and her American husband, Joe, have spent years building what I call a "cheeseburger in paradise" spot that includes a restaurant/bar, their house and a camping beach. They also rent out beachfront lots to others who, like Geary, have built homes. When Jenks and I were anchored there a few weeks ago, they were putting the finishing touches on a six-room hotel and I wanted to check it out as a get-away destination on weekends when I didn't go to Camp Chino and wanted a change of scenery.

Luckily we were so hungry we stopped for *huevos a la Mexicana* at Bertha's *tienda* on the way, because there would be no breakfast served at Café Olé this day.

Lines of large whitewashed rocks blocked the entrance to the entire place and seedy looking men with guns confronted us when we stopped in on that side of the highway and stepped from the pickup. Po Thang gave them a menacing growl, so they stopped short and yelled what sounded like a hostile warning to get lost. When we hesitated there was a show of firepower that needed no translation. We got lost.

Worried for the owners, Philly and Joe, we backtracked to Geary's and told him what was going on. He raised Café Olé on the VHF radio and was assured by Joe they were all right, if shook up. They were being allowed to walk out to the main road, but not take any of their vehicles. When they tried, the goons fired one over their heads.

"Check out our Facebook page," Joe told us, "and read all about it. We've gotten word to the police in Mulege, but so far no one has shown up. The cops don't like to get involved in property disputes and told us if they come all the way out here we'll have to pay for their gas and feed them lunch."

For some reason this sent Jan and me into fits of laughter.

Mexico, you gotta love it.

As we slowly passed by Café Olé again on our way south, I counted at least six armed men patrolling the road and beach. Then my heart almost went into full arrest when I spotted someone I knew and loathed strutting, like a preening banty rooster, along the hotel's front verandah.

It was that rat, Ricardo Lujàn, in all his Dickless glory.

Chapter 20

> Believe me, a thousand friends suffice thee
> not; In a single enemy thou hast more than enough.
> Ali Ben Abi Taleb

"You don't think Lujàn saw us, do you?" Jan asked as I hit the gas and sped around the bend and out of sight from Café Olé.

"Naw, but it was him, all right. No doubt about it."

"Well, at least now we know where he is. They say to keep your friends close and your enemies even closer. Looks to me like he's up to his old tricks of hiring goons and stealing property. I hope the folks from Café Olé are really okay. They gotta be scared. I sure would be."

I nodded. "A true *cacique* in action." Jan and I learned that word, *cacique,* the year before from Mexicans in Magdalena Bay. *Caciques* are large yellow and black birds known to steal other bird's nests rather than build their own, and the locals use

175

it as a derogatory term for people like Lujàn and his ilk. Human *caciques* are known to seek out properties in dispute, pay the *ejidatarios* a token fee to take the problem off their hands, then claim the land and anything built on it as their own.

Lujàn most likely has clerks at the county and state level on his payroll, always on the alert for something in dispute worth stealing.

It looked like Despicable Dickless was back in full *bandido* mode and I planned to stay far, far away from him. "Well, there goes any idea I had of staying in Conception Bay once in awhile, or bringing my boat down here any time soon. Looks like you're stuck with me at Camp Chino on weekends for the time being."

"And I plan to spend every weekend there and keep an eye on that Diane person. Speaking of, now that Rosario and she are alone for the weekend I'm hoping they're humping each other like those whales they count."

"You think? I know Rosario's smitten with her, but I can't quite see it as mutual. He's not in her league like Chino is."

Jan narrowed her eyes at me and growled. "Po Thang, how's about you and me throwing a big ole birthday party for Hetta. I'm thinking we should have it at Café Olé."

"You have a mean streak, you know that?"

"Yep. I got it from you."

"Well, then, you should be more grateful."

She shrugged. "Yabbut, you also taught me to be *un*grateful."

This set us cackling and when I caught my breath I told her, "About this birthday thing. If truth be known, I guess I'm afraid of not only getting old, but also being fat, short, alone *and* old."

"Well, hell, girl. Can't do anything about the *old* part, but you could stop eating, quit being a pain in the ass with the men who like you so they, namely Jenks, will stick around, and...uh...ya know, I saw one of those medieval racks on eBay. Maybe I'll get it for you for your birthday."

Seeing Lujàn again in Conception Bay rattled me. Now I knew where he was, and it was way too close to my boat. The question was, what could I do about it?

After arriving in Lopez Mateos, I put in a call to Jenks and as much as I hated to, I told him about Lujàn prowling around on *Raymond Johnson* and then seeing him at Conception Bay today. I didn't know who else to turn to for advice and even though Jenks was so far away, I trusted his judgment above any other.

He was not pleased. "I feel like I need to get on a plane. *Again.*"

Crap. Had I not promised to stay out of trouble? And had he not warned me he was getting a little weary of bailing me out? My spirits sank at his tone and tears blurred my vision.

Although the camera wasn't activated on Skype, Jenks somehow sensed my distress when I clammed up. Or maybe it was because I didn't say another word; that's just not like me. Normally a challenge like that *again* thing would have me cussing a blue streak, or at least hanging up on him after some smart-assed comment, but my silence must have spoken volumes.

"Hetta, I didn't mean that the way it sounded. I will gladly go anywhere, anytime, to help you out. I realize you had nothing to do with this...." I think he wanted to say *this time*, but thought better of it. "Look, enjoy your weekend in Lopez Mateos and don't give Dickless another thought. I'll think of something so you won't have to be looking over your shoulder. You have enough on your plate right now."

"But—"

"No buts. I'll come up with something, but until I do please be careful. And trust me."

"I do trust you, and I'm so sorry—"

"This one is not your fault, honey. I'm sorry I upset you. Last thing you needed was to feel any more alone than you already do."

I hung up feeling much, much better.

And that is why I love Jenks Jenkins.

Jan, Chino, Po Thang and I stayed with one of Chino's cousins who had a couple of spare rooms and didn't mind a dog in the house. Grans Yee said dogs are dirty, and besides that Po Thang might upset her own precious house pet, an ill-tempered, overweight goat named Preciosa.

My room was really a small office with a cot, but it was located right by the front door so Po Thang could be let out easily.

Carnitas was on the menu for dinner, so it's a good thing my cholesterol was running a little low.

This traditional Saturday night treat is to die for; probably more literally than I'd like to think about.

Huge chunks of hog are first boiled in (what else?) lard, then grilled over a mesquite fire for the best ever pork. Rolled into fresh homemade tortillas—making sure pieces of fat are included in the roll—and topped with Salsa Mexicana made with chopped onions, tomatoes, cilantro and lime juice, this culinary delight is beyond good. Po Thang, for the first time since we met, actually could not choke down one more bite.

Luckily we ate early, because Chino heard there were a few whales hanging out by the dunes and since it was a full moon, he suggested I go out there and listen to them sing. He had a domino game planned with his cousins and Jan said she'd heard enough whales for a lifetime, so around six I threw a kayak and a six pack of beer into the bed of my truck and took off.

I hesitated taking Po Thang with me, as I wanted to paddle out to the whales and figured he would be happier hanging out with the domino players at the house than locked in my truck. I was, however, overruled by everyone in the household when all those *carnitas* went to work on the dog's digestive system and he started letting go with some hellacious farts.

The full moon reflecting off white sand dunes and water was enough to justify the trip out, but whale songs were the topping on the cake. There were quite a few others out to see and hear the whales, so when I paddled out Po Thang took up with some campers. I needn't have worried he would try to follow me into the water; he took one look at me getting into the kayak and headed for the nearest nice warm campfire, welcomed by campers who had no idea how fortunate they were that he was full.

However, while I was relieved I didn't have to lock him in the truck, I was somewhat concerned about him getting too close to the flames and setting off a methane explosion big enough to wipe out a bunch of nice campers and an entire tour bus full of Japanese tourists.

It was chilly, as I was on the Pacific side of the Baja, but I was bundled up and the water was dead flat calm so I didn't get wet. Before I knew it, it was almost midnight and I was out of beer, so I collected my dog and headed for bed.

At least by the time we turned in Po Thang's flatulence had abated, but I have to admit those dog farts made me nostalgic for my dearly departed pooch, RJ. We used to refer to them as "Eau de Chein" or, as Jan preferred, "Oh, de dawg!"

Chapter 21

Those who set in motion the forces of evil cannot always control them afterwards.—Charles Waddell Chesnutt

Sunday morning after a big old bowl of *menudo*, that marvelous tripe soup the Mexicans have on weekends, Po Thang and I left for the boat, leaving Jan with Chino for a dusty back-road trek along the Pacific side of the Baja to their whale camp. I had considered taking that route myself, not wanting to pass by Café Olé and the dastardly Dickless again, but it was way out of my way and over unpaved roads for the most part.

I decided a baseball cap pulled over my hair, sunglasses and an unfamiliar pickup with a dog hanging out the window, blocking their view of the driver, were enough to camouflage me from Lujàn in case he was still around.

I needn't have worried, for the rocks blocking the entrance to Café Olé were gone, as were the goons. Despite my curiosity as to what had changed overnight, fear of running into Lujàn overrode my nosiness and I drove right on by, figuring maybe Geary would have the scoop.

Geary wasn't home, nor were his neighbors, so no luck on Dickless news. "Dang, dawg, guess we'll have to wait until we get back to the boat to learn the latest from Café Olé's Facebook page. By the way, do you have a Facebook page?"

Po Thang, who was happily perched in the passenger seat cocked his head and probably wondered if Facebook had anything to do with food. He'd recovered rapidly from his pig fest the night before and ate his own bowl of breakfast *menudo*. I was somewhat worried about the aftermath of innard soup on *his* innards, so I rolled my window down as a precaution.

A few miles down the road from Burro Beach, I spotted a lot of activity on shore when I rounded the curve at Posada, a Gringo community where the hot springs Jenks and I had recently steeped in burbled up from what I now considered a churning cauldron of unsettled volcanic activity. My nosy meter tweaked, so I turned into the entrance and parked.

Dune buggies, cars and pickups, as well as two Federal Police vehicles and a camo-painted military Hummer shared the beach. People milled about, all looking seaward. Whale shark sighting? I know there is often one in the bay and he always draws a crowd.

I found it ironic that when the Café Olé people were being held virtual hostage only a few miles away the day before, they couldn't even get the local cops to show up. But a whale shark? Now that's *important*.

I snapped on Po Thang's leash and we sauntered over to see what the fuss was about. Perched on cacti and rocks at the far end of the beach near the rock-lined natural hot tub were about a dozen buzzards. Seagulls wheeled and squalled, but other than that it was a pretty hushed scene considering the number of people milling about.

"So," I said to the first person I encountered, "what's so interesting?"

A tall guy I recognized as a resident of Geary's beach nodded a hello. "Dead guy."

"Drowning accident?"

"You might say that, if gettin' your ass boiled in a hot spring qualifies."

"Well, yuck. I sat in that pool a couple of weeks ago."

"Don't imagine anyone will be getting in there any time soon. Heard he's pretty much well done. Mush."

"Now there's an image to ruin one's whole day. Any idea who it is?"

"Nah, some Mexican."

We were both silent for a while, watching as the police backed a pickup down a beach which, under other circumstances, would qualify as travel brochure material. Now the picturesque sparkling turquoise water and white sand somehow made the tragedy of a death worse.

Another guy joined us and said, "They've been waiting for low tide so they can get the truck to the body. 'Course the lower the tide, the hotter the water and more tender the guy'll be. Wouldn't want their job right now."

Swallowing hard I was backing away from the beach when a waft of breeze carried the scent of cooked flesh at us, invoking memories of last night's *carnitas*. Po Thang whined and I had a gag reflex. To stave off the urge to urp I whirled, rushed back toward my truck and spotted Geary standing by the front bumper.

"Hey, Geary. I stopped by your *palapa*, but guess you've been here. Bummer about the dead guy."

"Hetta, I think you should beat feet out of here. Right now."

"Why? What'd I do?"

"Nothing. But that dead guy? According to rumor, he was involved in that hostage situation a Café Olé."

"Oh, please, please, tell me that salt-water stew is made up of Ricardo Lujàn."

Geary grinned but shook his head. "You better hope not. After all, you and this Dickless dude have a history, and the cops around here will be rounding up the usual suspects."

Crap, hadn't thought about that.

Geary told me to drive down to the next beach and he'd meet me there with more information about the dead guy. By the time I parked at Santispac, Geary caught up with me in his dune buggy.

Po Thang roamed the beach in search of generous campers while Geary and I sat in my pickup. He brought me up to date.

"Café Olé's Facebook page said they'd hired an off-duty cop to spend the night there last night. It was chilly out, so he was holed up in the restaurant trying to keep warm when he saw a couple of pickups pull in front of the hotel."

"With the full moon it was like daylight out there, so he probably got a pretty good look."

Geary nodded. "He figured the goons were bringing in reinforcements, so he woke up the owners of the place and alerted them. Philly, Joe, and the cop sat up all night, worried that maybe there would be an attack, but come dawn the hoodlums had vanished. Just like that, not a soul in sight."

"When I drove by a little while ago the rocks blocking the road were gone."

"Yep, Joe was on the radio this morning announcing that Café Olé is open for business as usual."

"And now maybe Lujàn is doing a slow boil?"

"Lucky for Joe and Philly they had that cop with them. A foolproof alibi if ever there was one, in case it turns out there was foul play."

"So, you think maybe one of the hired guns, after they left the hotel blockade, just got drunk and fell asleep in the hot spring? It happens, you know."

"Could be. Anyhow, I think it's best if you stay away for a while, until we find out more about whose body that is."

I didn't need convincing. The whole thing gave me the creeps, not because I was worried about Luján, but about *me* if he was dead.

I'd planned to stop in Mulege, hit Saul Davis's grocery store for some American goodies—Polish sausage and Alpo were on the list, and I'd heard he carried Velveeta!—but the Café Olé thing sent me straight back to *Raymond Johnson*, and the phone.

"Jan, Dickless might be dead!"

"You killed him?"

"Not that I wouldn't mind, but I was with you, remember?"

"Anything you want me to say."

I shot her the finger, even though she couldn't see it.

"I saw that, Hetta."

"Good."

"Anyhow, what happened to Lujàn?"

"Maybe nothing. I saw the police throw a body bag into the back of their pickup and Geary told me rumor has it that it was one of the perps from Café Olé, which, by the way, is goon free and open for business. The dead guy was found simmering in the Posada hot spring this morning, so hope springs eternal."

"That, Hetta, was a truly lame joke. But, uh-oh."

"What, uh-oh?"

"Well, you *do* have a history there."

"I know, I know. That's what Geary said, *if* it turns out to be Dickless. But I have an alibi. I was with you guys, thank the Lord."

"No, I mean a history of your men gettin', you know, parboiled."

"That's ridiculous. Okay, so my ex-so-called fiancé's body was found in the hot tub at my old house back in Oakland, but that was eons ago and even the police agreed I had nothing to do with it. Anyhow, like I said, I was in Lopez Mateos with you."

"Not exactly."

"What, *exactly*, Miss Jan?"

"You went off by yourself to commune with whales in the moonlight. You even said you might sleep out there until I told you those dunes harbored scorpions and that the last time, and I do mean the *last* time, Chino and I camped there we found at least a dozen under our tent when we broke camp."

"And that is exactly why Po Thang and I returned to the house in Lopez Mateos. I hate sleeping with critters."

"Oh, come on Hetta, you've slept with lots of critters."

Chapter 22

The body of a dead enemy always smells
sweet.—Titus Flavious Vespasian
NOT!—Hetta Coffey

As soon as I returned to the boat I'd rubbed Vicks vapor-rub in my nostrils to obliterate the stench of what I hoped was, at the same time hoped wasn't, Luján au jus.

If it was the jerk, I probably should have felt some bit of remorse for his family, but figured he probably hadn't gotten around to stealing one.

After I gave Jan the latest news, I called Jenks to let him know El Lujàn was maybe dead. Jenks wasn't exactly grief-stricken; after all, he'd launched a Molotov cocktail at the little creep once himself. "Couldn't happen to a nicer guy," he said. "How'd you do it?"

"Very funny. You're the one who said you'd deal with him when we talked last night. So, how'd *you* do it?

"Hey, I'm in Dubai, I have an alibi."

"Was that a very bad attempt at poetry? Gosh, between you and Jan I feel sooo supported." I told him what she said about my ever so slight connection to dead guys in hot tubs.

"Coincidence? You be the judge," he teased, using one of my favorite lines. "Just ribbing you, sweetheart. Well, if it is him, someone saved me a lot of time and money."

"How's that?"

"I was trying to hire you a bodyguard."

"You're kidding? I don't know whether to be grateful or pissed off."

"Stick with grateful, it'll make both our days go better. And as for you having anything to do with his death, do the math. Could you possibly have left Chino's cousin's house, driven to Conception Bay, found Lujàn, somehow lured him away from his armed guards and killed him in the time frame allowed? You and Jan saw him mid-morning one day and the next morning he's bouillabaisse."

"Oh, crap, Jenks, you have laid waste to any future desire for one of my fave dishes."

"Sorry about that. Okay, let's count the hours. You were with Jan and Chino's family until what time?"

"I left the house around six so I could get to the dunes in time to watch the moon rise. It takes around three hours to drive from there to Café Olé. So, say, six hours round trip, maybe a little less, but remember it was nighttime, Saturday night of Semana Santa, and even with a full moon Mex 1 is no picnic. I'm sure a racer from the Baja 1000 could cut that time in half, but not me, and certainly not in a Ford Ranger."

"Okay, let's say six hours. You left at six, that *could* put you at Café Olé at nine and then you're back in Lopez Mateos by midnight. What time did you return to the house from your whale-watching expedition."

"Rats. About midnight. We pussyfooted in, although Po Thang would probably take exception to the term. The lights were out and we didn't want to wake anyone. Ask Po Thang, he'll vouch for me."

Hearing his name, Po Thang sprang to his feet and stared at the fridge.

"Po Thang would have been a character witness for O.J. if there was steak in that glove. You might conjure up a more credible witness or two. Was anyone else out on the dunes?"

"Yes!" I pumped my fist into the air. "A busload of Japanese tourists. They even petted Po Thang. I told them I'd lived in Tokyo and found out one couple actually live in my building. Not when I was there, but they live there now. And, their tour guide translated when we got all fouled up between my lousy Japanese and their English."

"Well, there you go. Besides, that timeline of only six hours to drive round trip back to Conception Bay, off Lujàn and then get back to the house by midnight wouldn't hold up with the US cops, but I think Geary's right; cops, Mexican or otherwise, always go for the obvious suspect first. Is anyone at Conception Bay besides Geary aware that you know Lujàn?"

"Nope."

"See, no worries. Besides you have a perfectly reasonable alibi."

"Jenks, where I come from the phrase, some folks just need killin', is a perfectly reasonable alibi for people like Luján."

"Listen, Dorothy, you're not in Texas anymore. Write down everything you remember about that tour bus and any other people on the beach in case you need to find them. How come you went whale watching without Jan and Chino?"

"Jan said she'd seen enough whales for a lifetime and Chino had a hot domino game scheduled with his cousins."

"No wonder you left. You never win at dominos."

"Only when I play you, Jenks. I kick ass when challenging mere mortals."

He chuckled. He and I have played hundreds of games. I think I've won ten. One should know better than to play a game of chance with someone who spent twenty years in the navy, but playing against him had honed my skills tremendously, so I was hell on wheels with regular players.

We said our goodbyes and I longed to be beamed up and over to Dubai instead of spending a lonely night on the boat. At least maybe I didn't have to worry about Dickless Richard skulking around. That didn't keep me from activating my alarm and locking all doors.

Even with Jenks's reassurances, I tossed and turned all night, jumping up on occasion to jot down things like the name on the tour bus. Then I remembered the couple whose campsite Po Thang invaded saying they were staying there another week, and made a note to call one of Chino's cousins and ask him to locate the campers on the dunes and get a name and address. I also had one ear tuned for the sound of *federales* swooping down on the boat.

I finally drifted off, only to sit straight up in bed. Pictures! I'd given everyone at the marina a photo of Lujàn and told them to be on the lookout for him. Crap! So much for no one in the area being able to connect me to the dead guy, should it come up. Once again, lack of a local newspaper might prove useful.

Any chance of going back to sleep was long gone, so I decided to go to work at first light.

I'd cleared it with the head dude, Bert, to bring Po Thang with me to work this week, so long as I didn't try to put *him* on the payroll. It had crossed my mind; that dawg can *eat*.

A wildly thumping tail told me Safety had arrived at the office before he even entered the building. Po Thang's second favorite thing, food being first, seemed to be Safety. I had to admit that even though the man was still on my suspect list for the attempted murder of Rosario, those Robert Redford looks put the occasional wag in my own tail, as well. His obvious admiration of the lovely Jan, however vexing to the old ego, was probably a good thing considering Jenks was halfway around the world.

"Hiya, Hetta. How was your weekend?"

"Okay." *Except for some guy getting offed with me as a possible suspect.*

"Just okay? I thought you and Jan had grand plans."

"Jan had grand plans. I went along for the ride. What'd you do?"

"Went fishing."

"Get lucky?"

"Hetta, shame on you. A gentleman never discusses his dalliances."

"You dallied? You dog."

"Ha! You jealous? That sounded jealous to me."

"Safety, I'm taken, remember? How can I be jealous? Anyhow, get on with your story. Sounds like a good one."

"Since the fish weren't biting, I went ashore for some food and ended up at a dance on the beach. Great band, cold beer."

"Hot dames?"

"Some. Danced my "Boot Scootin' Boogie" off."

"Next time maybe I'll go with you. I love to scoot. Unfortunately, with Jenks, not so much."

"Your Jenks can't dance?"

"It's not that he doesn't, he thinks he *can*. It ain't pretty, but very endearing."

Safety found this highly amusing and when he quit laughing he said, "Can't wait to meet Jenks and tell him how lucky he is."

"That he thinks he can dance?"

"No, that he found you before I did. Wish you'd been at that do at Santispac Saturday night. We'd a cut a rug."

He winked and left me with my jaw resting on my boobs.

I'm not so sure what surprised me the most, that Safety said he wished he found me before Jenks did, or that Safety was at Conception Bay Saturday night, right down the beach from where that body was found.

Po Thang and I spent a blessedly quiet week together at the office, he sleeping most of the day under my desk between ball-throwing sessions with various mine employees on their breaks, and emptying the company fridge. Having an office dog boosted my popularity and gave me an opportunity to talk with employees I normally wouldn't, gleaning bits and pieces of job related gossip.

When I needed a break I took Po Thang with me on the hunt for treasures around the jobsite. I come from a long line of beachcombers, rock hounds and dumpster divers. When the personal metal detector first became available, my father was ecstatic, and he still always has the latest, snazziest model. When I was a kid he took me with him on various beaches and jobsites, looking for shark's teeth, old bottles, and anything else excavated by large construction equipment. One of our greatest finds was in a phosphate pit in North Carolina where we unearthed a nine-inch shark tooth that we later learned was from a megalodon about the size of a city bus. That tooth has had a profound effect on my snorkeling activities ever since.

I'd heard Geary mention he'd found Boleite in these hills when he was roaring around in his dune buggy, so I was on the search a couple of days a week. Boleite is a very rare silver species that is found only in this area, and was discovered in the late 1800's by a French mining engineer named Eduoard Cumenge who also found another mineral named after him, cumengite.

Boleite, even though it is technically a form of silver, is clear indigo in color and very rare and can, if you get the right one, be cut into a gemstone. Okay, so it is mostly found in a mine location nearer to Santa Rosalia and my chance of finding any of the little square rocks was nil to none, but then again, I still buy lottery tickets. At least I got some exercise and found other nice rocks, so it wasn't all for naught.

These little rock hunting excursions unfortunately emboldened Po Thang, who wandered off for his own dumpster dive into the mess hall garbage bin and returned smelling like old beans. After that I made him stay inside the office building with me unless someone was watching him. He sulked a little, but Safety took him for a pickup ride which somewhat restored his good nature.

Po Thang charmed everyone he met, even taking a liking to that turd in Purchasing, Osvaldo "Ozzie" Sanchez, which I thought at first was a lack of good judgment, then I realized that this dog doesn't give doodly-squat about who anyone is as long as they speak kindly and hand out treats.

I'm kind of like that myself.

While I looked for clues as to who was robbing the company store, Jan and Rosario did likewise from Camp Chino. Neither said a word in their emails about how Jan was coping with that little green streak she'd developed where Dr. Di was concerned, so I surmised peace reigned.

The Posada/Café Olé incident hung heavy over my head. It was a damned if you do, damned if you don't, situation. If the dead guy wasn't Dickless, I had to worry he'd come looking for me again, and if it was, the police might do the same.

I scanned the Mexican news agencies every night, both hoping to see something and fearing I would. After all, if Lujàn's ugly mug turned up on national television, someone working at the marina could see it and make a connection back to me. Of course, the Mexico City television stations were not exactly the best source for local stuff, but I worried that a murder (if that is what is was) of a local so-called big shot might get a mention.

We were nowhere nearer figuring out who dumped Rosario in the drink, either. Again, if that is what happened. Rosario was certain someone tried to kill him, but I wasn't a hundred percent convinced. I still held on to my cover-up theory, which in itself was bad enough.

Po Thang's popularity enhanced my chances for questioning my fellow workers about the incident, but although there was speculation galore, no one really knew anything. His position had not been refilled, probably due to budgeting problems, which brought me full circle: Follow the money and probably the entire mystery will solve itself.

Frustrated at my lack of progress and unanswered questions, I decided to make a job tour.

I signed out a truck and grabbed our orange vests and hard hats as company policy required. Po Thang looked quite jaunty in his vest and hard hat, but keeping the hat on him proved a losing battle. Safety had issued Po Thang's gear. His hat read: I BRAKE FOR ORES AND BARS

Chapter 23

BROAD IN THE BEAM (Nautical term):
Said of a wide vessel or a large-hipped woman.
I had the right of way.
Unfortunately the other gal had the widest
beam.

When Po Thang and I left the office for a jobsite tour I realized, as we climbed into a company truck, that I'd never driven into the busy part of the site. Up until then, someone else chauffeured me around and I now wondered, as I became more paranoid, if that was by design.

The administrative offices, man camp, mess hall and the like are all clustered near the entrance, whereas the actual mine construction area is set back at least a couple of miles. I was somewhat familiar with the busy roads from previous trips into the heart of what would, for a stranger to the ways of construction, look to be total chaos. Hundreds of vehicles of all sizes mill about in seemingly random patterns while hoards of worker bees armed with hand tools line roads and building areas. An ant farm I had as a kid comes to mind.

Having spent so much time on working sites, I knew there was a grand plan and everyone knew where to go and what to do, and that if I took precautions I could stay out of their way. Or so I thought.

I was stopped on the side of the road, double checking a plot plan for my location, when a cloud of dust caught my attention, especially since it seemed to be aiming right at us. Po Thang sat up straight and stared at the oncoming threat as intently as I did. We both let out what sounded like something between a squeak and a growl as it bore down on us, not slowing one iota as it neared.

Seconds later a huge piece of equipment, obviously totally out of control, outran its own dust. At the wheel was a wide-eyed woman who had apparently just spotted us and was desperately fighting the wheel and gears to either stop or at least slow down. She missed us by mere inches and careened past at nothing near a safe velocity.

Pissed, I turned around and gave chase, dead set on giving her a nasty piece of my mind. I had to drop back quite a bit in order to see the road through her dust, but keeping her in sight was hardly a problem since she left what looked like a tornado in her wake. Only when she made a two-wheeled turn—not easy with a piece of equipment that has six huge tires—onto an uphill grade did she finally roll to a stop. She was climbing from the cab when I caught up to her, and when she saw me stomping toward her she sank to her knees and set up a serious caterwaul. My anger dissipated when I saw her tear-streaked, terrified face.

Hustling to her side to see if she was hurt, I forgot about Po Thang in my rush. As we closed in on her she screamed and backed away, terrified. Mexicans, as a rule, are fearful of dogs, probably because until fairly recently dogs were for protection of property and therefore vicious.

I shooed Po Thang away while trying, in my best Spanglish, to reassure her that I hadn't loosed the hounds on her. Po Thang sat at a distance and whined, not understanding what he'd done to get a shooing.

"What's your name?" I asked her in Spanish.

"ChaCha," she sniveled.

"Okay, uh, ChaCha, calm down," I think I said, but I might have asked her for an order of clams.

She nodded and wiped her eyes. "I am fired?" she asked in English.

"No, no. Are you hurt?"

"No. My...what is the word? Stopping no work."

"Your brakes?"

"*Sí.* Is *always* happening," she wailed and started blubbering again.

I patted her on the head and glared at the big yellow monster that tried to kill both of us. Po Thang sauntered over and disdainfully lifted his leg on a tire.

Other than ChaCha's sobs and the killer machine's engine ticking as it cooled, the desert was silent. Reaching for my cell phone, I realized I'd left it at the office, so I headed back to the pickup and the company radio.

"Coffey to base."

A delay, then Laura answered and I told her where we were and to notify Safety, but he cut in on his own radio and said he was on his way. Five minutes later his dually came over a rise and Po Thang ran to greet him, but turned tail when he sensed fury.

Safety stormed our way, his face a mask of anger, which set ChaCha to howling once again. Po Thang joined in.

"What the hell happened here?" he shouted, then added, "For Christ's sake, ChaCha—and you too, dog—dry up."

They both dried up and I bulled up. "Listen here, you jerk. ChaCha, Po Thang and I were almost killed so *you* dry up before I stuff your ears up your ass!"

Safety stopped in his tracks, opened his mouth to say something, thought better of it, and grinned. "Let me rephrase that. Would everyone please stop the noise, and can I be of any help to you?"

ChaCha and I giggled, Po Thang relaxed and rushed in for an ear rub, and Safety saved his own ears.

Safety stayed with the oversized dirt hauler and I gave ChaCha a ride back to the equipment yard. She blabbed nonstop all the way, a mixture of English and Spanish, giving me an earful of the problems the women drivers were experiencing with their equipment. Oddly enough, I understood most of what she said because she kept repeating herself until I did. Yes, she admitted, they were newly trained, but they were *not* trained to handle large machines that continually malfunctioned. She also told me her husband was a car mechanic in Santa Rosalia and he said there were too many breakdowns so the mechanics at the jobsite must not know what they were doing.

After awhile, I started to tune her out because something she said was niggling at me. I wasn't sure exactly what it was, but something to do with the cost overruns we were trying to zero in on. I dropped her off and headed back to the office to check on some of Jan's findings. Maybe, just maybe, I was on to something, but it would take some major snoopery to find out.

Po Thang didn't know it yet, but we were in for some unpaid overtime. Well, he was. I planned to bill the hell out of the Trob.

The jobsite started shutting down at three and I was the only one left in the office by five. Safety left last, still in a huff over the possibility of yet another blight on his record. Even though there was no injury except to our nerves, any accident or near accident had to be reported and could possibly raise the need for a review of safety regulations, which in turn would go on his record because he hadn't thought to instigate the regulations in the first place. Safety, it seems, has a thankless job and it made me wonder why he did it. Back at the office after the Cha-Cha incident, I heard him yelling into the phone a couple of times, but couldn't make out exactly who he was talking to or what he said. I did catch a couple of choice words.

Once I had the place to myself, I locked the front door to make sure it stayed that way. I'd already sent Jan an email and told her and Rosario to get ready for a confab via live chat.

Me: Okay, no witnesses around here, but I'm still not gonna use the phone. You never know who is listening.

Jan: Ain't that the truth? Get this. Back when Rosario first told us his story, the one I wrote up and sent you? He said he "overheard" rumors of financial problems on the job. Well guess what? Our boy genius here planted a bug in Ozzie's office while he was working at the mine.

Me: And he's only now getting around to sharing this bit of info? Remind me to box his ears when I see him. So, is the bug still here?

Jan: He says yes, unless they somehow found it.

Me: Fantastic. Tell him I want to know how to activate that bug when we get through here.

Jan: Will do. What's up?

Me: I need you to look at the Heavy Equipment account. What we've bought, how much we paid, all that. And then what the maintenance costs are running, anything that might raise a red flag.

Jan: Roger. Give me an hour.

Me: Put Rosario on the computer.

Rosario: Hola. You wish to box my ears? What is that?

Me: It's something you do to bad kids when they act up. Why didn't you tell us about the bug before?

Rosario: I was afraid you would think I was a bad person.

Me: And now?

Rosario: Jan said you like bad guys, if they are *your* bad guys.

Me: Jan is right. Okay, no ear boxing. Tell me about the bug.

Rosario: You wish to listen to *Señor* Osvaldo's office?

Me: You bet your sweet little sneaky ass I do. Tell me how.

Lucky for me old Ozzie doesn't lock his office, although if he did I'm sure our little friend Rosario would know how to get in anyway.

As instructed, I looked under Ozzie's desk, located the computer, turned the tower a half-turn and removed what looked like a thumbdrive. Rosario had installed the bug the night before he disappeared, and he'd somehow fiddled with it, making it voice activated. He wasn't sure of its recording capabilities, in terms of longevity, as he was still tinkering with it when he left that last night, but I would soon find out. The bad news was I had to listen to the whole damned thing and return it before everyone showed up at the office the next morning.

I was dying to bug Safety's office as well, but it would have to wait until Rosario could supply me with another of those snoopery/thumbdrive/thingies (technical term). Turns out he had a stash with him at Camp Chino.

And while Rosario was my bad guy, I began to wonder what manner of person we had taken in and whether anything I owned was now bugged.

I took Po Thang outside for a potty break, looked around to make sure I was truly alone, plugged the bug into my own computer and settled in for a long night of eavesdropping on what would probably be the most boring recording ever. I listened with one ear while catching up on email to friends and family.

Knowing my veterinarian buddy in Arizona, Craig, is a late nighter, I caught him for an online chat and told him all about Po Thang and sent him a photo. Craig assured me my dog was purebred, asked if he'd been checked out by a vet. I told him Chino had done so. Then we talked about my alleged hate crime.

Craig: Nothing new, but I talked it over with Topaz Sawyer, that deputy you became friends with after the assault.

Me: How's she doing?

Craig: Fine. She couldn't believe the scuzzbucket was trying to sue you.

Me: Can she get into the jail and shoot him in the nuts again for me?

Craig: I think she'd like to, but nope. She did say she has vacation time coming and will come down there if you want her to.

Me: Fantastic. I'll pay her airfare and bill the Trob for it, as I could seriously use a real detective right now. I'll email her pronto.

I fired off an email to Topaz, gave her a little background on all the crap befalling me and invited her to an all expenses paid trip to the "charming seaside village of Santa Rosalia." I was hoping that description would lure her into thinking she was headed for the likes of Cancun instead of a dusty little mining town.

I was getting ready to catch Jenks for a chat when the ear I had tuned into the bug's playback caught my attention. I quickly hit the rewind key. Okay, I know it's not really a rewind key anymore, but what ever it is I hit it. I'm still struggling with the digital world here.

My computer announced the time, six-thirty AM the morning after Rosario almost lost his life, followed by the voice of Ozzie saying, "Good morning, baby girl. All ready for school?"

Osvaldo has kids?

The next twenty minutes damned near put me to sleep, as Ozzie spoke with what was probably his entire immediate family. I was nodding off when I heard a familiar voice. "Oh, sorry, didn't know you were on the phone."

Ozzie said, "Gotta go, sweetie. Bye. Love you all."

I heard his chair squeak, probably because he was swiveling to face his desk, then he said, "Good morning, what's up, Safety?"

"That kid who works for you? Rosario? We may have a problem."

"What kind of problem?"

"He and the company boat are missing."

"You're kidding. He was only supposed to fix the radio. What the hell happened?"

"I'm not sure. When I left him, he'd passed out on the boat and this morning he, and the boat, are gone."

"How do you know this? It's early."

"I stopped by to make sure he'd locked up, and *Lucifer* is gone. Then I stopped by the man camp and they said he had not checked in last night. So my guess is he took the boat somewhere."

"What should we do?"

"I guess someone ought to call the cops."

A heavy sigh. "I'll do it. After all, it is company property and he is not authorized to take it from the dock. You say he was passed out. I didn't think he drank."

"He did last night. Like I said, he was zonked, so I left him there. He...uh...said some things about the project. Things he shouldn't be talking about, or even know about."

"Like what?"

"Trust me, Osvaldo, you don't want to know."

Silence, another ragged sigh, then Ozzie says, "You are right, I do not."

Chapter 24

The guilty never escape unscathed. My fees are sufficient punishment for anyone.—F. Lee Bailey

"Po Thang, you are an incredibly bad judge of character. Your BFF, Safety, is indubitably guilty of something. I'm just not sure what yet."

Raising his head from his blankie, he cocked it hopefully, one ear raised. He had been sleeping for six hours while I listened to the entire recording from Ozzie's office. Absolutely nothing interesting happened after Safety told him about Rosario and the boat, and Ozzie called the port Captain instead of the police, which is exactly what I would have done in the same situation.

It was hard to keep my eyes open while hearing those long hours of droning conversations with vendors, calling the home offices in Mexico City and Canada, blowing his nose, chomping on lunches, farting, singing off key (Julio Iglesias fan, so he can't be *all* bad) and talking to his kids every morning. After two days, the bug thankfully reached capacity.

Boring or not, I downloaded the whole thing into my computer as Rosario instructed, erased the thumbdrive and plugged it back into Ozzie's computer.

Well after midnight Po Thang whined to go outside. I knew he was bluffing because in the short time I'd had him he'd slept through the night, but what the heck. We walked outside and while he sniffed around and gave a rock a half-hearted squirt, I admired a starlit canopy seemingly within touching distance and marveled at the intense luminosity of the Milky Way. On the horizon glowed the lights of Santa Rosalia, as well as El Boleo, that nearby mine. Across the Sea of Cortez, some eighty miles away, Guaymas lit the sky despite a moon just a slice off full.

Much too close, a coyote cut loose and was answered by what sounded like an entire pack, sending a shiver down my spine and raising the hair along Po Thang's. "It's okay boy," I whispered as I bent down to rub his trembling back and latch onto his collar in case he decided to do something stupid as dogs will when frightened. I wondered what his nights out on the lonely highway were like and whether he ever had to defend himself against critters out there.

I began backing into the office building, hauling Po Thang with me, when I spotted what looked like headlights jouncing along between us and El Boleo.

"Po Thang, there's a vehicle out there. I didn't even know there was a road."

The dog stared at me, evidently forgetting about the coyotes and wondering whether there was food involved in this one-way conversation.

Once inside, I pulled up Google Earth, pinpointed both Lucifer and El Boleo, then zeroed in and found not only one road, but dozens of them crisscrossing the desert like spider webs. From previous experience I knew some were little more than goat paths, and the vehicle I saw could belong to anyone. Drug runners came to mind, but I dismissed that; why would they be back in these mountains that had so much mining activity? Some small time miner still eeking out a little gold once in awhile? These mountains had been mined for centuries by locals and abandoned tunnels and pits honeycombed the region.

I made a note to ask about those lights and roads, then yawned and shut down the computer. As much as I wanted to go home, there was no way I was going to drive down *Cuesta del Infierno* in the dark, so I stretched out next to Po Thang on his blankie and conked out.

That dog is a cover hog.

"Hetta, what in the hell?"

Po Thang's exuberant tail slapped me in the head several times before I fully woke. Safety was standing at my office door, hands on hips and a sardonic grin on his face.

I was tempted to say something I would regret when thinking back to what sounded somewhat, but not exactly, incriminating on that bug the night before. Instead I asked him to take Po Thang out for his morning constitutional while I went to the Ladies and brushed my teeth. By the time they returned I had coffee made, something I badly needed. I felt like, well, I'd slept on the floor with a dog. I fished a dog hair from my coffee, finished it off and set it down on a low table where Po Thang slurped the dregs and whined for his breakfast.

"Sorry, Buddy, I ain't got no food for you this morning. We cleared out the fridge last night."

Safety looked surprised. "You two stayed here all night?"

"Yep. Didn't want to drive down the hill after dark."

"Well, then, let's go over to the mess hall and get you and Po Thang some victuals."

"Okay," I agreed lamely.

I know, I know, here was a guy high up on my suspect list and I was driving off with him, but hey, we're talking *breakfast* here. Besides, I had a dog to think of.

Po Thang was not welcome in the mess hall, so we scored him his breakfast first, then left him asleep in the pickup while I devoured a breakfast for two. As we ate *huevos a la Mexicana* it was hard to ignore Safety's baby blues. My resolve not to trust him took a little setback when eye-to-eye with this Robert Redford look-alike, but that didn't mean I wasn't going to investigate anything he touched on this project. I wanted to start with something he had a large hand in: Equipment.

"I suppose ChaCha has recovered from her scare yesterday," I said casually, easing into where I was headed.

"She's fine. The shop is checking out the hauler's braking system, trying to see what went wrong."

"Isn't that a pretty new rig?"

"Just been on the job six months."

"I mean, new, new. A new model straight from Caterpillar?"

"Um-huh." I'd caught him with a mouth full of eggs, a timing talent that waiters and waitresses worldwide must learn in serving school.

"Could I get a ride in one? I've been trying to imagine how a little gal like ChaCha can handle a monster machine like that."

"It's really an oversized truck. Hydraulics help a lot. In this case, size really doesn't matter."

"On the truck, or the operator?"

He grinned. "The driver."

"So, how about a ride, cowboy?" I said this with a purr. I've learned a thing or two from Jan over the years.

Safety actually broke out in a blush, which on a redheaded man I've always found endearing. "Uh, sure. I can set it up with the heavy equipment manager. When do you want to go?"

"Too tired today. Tomorrow? I may work from the boat the rest of today. I feel like I've been run over by one of those dirt haulers after sleeping on the floor. And Po Thang snores."

"Don't blame you for wanting to head for your nice soft bed. I mean, I guess your bed is soft." He blushed again and cleared his throat. "I'll send you an email later, after I've set up something with the equipment guy. Shouldn't be a problem. I doubt he'll want to send you out with ChaCha, however. And Po Thang can't go."

"Just as well, he'd probably want to drive. I'm stuffed, please dump me at my pickup so I can head for a nap."

"Want company?"

My mouth fell open, but before I could say anything—I had, after all, been flirting seconds before—he reddened again. "Uh, I meant later, uh, this week after work. Maybe for a beer and some dinner?"

"Sure, why not."

What exactly was happening here? I needed the complication of a flirtation with Safety, even an innocent one, like I needed an altimeter for my boat.

Once back on the boat I called Jan and Rosario, asking them to return to Santa Rosalia later in the week. We needed a serious powwow and work session. Meanwhile, Jan forwarded that bunch of info on heavy equipment purchases, operating costs and the like.

Then I called Jenks, because this thing with Safety was getting a little weird and I needed reassurance from Jenks that we were still in love. I know, how fickle does that sound? But when your sig-other is thousands of miles away and you are being wooed (I think) by Robert Redford for crying out loud, what's a gal to do?

Even though I knew for sure Safety was at best a lying skunk, I still didn't know *why*. Not that being a lying skunk is always a *bad* thing; it has worked for me many a time.

What I didn't get was that Safety knew me through the Trob, so that must mean Wontrobski wanted Safety to know what I did. If Safety is dirty, wouldn't knowing my mission give him an insider's ability to lead me down the old proverbial garden path? Maybe that was exactly what he was doing.

Two can play that game.

I talked with Jenks for over an hour, after which I felt empowered to lead Safety a merry chase without any danger of makin' whoopee. I'm such an amazingly simple person when it comes to men: one at a time, so long as I feel secure.

Safety was in for a bumpy ride, but not, if I was reading him right, the kind he evidently hoped for.

It's women like me who give women like me a bad name.

Jan's latest info arrived with a ding on my computer just as I woke from a two-hour nap, which was interrupted several times by Po Thang trying to sneak into bed with me. I guess he figured since we'd shared a blankie the night before, I owed him. Males! They are all the same.

I spent the rest of my day poring over equipment purchase orders and researching prices on the Net. I zeroed in on the heavy duty off-road haulers like the one ChaCha almost flattened me with.

The Caterpillar 777G, I found out from the company's website, is the newest star in 100-short-ton size class. According to the blurb this huge yellow Cat is a workhorse for mining and large earthmoving application and "delivers greater levels of production and fuel efficiency as well as enhanced safety, operator comfort and service convenience" than earlier models. Evidently they never met ChaCha.

After reading the glowing reports on this big baby, I was really looking forward to my ride the next day. Maybe they'd let me drive? After all, I do operate a forty-five-foot yacht with Caterpillar engines.

Chapter 25

Never drive faster than your guardian angel
can fly.

I was next to a tire, looking *up* at the tread.

No I wasn't lying on the ground, but standing fully upright, or as fully upright as someone five-four gets.

The Caterpillar 777G, as its black and white cab insignia declared, was a yellow behemoth covered in dust and mud, but still had a few shiny places showing through despite the best efforts of ChaCha and her fellow drivers. Because only a limited amount of mining from the old strip mine site was underway, this big baby was being used as a dump truck for building roads and the like, so it hadn't suffered the dings it would later, when serious stuff began. Not that the women weren't doing their damnedest.

The front tire I was standing next to was over six feet high, which is pretty danged impressive. I knew, from the purchase orders we'd downloaded, that the base price was over a million and a half dollars and then there were extras, bringing it well into the 1.7 million dollar range. And they had five of them already on site, with another five due in any day. They were arriving in pieces for the most part due to the impossibility of driving a completed one down Mex 1. Reassembled on site, they were just getting broken in by now and, unfortunately, broken down, reportedly because of the novice operators.

My driver, an American I'd met in Pedro's van my first day on the job, was both the site's heavy equipment manager, and driving instructor. I couldn't help but admire his hard hat slogan: NOTHING BEATS A GOOD DUMP! I requested one of those stickers for Po Thang's hat.

I didn't recall his having such a headful of bright white hair when we'd met, but I could see where a daily commute with Pedro could have that effect on a person. Or maybe it was ChaCha and the ladies' dubious driving skills taking a toll on Mr. Warren. Teaching a bunch of Mexican women, most of them first-generation drivers, to operate these huge trucks had to be a nerve-wracking experience. No, I am NOT being anti-feminist here, I happened to have almost been flattened like a tortilla by one of his students.

"So, John, did you figure out what went wrong with ChaCha's brakes the other day?"

He looked startled. "How did you know about that?"

"Unfortunately I was in her path."

"Oh. Sorry about that. But no harm no foul, I guess. Looks like a brake line suffered fatigue."

"Fatigue? These are brand new machines."

"I think they use that term, fatigue, when they can't figure out what went wrong. Maybe one of the operators whacked into something and didn't report it. Who knows? I'm thinking of installing cameras on these big guys, what with all the problems we're experiencing."

"This one looks good on the outside, anyway. Where are we going?"

"Where do you want to go?"

"Maybe on a typical run? Take on a load of dirt or whatever it is you're hauling? I like to get a feel for the daily happenings on jobs I'm on."

"You're the boss."

"I am?"

"Safety says you are, so you are."

"Gee, I didn't know he is so important."

John grinned. "Oh, you have no idea."

I let that slide. I might not have any idea, but you can bet your sweet bippy I was gonna find out just how important Safety was, and why.

"You ready to saddle up?" John asked.

When men ask me something like that I usually bop them one, but I detected nothing untoward in John's question. I eyed the two-step swinging ladder leading to a set of steel steps and lamented not having done squats of late. "Uh, does that first ladder lock down? It looks like it's kind of dangling there."

"Don't worry, it won't move until we get aboard. Then I'll get her folded up and out of the way. Up you go. Follow me and put your hands and feet where I do."

One thing I hate about climbing anything is my feet leaving a good solid base. I'm not so much afraid of heights as I am uneasy when both feet are on a rung. Ladders, as you might surmise, are not my favorite things, which is one reason I love the real steps on my boat. Many boats have ladders instead. Jenks, having been in the Navy and on large ships can clamber down a twelve-foot ladder, facing away from it, with a cup of coffee in each hand and never spill a drop. Me? I do one rung at a time, facing the rungs, and make sure both feet are firmly on one before attempting the next, all the time hanging on for dear life with both hands. I also use this method when climbing. I might look like a five-year-old, but I sure as hell wasn't going to fall.

I needn't have worried about this particular ladder. Made of solid steel, the fold-up steps on the big earthmover's were about as secure as any can be, so I was quickly (for me) up the more user-friendly perforated steel stairs, and the cab's entry level. I held onto a railing and looked down, which might have been a mistake as a bit of vertigo set in. Or maybe I had one little bitty glass of wine too much the night before. I couldn't get into that cab, and my seat, fast enough.

Once settled into what I learned was a fold-down instructor's seat I buckled my lap belt. As jump seats go, this one wasn't too bad in the comfort department. I took in my surroundings. "Wow, this is freakin' huge!" I exclaimed. I have a flair for the obvious.

"Actually there are much larger models, but this one is no slouch. It's over five thousand five hundred millimeters wide, just for starters."

I did a fast calculation in my head. Okay not so fast, but I broke it into meters and did some rough division and came up with a number. "Eighteen feet?"

He nodded.

"No wonder it arrives in pieces. No way would this get down Mex 1. I figure both lanes can't be more than twenty feet wide, with no shoulders, and there are places where even that's being generous."

"You're right. And at over fourteen feet high, that's another problem. Ready?"

We started the day by picking up a load of rocks, taking them to a drainage ditch project and dumping them. The ride was amazingly smooth and quiet for such big diesels.

"Want some music?" John asked me.

"You have a stereo on this thing?"

"Yep. Far as I can figure, that's about the only thing different from the older models I've operated, but the powers that be wanted newer and better, so you're riding in it."

"I like it. Maybe I'll consider a new career."

"You couldn't do much worse than the trainees."

"Oh, I think I can do much better. My dad taught me to drive a D-8 when I was ten. And, after all, I do operate a forty-five foot motor yacht with Caterpillar diesels not unlike the ones on this machine, *and* without the benefit of brakes. So you gonna let me operate this big boy today?"

John looked doubtful, but when I reminded him that Safety said I was the boss for a day, he reluctantly showed me how to run through all seven forward gears, using a digital readout telling me when to shift. We were far away from anything remotely dangerous, in a flat field that was being prepared for a building. No ditches, rocks, trees, or even a cactus in the way of a threat. I drove around in circles for twenty minutes until I was familiar with all of the levers—and there were a lot. I even practiced dumping the bucket, even though it was empty.

After driving the big Cat I couldn't wait to get back to the office and tell Jan all about it. She commented it was a miracle the machine was still in one piece, a dig I chose to ignore, but stored in my *get even* file for later.

She and Rosario were getting ready to leave Camp Chino for the boat, she said, and should be there by the time I was. "We're packing up right now. Chino's so glad to get rid of me he's driving us over instead of making us take the bus."

"I've felt that way a time or two myself. What have you done?"

"Nothing, honest. Well, to *him*."

"Let me guess, Doctor Dropdeadgorgeous has had a bad week?"

"You might say that."

Chapter 26

At this point, no one is above suspicion.—
Hetta Coffey

Before I even stepped onto the boat I knew
Jan and Rosario were there; the mouth-watering
aroma of something wonderful cooking greeted me
as I walked down the dock.

Po Thang raced ahead, ecstatic to see his
friends again which gave me a twinge of jealousy.
After all, we *had* slept together. But I needed not
fret, for after his brief display of joy he headed for
the galley, went on point at the oven and held his
pose until Jan's Venetian-style lasagna came
bubbling toward the dining table. Her recipe, made
with spinach lasagna noodles—the last of our stash
brought down from the States—and layers of garlic
and parmesan-laced béchamel sauce, mozzarella,
and a savory marinara sauce is, in my humble
opinion, the best on earth.

After enjoying his freedom at Camp Chino,
Rosario was less than pleased to be back under

house arrest, although with that blonde beard and hair I don't think his own mother would recognize him. However, now that I knew for certain that Safety was hiding something we couldn't risk a chance encounter.

After dinner I called a strategy session.

"So here is what we know for sure," I told them. "Not a damned thing."

"I like this kind of meeting," Jan said. "Can we go to bed now? I'm stuffed and tired."

"Meeting adjourned."

Did I mention that I positively abhor meetings?

It has been my experience that the only person who enjoys a meeting is the person who calls it so they can look important and boss everyone around. While I do like bossing people around, I prefer a more informal jawboning session, say, at a bar.

Because Rosario couldn't be seen in a local cantina, we gathered around the dining table the next morning to try figuring out where we were in our investigation, which was pretty easy: nowhere.

Jan had walked into town early and secured fresh *torta* rolls from the famous El Boleo bakery, or *panaderia*. Baked in century-old mesquite fired ovens, these sandwich rolls, when split and lightly toasted, make the perfect base for Jan's Mexican-style version of eggs benedict. Lemons being hard to come by, she subs lime juice in the sauce and throws in finely chopped cilantro. Luckily we still had canned Canadian bacon left in the larder, and a chilled bottle of not very good but better than nothing champagne in the fridge.

"Ya wanna know what I think?" Jan asked between sips of champers and bites of her perfect hollandaise sauce.

"Not really," I teased, "but someone has to come up with something."

"Somebody is doin' some creative financing."

"Really? Like how?"

"I don't know for sure, but if you want to hide spent money, you don't spend it all from one account. Too obvious."

I thought about that. Accounting is not my long suit. "Wouldn't that take someone high up the organizational ladder to pull that off?"

"Yep."

"Then no one is above suspicion. Want to stake a wild guess as to how high this mess can go?"

"Chief Financial Officer or someone like him with pull and power."

"But he's in Canada, right?"

Jan nodded. "Yeah, I'm putting him on the list anyway, but this looks more hands-on, so my money is on someone in Mexico, either right here or in Mexico City. Someone with, what is it they say about murder suspects? Means, motive and opportunity."

"What does this mean?" asked Rosario.

"It simply boils down to someone, or in this case probably several someones, with the ability to commit the crime. This means the perp has to have the *ability* to steal money and hide where it came from and went to. That rules out people like you,

Rosario, who have no opportunity to finagle things on the project. Although, after seeing what you've been up to, I may have to change my mind about that."

He pointed to himself. "Me? I was the one they tried to kill."

Jan used her fork to wave away his protest, thereby snagging Po Thang's attention. He'd run through his eggs and was looking to clean the plates and flatware. "Oh, for crying out loud, Hetta, you read way too many cop novels. Perp? Anyhow, we know the motive: moola."

Rosario opened his mouth, but I quickly explained. "Money."

"Oh. Moola. I have never heard that word."

I had folded down two fingers of the three I held up when listing what it takes to commit a crime. I wiggled the one left. "Opportunity. Far as I'm concerned in this case, it is the same as *means*. We have to zero in on who has the ability, and how."

Jan brightened. "If we find the *how*, we can find the *who*. So, let's get back to work on the paper trail, even though these days it's more of a data trail."

"Okay then, Ms. CPA, if you were able to, how would *you* somehow add hundreds of thousands of dollars onto a project and then steal it."

"Easy-peasy. I'd set up a phony baloney purchase order or two. Make one out to, say, Hetta Coffey, LLC. Then you would submit invoices for services *not* rendered, and we'd split fifty-fifty."

"Seventy-thirty."

"Sixty-forty, and that is my last offer."

"What a cheapskate."

Rosario held up his arms. "What are you talking about?"

Jan and I had a good laugh, but we knew we were on to something.

Maybe.

After several hours of comparing estimated costs for each and every department on the project, we found no real red flags, only a steady twenty-percent or so overrun for each one. Which, in itself might not be all that suspicious, except that the cost overruns were being blamed partly on gasoline and steel prices, so why the overspending in, say, office supplies? Seemed a tad too tidy.

If, for instance, the monthly budget was estimated to be a cool million, to take a number, twenty-percent is a substantial overrun. In one year, you are looking at two and a half million bucks.

I'd heard El Boleo, the big mining project over the hill, was also having money worries, but it was more understandable because they were building in El Vizcaíno Biosphere Reserve, Mexico's largest protected area. I was amazed they even received a permit to mine there, but El Boleo was taking drastic, expensive, measures not to cause environmental problems. I'd gotten a tour of the project and was very impressed with the steps they were taking.

All the water used at that mine came from a massive desalination plant so no ground water is tapped, and they even use the brine byproduct to salt roads so no excess salt is pumped back into the sea.

My project, Lucifer, had a much smaller scope and is outside the protected area by mere miles, but because of that we have far fewer constraints, but there were some similarities in the rising cost of steel and fuel.

This was really boring stuff to spend much time on, so I took a break and called Deputy Sawyer in Bisbee to see if she received my email invite and was coming over. Even if the boat *was* getting a little crowded.

"Hetta?" she said, "How good to hear from you. And before you even ask, I haven't managed to break into the prison system and plug that piece of crap for you."

"Well, dang. If you can't do it can we hire someone? Surely you have friends in low places, what with your job and all?"

"I arrest them, Hetta, I don't drink beer with them. And speaking of beer, if you'll ice down a case or two I might take you up on your generous offer of an all-expense paid trip to sunny Baja. I could use a break, it's still cold up here and I have vacation coming. How about next week? How do I get there?"

"It ain't easy, but the best way is to drive to San Carlos, stash your car in one of the storage lots and fly over. Unfortunately on the way down you almost have to spend the night in San Carlos because the plane leaves really early out of Guaymas, but on your return trip it's a one dayer."

"That's okay, I want to visit San Carlos again anyway. What airline?"

"Aero Calafia. You better go online, check the schedule and book if you can. If for some reason you can't do it that way, I'll buy your ticket from here. Just let me know when and I'll be ready for you. By the way, there's a shuttle from the Santa Rosalia airport to my marina. Jan will be here on the boat."

"Okay, then. Chill down that Tecate, and *hasta la vista*, baby."

"We're gonna have company, guys," I told Jan and Rosario. "Well, Jan and I are going to. Rosario, you'll have to go back to the fish camp so our friend Topaz can have the guest cabin."

Rosario tried to hide his glee, but I had a sneaking suspicion he couldn't wait to get back to Doctor Delish and more freedom. I wondered if the pretty marine biologist had any idea Rosario was smitten with her. And speaking of smitten...."So, Jan, have you managed to divert the lovely doc's amorous attentions from your beloved Chino, or does she still want to play doctor?"

Jan's face clouded. "I knew you couldn't leave that alone. And, it's none of your bidness."

Rosario looked stricken. "You think Doctor Diana is really that interested in Doctor Chino?"

"Don't tell me you haven't noticed?"

"No." His short and gruff answer spoke volumes.

While Jan and Rosario lapsed into separate pouting sessions over the same woman, I marveled at the human capacity for attraction to, and dislike for, others. I was really pissed at Safety, but he still held a strange appeal. Jan was ready to call it quits with Chino until Doctor Devine showed up. I am in love with Jenks, but once in awhile someone like Safety, or the elusive and mysterious Nacho, comes sniffing around and I get an itch. Lucky for Jenks I have scads of Benadryl onboard.

I could understand Rosario's infatuation with the doc, considering his youth, but the rest of us? Aren't we getting a smidgen long in the tooth for this crap? I sometimes feel like I'm living my life in Soapoperaland, and none of it is real.

Reality, however, has a way of biting you in the butt, as it did when I opened a good news/bad news email from Geary.

The good news was the well-done bod was not that Dickless Luján.

The bad news was the well-done bod was not that Dickless Luján.

In my mind the really good news was that now I would maybe have an opportunity to off him in person one day.

However, Geary had even more worse news. Evidently one of the other players in the Café Olé incident had been arrested, and he told the local cops that their boss had warned them of a dangerous red-haired Gringa with a yacht before his fellow thug ended up boiled.

If we were in the States, the authorities would be referring to me as a "person of interest".

Chapter 27

Lamont Cranston: We're going to need help on this, m'lady—help from an old friend.

Margo Lane: The Shadow?—From a 1954 Radio show.

After telling Jan I was a "person of interest" in a death I had nothing to do with, I whined, "I feel totally helpless. If they come after me, even though I have an alibi, it probably won't make one damned difference."

Jan nodded. "Mexican cops don't give a big rat's rump about alibis. They toss you in the local clink and wait for things to get sorted out."

"Then we need things sorted out *before* they come for me."

"Does Geary think the cops know where you are?"

"He doesn't know much. Conception Bay and Mulege are gossip mills on steroids. He says he overheard this latest tidbit during a Texas Holdem tournament."

"Well, that's appropriate. They actually *named* you?"

"Not exactly. This guy he was playing cards with said the cops were nosing around the Gringo community, asking about a red-haired woman with a boat."

"Well, heck, you're safe. You ain't no real redhead."

I tossed and turned most of the night, imagining heavily armed *federales* in balaclavas swarming my decks. Jan and Po Thang—who had wormed his way onto Jan's side of the bed—growled at me several times for waking them up with my fretful writhing, so I moved out to the settee in the main saloon. Still unable to sleep, I decided to try raising Jenks on Skype.

Before I called I brushed my teeth and hair. Like Jenks can smell my breath on Skype?

"Whatcha doing up, Hetta? It's your middle of the night."

"My dog threw me out of bed, and don't even think of making some smartassed remark."

"Sounds like he threw you out on the wrong side of that bed."

"Sorry. It's been a long day and longer night. We've been going over really boring accounting crap trying to find the black hole of pesos. You know how I hate that."

"Good thing you have Jan working on it with you. Okay, so what's really bugging you?"

Jenks is getting to know me all too well. "That rat bastard Lujàn."

"I thought he was stewed, so why are you stewing?"

"Clever. You have razor blades for lunch? Here's the deal, he ain't dead. However, one of the other goons from the Café Olé thing *is* dead, and I think someone is trying to finger me. I smell a set up of Lujàn's doing, because now the local gendarmes have been nosing around the Gringo community, asking about some redhead with a boat."

Dead silence. From his frown he was either stifling the urge to remind me that my hair is so red by the grace of L'Oreal, or he was working up a worry.

"Still waiting for a profound statement here," I prompted.

"Sorry, I'm thinking."

"I hate it when that happens. I *thought* I saw smoke wafting from your ears."

We shared a chuckle at our old joke. It made me feel much better just knowing I had him in my life.

Finally he said, "I can't believe I'm going to say this, but I think you need to contact Nacho."

"What? You told me Nacho is dangerous. That he's bad news. And to stay away from him."

"All that is true, and on top of that every time that man gets near you I get a bad feeling."

"Would that bad feeling be jealousy by any chance?" I teased.

"Yes. But desperate times, and all." He sighed. "Look, here's the deal. I talked to Nacho after you called about Luján nosing around and then pulling some stunt at Conception Bay, and asked him if he could find you a bodyguard. I have a sneaky feeling he decided to take care of the problem himself."

"You talked to him?"

"I felt you needed someone in your corner, even if it is a rival for your affections."

"Oh, come on, Jenks. You have nothing to fear in that department. He holds zero appeal for me," I prevaricated. I do not lie outright, I fib and prevaricate. It sounds so much better.

"I'm not sure that works both ways. I've seen how he looks at you. However, right now I think it's more important to have friends in low places on your side."

"Funny, I just asked Topaz Sawyer, our sheriff's deputy buddy in Bisbee, if she had some of those people around so we could deal with that sleazebag I shot in the nuts that's trying to sue me."

"Hetta, does it seem at all strange to you that we're having a conversation that most people would not experience in a lifetime, unless while brainstorming a Hollywood screenplay?"

"Jeez, Jenks, a little murder, mayhem and gunplay put a little spark in a romance, doncha think."

"Just make sure *whose* romance."

I changed the subject and told him Topaz was on her way to Santa Rosalia, so Jenks was somewhat mollified. Maybe he viewed her as a chaperone? He still urged me to contact Nacho, pronto.

I removed the mystery man's card from where I had taped it underneath a drawer. Which, according to Jenks, is the first place someone would look. I thought it was safer than burning or eating it, what with my lousy memory for numbers. Conversations I remember for decades, but numbers? Not so much.

Now that I looked at the card again, I felt foolish. Who in the hell could forget *this* phone number?

L. Cranston Pest Control
1-800-got-bads?
We get what's bugging you.

I wasn't all that sure what he could, or would, do to help me out, but he had gotten me into, and out of, several dustups in Mexico. Jan and I have spent a great deal of time talking about him, speculating on who he worked for or what he did exactly.

We both agree on one thing; Nacho is handsome in a criminal sort of way.

Right now it was looking like I needed someone with his skill sets (murder and mayhem) to deal with this Luján thing, and figured while I was at it I might as well let him know about that scuzzbucket in the Arizona prison who was messing with me.

Killing two birds with one stone in Nacho's case could be taken quite literally.

There was, of course, no answer at that 800 number, so I left a voice message. "This is Margo Lane. Uh, Help?"

Po Thang obligingly ate the card.

Monday morning we timed our departure from the boat to coincide with first light, but even then we took no chances and stuffed poor Rosario into the back jump seat of my pickup with Po Thang perched on top of him when we drove through town.

We had arranged for Chino to pick them up at a truck stop a little past Lucifer, on Mex 1, so I could scoot back to the jobsite with plenty of time to bug Safety's office before anyone else arrived. This spy bidness is exhausting work.

I posted Po Thang on the front porch of the office building to make sure I was left alone to my devices, literally. Not that Po Thang was worth a damn as a guard dog, but no one got by him without giving him at least an ear scratch, so I knew I'd hear his pleading whine in time to scoot back to my office.

I first inserted the fake thumbdrive in Safety's computer, making sure the side of the tower containing the bug was turned to the wall. Satisfied with that job, I hurried to Ozzie's office, removed his bug, downloaded it into my computer, and replaced it just as Po Thang's *pet me* whine announced company.

I was back at my desk, looking quite innocent I thought, when Laura opened the door and she and Po Thang entered, she holding her lunch bag above her head to avoid pillaging. When she threw the bag in the fridge and slammed the door, Po

Thang, rebuffed, deigned to grace me with his presence. Mainly because he knows I keep dog biscuits in a desk drawer.

Laura returned to my office with a post-it in hand. Bert Melton, the project manager, wanted to see me in his office at nine. Dang. I'd been on the job for over a month and had zip-all to report. I'd been avoiding him for that very reason.

Worried that he might be considering giving me the old heave ho—and I had decided I wanted to ride this one out, if for no other reason than to nail whoever tried to do in Rosario—I resorted to a ploy that has worked well for me in the past; when you don't have snot, make a graph.

The thing I love about graphs is that, depending on the scale, you can make them project whatever slant you desire. Of course, you never want to leave a copy with anyone, lest they figure out that a squished graph can look ominous, with huge jagged peaks and valleys, while a lengthened one with gently undulating ups and down doesn't look all that bad.

By the time I reached Bert's office for my meeting, I had devised a graph making the cost overruns look much worse than they really were, dragging the timeline out a year to show a line climbing off the upper right hand corner of the page.

"And so you can see, Bert, without cutting back somewhere, this project's cost overruns are destined to soar into the ionosphere." That much was true, but I figured an overly sharp climbing visual would prompt him into thinking he really, really needed me.

He did seem suitably impressed, but said, "I think that goes without saying. My question to you is, where are you in this? I have to justify you to the home office, you know. You *and* Miss Sims."

Damn. I had to throw him a bone. "We are making progress, but if I tell you how you have to promise me it never leaves this office. One leak and my investigation could go south, along with any money already stolen, if in fact it has been. Stolen, that is."

"So, what you're saying is that if you tell me you'll have to kill me?" he asked, his face a study in barely concealed amusement at my overly dramatic warning. "My lips are sealed."

"Okay, I can't say much for sure right now, but we think it's something to do with..." I lowered my voice to a whisper, "purchasing."

When I first met Bert Melton I had marveled that a man with such a seemingly gentle demeanor attained project manager-hood on a job of this caliber. Of course, then I reminded myself of the location. Lucifer is not what one would consider a plum assignment. Then he told me he'd asked for this job. He had, after all, been here for five years, even *before* the project's construction ground floor, as one of the scientists on the exploration team. He said he planned to retire after this project. All in all, he seemed unruffled by possible project cutbacks, probably because he figured no matter what, his job was secure—a naive notion in this bidness.

He also did something that my father never did; he bought a house near a jobsite. Most in the ever-changing engineering/construction field, being self-proclaimed vagabonds, do not buy homes predicated on staying employed on a particular project. What they do is buy a place where they plan to live someday when they retire. Did Bert plan to retire in Santa Rosalia?

Okay, Santa Rosalia is a cute little town, but wouldn't even make AARP's top *million* retirement destinations. Again, though, he is fluent in Spanish, loves to fish, and seems quite content here. Maybe that accounts for his kind demeanor?

That had been my assessment of him, right up until the moment he blindsided me with a furious outburst. He turned a worrisome shade somewhere between puce and purple and growled, right after I said, *purchasing*: "Miss Coffey, I don't know who you think you are dealing with here, but you are way off base and I suggest you get back on track, or off my project."

Stunned at not only his outburst, but his vehemence, I was literally blown back in my chair, speechless. For some reason, instead of tossing me from his office, he stormed out himself, slamming the door shut behind him and leaving me sitting there with a dropped jaw. I was, for one of the few times in my life, totally bumfuzzled.

A timid knock on the door drew me out of my stupor, and I managed to say, "Yes?"

Laura, white-faced herself, peeked around the door. "Miss Coffey, are you all right?"

I pushed myself out of the chair and tried to smile, but it wasn't easy. It felt like someone had gut-punched me and I couldn't quite catch my breath. "Y-yes, Laura, I'm fine."

Back in my office, I rued the day I removed the door. Laura brought me a cup of tea and a bottle of water. Po Thang sat on my feet, his way of letting me know he was there for me in case I dropped a steak or something. I rubbed his ears, which was a comfort to me, and he nuzzled my hand. Maybe dogs just know when we humans have been stupid?

Chapter 28

Thou canst not joke an Enemy into a Friend;
but thou may'st a Friend into an Enemy.— Benjamin
Franklin

The rest of the day, after Bert blew up at me
and stormed out, passed without further kerfuffles.
Still, I remained on edge; too many things hung
heavy over my head, and I felt embattled on all
fronts.

Still smarting over Bert's unexpected
admonishment, I also stressed over the possibility
that Safety would somehow spot the bug I'd placed
in his computer tower. He was in and out of the
office most of the day, so I doubted my plant would
glean anything of interest, but I didn't want it found.
He did stop in and volunteer to visit the boat later
and bring beer, and I gratefully agreed. Bert's rebuff
was painful and I needed a friend. Any friend.

Now that I'd gotten reassurances (how pitiful and needy does that sound?) from Jenks, and sent that plea for help to Nacho, I really had no room in my life for another man, but he did bring the beer, so what's a gal to do? He also brought Po Thang a big old greasy knucklebone, which the dog wanted to drag around on my carpet, but earned him the boot onto the dock. I had everyone trained to close the gates onto the docks so Po Thang, even if he wanted to, couldn't escape the marina grounds unless he jumped into the water and he showed no inclination to do so.

While Po Thang worried his bone, Safety and I retired to the sundeck with beers. Once we settled in, he said, "Boy, did you ever punch Bert's buttons today. What did you say to him?"

"I really don't know, exactly. Well, I know what I said, but not why it upset him so much."

"What exactly did you say before he blew?"

"Lemme think. I simply told him that Jan and I think the cost overruns might have something to do with purchasing."

His beer stopped at half-mast. "You're accusing Osvaldo?"

"No, of course not. I simply meant we are delving into purchasing anomalies. I didn't get a chance to explain what."

"Ah."

"Ah?"

"Look, Bert hired Osvaldo, despite other candidates suggested by corporate, so if he thought you were saying Purchasing with a capital P, as in

Osvaldo's department might be guilty of something, he may have taken it personally."

"Have you talked to him since our dustup?"

"No, I wasn't there, remember? I heard about it later."

I wondered if I should try to find Bert's house and attempt to rectify the situation, but wasn't exactly sure where he lived. It shouldn't be hard to figure out, however, because he said it was near the hospital, on the hill, and since his company truck couldn't be driven after dusk, it should be easy to find. I had seen very few garages in town, and certainly none that would house a truck the size of Bert's. Almost everyone parked on the street. I decided to go on a little foray later, but felt it best not to share my plans with Safety.

Instead, I changed the subject, once again bringing up the night Rosario vanished and once again getting nowhere.

"Why are you so interested in Rosario, Hetta? You didn't even know him."

"I don't know. Like Jan, I have this feeling his disappearance might not be an accident." As soon as I said it, I wanted to give myself a swift boot in the butt. I'd already alienated Bert today and I needed to keep someone on my side. Nothing like needling your prime suspect.

Safety looked annoyed. "You're beating a dead horse. Why on earth would someone want to do harm to that kid? I mean, on purpose."

Hmm, that *on purpose* part sounded sneaky. "You tell me, Safety. I wasn't there."

"There, where?"

"On the boat. You said you were, didn't you?"

Safety's eyes narrowed. "Not that I recall."

Oops, now *I* recalled. He had told Ozzie, and I got it from the bug Rosario had planted. *Way to go, Sherlock. You're batting a big fat zero today.*

"Oh, um, don't know where I got that idea. I guess because you said he was fixing the radio on the boat?" *Lame, Hetta. Better keep your day job. Oh, wait, I'm doing it. Albeit badly.*

I didn't like the way Safety was looking at me, so I changed the subject, once again. "Say, when I stayed over at the office the other night, I took Po Thang outside and saw headlights to the southeast, on what I'd call a back road into the site. There's a road there?"

"Many. But what you saw was probably the brine truck. For some reason he usually comes at night."

"Brine truck?"

"Yeah, there's an old man and his son who own land on the back side of El Boleo and he has this dilapidated water truck he uses to haul brine to our site. Makes a little money that way, and we use the brine on our roads to keep down dust."

"Ah, the byproduct water from El Boleo's desal plant?"

"Yep. He can't haul it over the *Cuesta*, so he's forged a road that turns less than twenty miles into about fifty by following zigzag goat paths, a dry river bed and heaven knows what else, but he manages to get here every few days. How he keeps that old truck going is a freakin' miracle. I'm always amazed at how much work, and I mean hard labor, Mexicans are willing to do to make a peso."

"They are very inventive, that's for sure. You ever drive that road?"

"I rode with him once and believe me, once was enough. I did it to mark the road, in case we ever need to use it."

"How'd you mark it?"

"The Mexican way, with rocks and a bucket of whitewash. The old man helped me. Took us all day, but we got it done."

"I know about painted rocks. I once took an off-road vehicle across the peninsula and learned the system in a hurry. A line of rocks across the road means don't even *think* of going here." What I didn't mention was at the time I was driving an off-road 4X4 Toyota, or that I had stolen said vehicle from Nacho. Hopefully Nacho didn't hold a grudge, now that I needed his help.

Safety brought me back from my thoughts of Nacho, saying, "The Mexican system of lane control works. I hadn't realized how many roads, if you can call them that, are all over the place here."

I knew, because I'd checked them out on Google Earth, but I had decided not to share anything with Safety that didn't get me more answers.

"Anything else you want to know before I leave, Detective Coffey, or am I free to go?" Safety said, rather sharply, as he rose.

I shook my head, knowing I had annoyed him enough for one evening.

He finished his beer and left, no mention of the previously mentioned dinner.

So, in only one day I managed to almost lose my job, goad one perfectly placid man into apoplexy, and alienate another.

I must be losing my touch.

Chapter 29

I've traveled far and wide, always alone, so therefore I've never been in Cahoots. —Anonymous from the Internet

After Safety left in somewhat of a snit and I had an evening to kill, I decided I'd go on that house hunt and maybe clear the air. When I'd told Bert Jan and I suspected the problems might lie with some purchasing ploy, he evidently thought I meant Purchasing, with a capital P, meaning Osvaldo. And now that Safety told me Bert had hand-picked Ozzie for this job, I guess my speculation came off as a reflection on him. I can understand his getting steamed. Still, that Jekyll and Hyde outburst was odd.

Since we hadn't had dinner, Po Thang and I hit our favorite taco stand and indulged in a few. The owner didn't mind Po Thang, since the entire place is outdoors, but after my dog successfully stared down a few diners, willing them to toss a taco his way, I put his Rasputin self back in the pickup. He was still fixated, but from a distance and through the window he was less the hound from hell.

After our tacos I set out for Bert's house. Once on hospital hill, I drove a quadrant zone search pattern starting with the Clinica Hospital Santa Rosalia as my base. I had a map of town in the pickup, but since I only had about six streets no more than three blocks wide to cover, I didn't think I'd need it. Sure enough, I turned down the second street and there were four white trucks parked at the curb, three of them stenciled with the Mining Company logo and, to my surprise, the white dually belonging to Safety. All sported the required safety whips flying orange flags required when on site.

I parked a block away and left a sulking Po Thang in the truck. Backtracking on foot, I stuck to the street side instead of the sidewalk figuring, I could duck for cover behind a vehicle if need be, but also because Mexican sidewalks are notoriously booby-trapped with holes and pieces of rebar sticking up for no apparent reason. Walking on one after dark without benefit of street lights is a good way to break a leg.

In the center of the block sat a fairly large, by Santa Rosalia standards, Victorian style home with a wraparound porch. Since the street climbed a hill, it was obvious the home would have a great ocean view during daylight hours.

The interior was brightly lit but, unfortunately, gauzy drapes were pulled closed, hampering my vision. I could see there were people inside, but not exactly who or how many.

Company trucks not only have a logo, they are also numbered. I went back to my pickup for a penlight and my cell phone and left Po Thang even grumpier than before after raising his hopes with my brief return.

Back on the street in front of the house I was almost certain belonged to Bert, I called Jan.

"Hey, Hetta, how's things?"

"Fine, but I need some info, pronto."

"Why are you whispering?"

"I'm on surveillance. I've spotted some company pickups and I need to know who they're assigned to."

"Standby, I'll go get Rosario. He knows how to check on stuff like that. Want me to call you back?"

"Please. I'll put the phone on vibrate."

"Yeah, well don't even tell me where you're gonna stick it."

Santa Rosalia is a small town, with nosy neighbors. I stood out like, well, a redheaded Gringa in a sea of Latinos, even on a dark street. In spite of all the people milling around outside the hospital a half-block away, I was sure to be noticed if I loitered, so I went back to my pickup and moved it a block. I still had a clear view of what I guessed was Bert's house, and the pickups parked outside it.

Po Thang was thrilled to see me and whined for a walk, but I knew he was bluffing. Realizing I wasn't falling for his ploy, he finally curled up in the passenger seat and went to sleep. I must have dozed off, as well, because the vibrating phone in my bra jarred me awake. As I dug out the phone, I glanced out and was gratified to see all four pickups still in place. Some sleuth I am. My first stakeout and I fall asleep.

I gave Rosario the numbers and after a very slight delay, got my answers. "These vehicles are assigned to Osvaldo, Bert Melton and John Warren."

"Thanks. One more question. Do you know why Safety is allowed to drive his personal vehicle on site when no one else can?"

"Yes, I do. His dually is rated as a 4X4 and his job requires such a vehicle. There is one on order, but it had not yet arrived. At least while I was still there."

"Okay, thanks. Can you put Jan back on?"

"What are you up to, Hetta?" Jan demanded when Rosario handed her the phone. "Whaddaya mean, surveillance?"

I told her about my crappy day with Bert and Safety and how I'd gone looking for Bert's house and found all the pickups out front.

"And how is this your concern?"

"I don't know. Seems fishy."

"Or a weekly poker game?"

I hadn't thought of that.

"You're probably right. It's just that—oops, gotta go. Someone opened the front door. Call you back later."

I hung up and slid down into my seat. Po Thang, however, thumped his tail and woofed softly. I put a warning finger on his nose. "Do the words, *dog pound*, mean anything at all to you?"

He stopped woofing, but that tail still let me know he'd spotted a friend.

Sure enough, Safety, Ozzie, Bert and John Warren, the guy who'd taken me for a ride in the big dirt hauler, walked onto the porch. I couldn't hear what they were saying but tension practically resonated off the group. Safety said something to Bert, poking his finger at the project manager with each word, then turned and strode off the porch.

Po Thang's tail went berserk so I clamped his muzzle with both hands hoping Safety would leave quickly. Instead of heading for his truck, though, he walked to a small house next door, used a key for entry and went inside. Lights came on. A couple of minutes later, Ozzie and John went in the other direction and into another small house.

Bert reentered his own home and shut the door.

Po Thang snorted and I realized I still had his nose in a death grip. "Sorry, boy," I told him and gave him an ear scratch apology. He licked my hand in forgiveness. "So what do we have here? A gang of four?" I asked him. He twitched an ear.

My phone vibrated. "Jan, I told you, I'm on sur—"

"*Corazón*, have you missed me?

"N-Nacho?"

"You rang?"

"Yes, but I can't really talk right this minute. I'm kinda busy."

Po Thang went berserk at the same moment as someone tapped on my window.

Crap! Busted!

Chapter 30

The ordinary man is involved in action, the hero acts.
An immense difference. —Henry Miller
I need me a hero!

The tap on my pickup window frightened me only slightly less than Nacho's phone call. How can a guy who calls you *corazón*—literally *my heart,* but really meaning *my love*—instill such a frisson of both fright and lust just with words?

Dreading I'd been busted by one of what I now referred to as the Gang of Four, I yelled at Po Thang to shut up and reluctantly turned to see who was out there. I knew it wasn't Safety from Po Thang's frantic reaction.

Nacho waggled his cell phone at me and leaned down, an irresistible macho Latino smirk on his criminally handsome face. I hit the window button and it slid open as Po Thang lunged across me, came face to face with Nacho, cowered, and jumped into the back seat, all his bravado gone.

"I see you haven't lost your touch, *Ignacio*," I snarled, using the given name I know he hates. "You can still terrorize helpless women and dogs with a single look."

He laughed softly. "You do not look terrorized and surely you do not refer to yourself as helpless. Although, I am always pleased when you require me."

I sighed and unlocked the passenger side door. "Get in. I can't be seen lurking out here."

Nacho walked around to the other side of my truck, opened the door, and poked a warning finger at Po Thang, who had summoned the courage to let go with a less than hearty growl. He used the same finger to point to my missing overhead bulb. "I see you have been reading mysteries and taking notes."

I started the truck and rolled down the hill, away from prying eyes in the houses lining the street, especially the three housing my Gang of Four. At the bottom of the hill, I stopped and killed the engine.

"How did you find me? Are you following me?" I demanded.

"Always."

"Oh. Uh, Nacho, Jenks said I should contact you because of Luján, the guy he called you about. One of his men is dead, and I think he might be trying to frame me for it. A friend heard the police are asking around about me."

He smiled. "Rounding up the usual suspects?"

"I guess, and I'm scared."

"A rare admission from Hetta Coffey. But, *mija*, Lujàn will no longer be a problem for you."

The pit of my stomach went a little wonky, whether from fear, or maybe hope? "Did you do him?"

"Such talk. No, the *cabrón* still lives, but he has relocated rather than face murder charges of his own man."

"Luján killed the guy in the hot spring?"

"I cannot say. However, if he agrees to stay far away from you, his henchman's death will be ruled an accident."

"You can do stuff like that?" Despite my best efforts tears of relief stung my eyes.

Nacho took my hand. "For you. What happens in Mexico stays in Mexico."

I jerked my hand from his. "Well, nothing is going to happen with you and me, so there."

"You wound me, *corazón*," he gently brushed a tear from my cheek with the back of his hand, "but I see a fire for me in your eyes."

Doodness dwacious.

Jenks. Jenks. Think Jenks.

I was back on the boat, full of burning questions. Well, something was burning. My cheek, for instance.

Holy Moly, how can Nacho have such an effect on me? I'm in love with Jenks, for crying out loud. No wonder Jenks doesn't want Nacho within ten miles of me. However, Jenks was the one who told me to call him, right? And what harm can a little lust do, so long as I don't act on it?

After I jerked my hand away, Nacho had stepped out of the pickup and vanished into the shadowy night from whence he came.

I had one more thing to do before this extremely long and eventful day and evening ended, for when I opened my email I found out I was an aunt, sort of.

"How's daddyhood?" I asked the Trob when I called. I'd poured a large glass of wine for myself, and a small amount for Po Thang, to settle our nerves. Po Thang was still trembling after his encounter with Nacho, and so was I.

The Trob sounded like he was stifling a yawn when he answered. I know he stays up late, so I was surprised when it sounded as if I woke him. "Babies are cute, but they sure make a lot of noise."

"Earplugs and nanny," was my advice; what do I know about babies?

"Allison doesn't want a nanny. Says it's not good for bonding."

I could not believe the word, "bonding", came out of his mouth. Next thing you know, he'd be trying to get in touch with his feminine self. "Uh, well, send me pictures, okay?"

"I will, but she's not very pretty."

"What? Allison would murder you if she heard you say that about your own baby."

"She says it, too. She says the baby looks like me."

Now that *is* unfortunate. At a loss for something to say other than, *well at least she'll be smart*, I changed the subject to why I called. "What can you tell me about Safety?"

"Who?"

"Joe Francis, here on the site. The Safety Engineer."

"Never heard of him."

"What? When I met him my first day on the job he gave me the definite impression he not only knows you well, but also that he knew you had hired me and why."

"Sorry," Wontrobski said as he yawned into the phone. "Don't know him."

"Interesting. By the way, I'll be billing you for Topaz Sawyer's visit to Santa Rosalia. She's a cop and I want her here to pick her brain."

"Whatever."

Sometimes I love my job.

I hung up with the Trob and replayed in my mind the conversation I had with Joe Francis, a.k.a. Safety, that first day on the job. I have the ability to do that, almost to the very words spoken. I had warned Jenks when we first met that I rarely forget a conversation and if I get two pieces of information that do not match, my brain receives a flashing TILT signal like the one you get when you shake a pinball machine too hard. So far Jenks had never given me one single reason to doubt anything he told me. However, I now knew for certain the same could not be said for Safety.

When I'd thankfully exited Pedro's shuttle of doom on that first day at the Lucifer mine, Safety was waiting, and walked toward me. I immediately noticed he was tall and lanky, like Jenks, but with reddish hair worn long and curling out from under a gold hardhat plastered with stickers like MINERS DO IT IN THE DARK and MINERS DO IT DEEPER.

His freckled face was painted with a welcoming smile, and I couldn't help but notice his orange vest almost matched his hair. According to the name on his hat, he was Joe "Safety" Francis. I also recalled the frisson of surprise, and okay, the tingle of a warning, when he removed those sunglasses and momentarily transfixed me with bright blue Robert Redford eyes.

I recovered quickly and resorted to my usual smart mouth. "Let me take a wild guess here, Joe. You're a miner?"

He'd grinned crookedly—perhaps purposely bolstering that Redford personation?—stuck out his hand and told me everyone called him Safety. Then he said, if I remember correctly, "He said you were a fast study."

When I asked who he meant, he said, "Your boss."

I said something snarky in return, but then I shook his hand and followed him back to that big old dually truck of his, where I found a hard hat on the passenger seat. My hat was white, with only my name and no clever stickers.

When I made some smarty pants comment about why my hard hat was white while his was gold, he offered up an equally quick, "Because I'm a guy?"

I countered with a zinger which brought another grin and he said, "Your *jefe* also said you could be a pain in the ass."

I told him the Trob was always right. And now that I thought about it, Safety never said the name, Wontrobski. He said "boss" and "*jefe*", which is boss in Spanish. I was the one who mentioned the Trob by name.

Oh, yes, the lowdown snake had, without a shadow of a doubt, intimated he not only knew the Trob, but was on the Trob team. When I'd told him that despite my job title of Liaison Materials Engineer, I don't liaise well with others, I think he thought I was joking.

Well, buddy, the joke's on you and it starts, right now.

Chapter 31

The trouble with conspiracies is that they rot internally. —Robert A. Heinlein

I called Jan immediately after talking with the Trob. It was late, but I'd promised to let her know I was safely back onboard.

After sharing my suspicion that not only one, but four men from the project were somehow in cahoots, I ended with, "And now that I think of it, Safety looks more like Howdy Doody than Robert Redford."

"Oooh, someone almost had a crush, didn't they?"

"Certainly not," I huffed.

"Did too."

"Did not."

"Okay, enough about Safety, then. Let's discuss your *big* birthday party."

Jan's parting dig didn't put me in the best mood the next day at the office. I'd get back at her later when she returned to the boat for Topaz Sawyer's visit, but for now I had bigger fish to fry.

I once again left early to beat everyone into the office, and downloaded both Ozzie and Safety's bugs and replaced them. Rosario had given me a set of earphones for my computer so I could listen to the bugged conversations with no fear of anyone overhearing, so I put off dealing with both until later.

As Safety had been out of the office most of the day before, I didn't expect much from his side, so I played back Ozzie's bug first. Nothing new there, except one little tidbit where he seemed to be arguing with someone. I had no way of knowing who that someone on the other end was, as I didn't have the phone bugged, just the office, so I only heard half the conversation. And, it was in rapid-fire Spanish.

I forwarded the conversation to Rosario for translation and also asked him if he could do something about getting me phone bugs, as well.

I did find some good news when I checked my Facebook page. Russell Madadhan, the guy we were pretty sure was Rosario's long lost father, had friended me back. Now I was able to check his friend list, maybe get more info on his family and the like. The last thing I wanted to do was scare him off. Eventually I'd let Rosario know, if in fact this guy was his dad, but for now I was still checking him out.

Most of Russell's one-hundred and seventeen friends were men and when I had time I'd see what they were all about, maybe find that all important link to a misspent youth in Mexico. My hope, of course, was to ultimately reunite him with his son, Rosario, but since he didn't know he *had* a son, I thought I'd better tread lightly rather than do something like post a photo of Rosario on his Facebook page and say, "Look familiar?"

Checking his timeline, I was relieved not to find any messages like, "Yo Russ, we miss you back here in San Quentin," or the like.

I decided, now that we were such good friends, to send him a private message: *I am living and working in Mexico right now, so Facebook is my lifeline back to the Bay Area. Thanks for being my friend. I love Mexico, but where I live there are few Americans.* He didn't post often, so I didn't have great expectations of an answer anytime soon. I hoped, since we had zero friends in common, he didn't think I was some nut case and get me suspended by the Facebook police.

I also had an email from Topaz Sawyer saying she'd arrive on Monday and was *so* excited about a trip to sunny Mexico. She wanted to know if she should bring her bikini. I'd checked the water temp the day before on my boat's depth sounder: 69.5. It looked like a trip to Conception Bay was in order while she was visiting, as Geary was reporting seventy-three degree water, which is still too cold by my standards.

I guess a warm up in the hot spring was still way out of the question?

I fired off an email to Jan telling her of Topaz's arrival and asking her to beat feet over here by Thursday night and bring extra bugs I'd try to place on Friday morning. And to put Rosario on a mission of digging deeper into the backgrounds of my Gang of Four.

Now that I'd handed out assignments, I listened to Safety's bugged conversations and gleaned very little except that it was working.

Not knowing what to expect as a result of the tiff with Bert the day before, I was dreading his arrival. I was ready with an apology, but hoped Safety, when he'd seen Bert the night before, had explained I hadn't meant Purchasing with a Capitol P, thereby not besmirched Ozzie, a guy he'd personally hired. I'd seen what looked like Bert and Safety having their own set-to on the porch and wondered what that was all about.

Much to my relief, Bert headed straight for my office, said he was sorry he'd been rude and asked me to please forgive him. After he went on to his office I let out the breath I'd been holding.

I glanced out to see that Laura had visibly relaxed as well, and Safety gave me a smile and a thumb's up. The tension in the building disappeared like magic. Even Ozzie offered a cheery good morning greeting.

Of course, all of this nice stuff raised my suspicion level a few notches, so I fired off another email to Jan, urging her to help Rosario expedite those background checks.

All I had at my fingertips were the standard resume-type stuff companies print on brochures for investors and for bidding on jobs. Useless fluff meant to impress. For example, mine reads:

Hetta Coffey holds a BS in Civil Engineering from ULB (Université Libre de Bruxelles) and has over twenty years of experience in the Materials Management field. She has been responsible for multimillion dollar Petrochemical and Mining projects in Japan, Mexico and the United States.

The way it should read is: Hetta Coffey can BS almost anyone and graduated from ULB by virtue of them giving her a degree to get rid of her. Since then she has managed to piss off people in Petrochemical and Mining projects worldwide, and five of those so-called twenty years of experience she worked for Daddy during the summer.

Like I said before, being nice in this industry is the kiss of death and that is why I was surprised Bert climbed as high as project manager for such a large job. Not that he isn't, on paper, qualified. And he had certainly showed me a not-so-nice side the day before. I anxiously awaited Jan and Rosario's report on him and the others.

Meanwhile, I decided to check out Rosario's alleged dad's friends.

One by one I looked at their Facebook pages, finding that most worked in high-tech. Some were married, some single. None of his friends seemed to be relatives. Bored silly with his friends' pages, I was about to chuck it when I hit on something interesting. The word, Baja, caught my attention, so I took a look at that friend's page.

Baja Gamer's photo was an Avatar, with the cartoon-like image of a Don Quixote character taking on what looked to be an army of mechanical creatures. Most of the posts had to do with gaming, none of which I understood. However, the fact that Rosario was also a gamer made it apparent the apple hadn't fallen far from the tree. Wondering where this Baja dude hailed from, I opened his album containing ten pictures and received a jolt; one of them was the faded snapshot Rosario had shown me of two love-struck teenagers, his mother and father, in Puerto Vallarta those many years ago when Rosario was still a twinkle in Russell's eye.

WTF?

I called Jan immediately and told her to pack a bag and that I'd be there in two hours to pick her up.

"What's the sudden rush, Hetta? I said I'd be there by Thursday."

Jan and I have a code. When there's trouble nearby, revert to pig Latin. "At-ray. O-nay English." I've never quite mastered pig Latin words when they start in a vowel. Besides, saying English-way didn't obscure a danged thing.

"And-stay eye-bay."

I heard a rustling as she moved about, then a door closing. "Ood-gay."

"Ug-bays! Ug-bays! End-fray ot-nay end-fray."

"Gotcha."

I picked up the conversation in plain old English. "I need those bugs so decided to drive out. Start packing. I'll explain later."

In a daring daylight raid, I removed the bug from Safety's computer while he was out of the office, then told Laura I would be back, but much later. If I were to pick up Jan, stop back by the office and get us to the boat before dark, I had to get a move on.

Jan and Rosario were working in the office Jan set up in her and Chino's spare room. Rosario was staying in the other large trailer, while Doc Di now had her own, smaller RV. The place was starting to look like a trailer park.

Rosario gave me the thumbdrive bugs and lamented he didn't have anything to plant in a telephone. "That's all right, these will do. Thanks. Okay, Jan, we have to get on the road. We're burning daylight."

"I sent you the information you wanted on Bert, Ozzie, John and Safety," Rosario told me, "When you return to the boat, it will be waiting."

"Nice work. Okay Jan, let's load up your laptop and roll. We have work to do. Rosario, would you get Po Thang rounded up for me?"

As soon a Rosario left the office I plugged the bug I brought from Safety's office into Jan's desktop tower and shoved it further under the desk.

Jan gave me a two thumb's up.

Ten minutes later we were back on the washboard road from hell, headed out to Mex 1's blessed pavement.

"Okay, Hetta, talk."

"Rosario is scamming us. I don't know how yet, but he is." I told her about the Facebook thing and that I suspected Baja Gamer was none other than our boy Rosario.

"But why would he tell us that fairy tale if he'd already found his father?"

"I have no idea, but one thing is for sure, he can't be trusted. Did you manage to get those files he has on our Gang of Four?"

"He copied me, so yes."

I thought about this as we bounded along at a kidney scrambling speed. We had four computers involved, five if you count my office desktop. "I have a sneaking suspicion Rosario has much more on his laptop than he's shared."

"I've had that feeling ever since you called a couple of hours ago. Which is why," she gave me an evil grin, "I sent our at-ray end-fray out to find Chino and tell him I was leaving."

"What's that got to do with the price of rice in China."

"Hetta, Hetta, Hetta. After all these years under your tender tutelage in wickedness, do you think I've learned nothing?"

"You raided his computer?"

"Faster than Po Thang can clear a fridge."

We stopped back by the office and found everyone gone for the day. I couldn't do anything about bugging John Warren's office, because he was in a small trailer attached to the Mechanics Shop deep within the project's interior. That little visit would have to take place on the morrow.

However, I downloaded Ozzie's bug and rebugged him and Safety before we headed to Bert's office. We were surprised to find it unlocked.

Canadians, you gotta love their trusting little souls.

Since I didn't have to get to the jobsite at the crack of dawn to download the bugs, Jan and I worked late into the night. As promised, Rosario had forwarded the dirt on our men. Or rather, he forwarded his version.

Then we compared what he sent with what Jan stole from his computer.

TILT!

Chapter 32

It is discouraging how many people are shocked by honesty and how few by deceit.—Noel Coward

"We should have seen this one coming," Jan said. "No man is that honest. Well, except Chino and Jenks."

We were enjoying a relatively late breakfast of Jan's famous pecan waffles. "So, do we now have a Gang of Five? You think Rosario is a colluder in this scheme and for some reason they tried to off him?"

Jan shook her head. "I don't see it that way. From some of the file dates I found in his computer, Rosario started digging stuff up on the other four as soon as he arrived at the jobsite."

"But why? Job security? Or blackmail? And maybe that's why they tried to kill him? And why would they? Okay, Bert hired his friends and while that's not exactly ethical, it isn't a crime. Yet. A handpicked clique, as it were."

Jan nodded. "A cahoots clique."

We went onto the sundeck with our coffee and watched pangas speed out of the harbor to check their nets. They were trailed by pelicans and gulls looking to steal an easy meal. A huge blue heron glided in and landed less than daintily on my swim platform, prompting Po Thang to bark furiously and lunge toward the bird. The bird totally ignored him, which drove the dog more nutso.

Jan shushed him and laughed. "How do you think that bird knows Po Thang can't get to him?"

"Oh, but he can. All Po Thang has to do is jump onto the dock and out onto the swim platform. He hasn't figured it out yet."

Po Thang reluctantly gave up his barking and returned to Jan's side. She rubbed his ears and said, "Or, maybe he doesn't *want* to figure it out."

"Like Rosario doesn't want us to know that Ozzie is deep in debt due to hospital bills for his youngest kid?"

"Or that Safety couldn't get a job anywhere else because he's committed a felony? Never mind that the felony was driving related and no one was badly hurt."

We were on a roll, so I added, "Or that John Warren is stuck with an underwater house that is only worth one third of the seven hundred grand he paid for it?"

Jan gathered the breakfast dishes Po Thang had so graciously cleaned. "And then there is Bert. His wife has left him and is cleaning out everything he worked for. His dream of retiring in Mexico is quickly biting the dust."

I followed her into the galley and grabbed my backpack. "Thanks for the great breakfast. Wish I could stay, but I have the devil's work to do. I'll be late. I have to wait for the office to clear so I can download bugs."

Po Thang, when I grabbed my pack, ran for his leash. "Not today, boy. You stay with your Auntie Jan." He didn't look all that disappointed.

"Call me if you come up with anything new, okay?"

"I will, but Hetta, we already know something very helpful. Those four have at least one thing in common. They all need money. Badly. And a lot more dough than working at the mine will earn them. All we have to do is find out how they're stealing it."

"Gee, that's all?"

"I do know another thing."

"And that is?"

"Why are they still here?"

"Jan, you said that you knew something, and then asked me a question."

"Think. If you had somehow managed to steal, say, a half-million bucks, would you take it and run? After all that's only a little over a hundred thou each when you divide by four and that's chump change. We know they need much more to bail themselves out or retire."

A bright ray of light penetrated my heretofore thick skull. "They're waiting for a big payoff of some kind!"

"Bingo."

I put down my bag, called Laura and told her I'd be late and we went back to work on the computers, searching existing purchase orders for any pending cash layouts of mega proportions. It didn't take long to zero in on an agency in Monterrey supplying the big Caterpiller 777Gs. Five of them, to be exact, at 1.7 million each.

"And," Jan added, "get this. A wire transfer for almost seven million bucks was approved by Bert yesterday."

"Whoa, no project manager can approve a cash layout like that. What are the rules for who signs for what amount on this project?"

"Hang one." She attacked her keyboard with enviable speed while I refilled my coffee cup. "Okay, got it. Over ten thousand requires three signatures: the Purchasing Manager and Project Manager on site, and the Comptroller in Mexico City."

"Okay, there's two of our Gang of Four. Who signs the delivery ticket and writes up the Material Receiving Report here for large equipment."

"It's a joint effort. John Warren, the equipment manager and your BFF, Joe "Safety" Frances, who wears two hats: Safety Engineer and Operations Manager."

Later that day while Jan continued following the moola, I went to work with a mind to visit the equipment yard. My mission was two-fold: place a bug in John Warren's computer and take a look at those brand new 777Gs listed on the material receiving report.

As soon as I reached the office, I checked out a company truck and drove to the Mechanics Shop, all the while keeping out a sharp eye for ChaCha and her friends. Lucky for me, they were working on another part of the site, or perhaps were all in traction.

John Warren was surprised to see me when I walked into his office, but he didn't seem at all upset. Why should he? He had no idea I was on to his gang. He offered me coffee, which I quickly accepted because on my previous visit I'd noticed the break room was out in the shop. As soon as he left I planted the bug and was seated and browsing through a brochure for the 777G when he returned.

"So, Hetta, to what do I owe the pleasure of your company?"

I had a story ready. "You remember my friend, Jan? You met her at the dock awhile back."

"Who wouldn't?" he said with a smile. "Not often you run into a tall blonde around here."

"Well, I told her about my ride in one of these," I shook the brochure at him, "and she wants to know if you'd take her for a spin."

He frowned. "I don't know. You'd have to clear it with Bert."

I stood and put my empty coffee cup in the trash. "Great. I'll ask him. Well, gotta run."

I left him with a puzzled look on his face, he probably wondering why I drove all the way out there to ask a question I could have asked on the phone. Purposely taking a wrong turn, I entered and circled the large fenced equipment yard looking for those new machines. Not there. On my way out, John waited by the gate.

Rolling down my window I tried to look sheepish and said, with an eye-roll, "Jeez, I'd get lost going around the block." I gave him a wave and sped off.

Now I had to figure out how to retrieve that bug from his office.

Back at my desk I pulled up the overall organization chart and identified the Comptroller, that third guy who had to sign off on a multi-million dollar cash layout. Julio Vargas was based in Mexico City and when I fired off that info to Jan, she answered back she was way ahead of me and was on Vargas's tail. Maybe I should give her a raise.

With time to kill before everyone left me to retrieve all three bugs in my office building, I decided to do a little more looking into Rosario's Facebook connections. Convinced that Baja Gamer and Rosario were one and the same, I looked at Gamer's friends. There weren't many, only fourteen including Russell. Most were gamers from different parts of the States with one exception: Julio Smith, Mexico City. Julio Smith?

Julio's avatar was a Neptune-like, King of the Sea character. He had twenty-eight friends scattered all over Mexico and the States. One of them was Russell Madadhan and another was a little sister, Isabel Smith Vargas. ¡Carumba!

I sent another email to Jan: the comptroller is Julio Smith Vargas. Mother's name is Vargas, father is the Smith. BTW, he's a Facebook buddy of Baja Gamer and Rosario's dad.

And they say the social media is a waste of time.

Over a fabulous dinner of beef Stroganoff with homemade noodles and fresh asparagus, Jan and I discussed this ever more confusing situation.

"Okay, who is scamming whom here? And how?"

Jan shook her head. "Danged if I can figure it out. The more I learns the confuseder I gets."

"After dinner, let's make boxes. You know, like connect the dots. Sometimes that helps."

"Can't hurt. By the way, Rosario called today. Wanted to know what he should do next."

"I'd like to tell him, the little rat. We now have seven men, if you include Rosario's father, possibly all involved in an undefined criminal activity, who are either working together...or not."

She shook her head. "Not working together. They think Rosario's dead."

"The Gang of Four think he's dead because they most likely are the ones who tried to kill him."

"What if they didn't?"

"Huh?"

"What if the little turd faked his own death?"

"Jan, you are a genius. I think you just solved the whole thing."

"I did?"

"Think about it. If you are dead, how can you possibly be accused of stealing something after you died?"

"You think Rosario is gonna steal the money himself? How can that be? He was a fairly low-level clerk."

"Yabbut, maybe a high-tech clerk with a buddy way up in the organization? Someone in the financial end, like Vargas. How did Rosario get his job in the first place?"

"Good question. Let's get to work."

We were on a roll.

Rosario was hired out of Mexico City.

In Mexico, all roads, especially the crooked ones, lead to Mexico City.

And there is nothing they like better than to play a little game called Get the Gringo.

Chapter 33

Life is a dead-end street.—H.L. Mencken
And we rolled to a stop.—Hetta Coffey

ChaCha's husband's shop was easy to find. She'd told me it was on the hill not far from the hospital, and on the road leading back to Mex 1. She said they lived next door.

I showed up on her doorstep unannounced, but in Mexico that doesn't mean anything. She had told me to come by sometime and now I was here. Mexicans don't ask why you came, they just seem glad to see you.

Ushered into a spotless living room that shall remain spotless into the next century because the white furniture and white carpet were entirely covered in plastic, reminiscent of my grandmother's house in Texas. Grans didn't go so far as to cover the floor in plastic, but lamp shades and chair seats remained factory fresh until the day she died.

When ChaCha's husband wandered in, I saw the need for plastic. Lots of plastic. He was covered, head to toe in black grease and smelled of gasoline and diesel fuel. When I held out my hand in greeting ChaCha slammed a clean towel into his greasy mitt and wrapped it up before he could shake.

He escaped back to his shop, leaving us girls to chat. ChaCha made limeade and placed it on the glass coffee table along with some cookies— thankfully not wrapped in cellophane—then sat back with a crackle and waited for me to say something. Like, why I was there.

"Your work is *buena*?"

"*Sí.*"

"*No mas problemas*?"

"*No.*"

Okay, in for a penny, in for a pound. I reached in my pocket and pulled out a thumbdrive. "Do you know what this is?"

"*Ah, sí. Memoria Ooh Esse Bay.*"

"You're sending that nice woman into the lion's den to do your dirty work?"

"Oh, come on, Jan, John Warren isn't exactly Hannibal Lecter. He's just a thief."

"How did you talk her into it?"

"I asked her to retrieve the *memoria ooh esse bay*—that's USB thumbdrive in Spanish in case you ever need to buy one in Mexico—from John Warren's office next week. When he isn't looking, of course."

"And she didn't question your motives? I mean, she could lose her job if she gets caught."

"I promised her a promotion. She really hates driving all day and would like to work in the office.

Or maybe train other women to operate those big machines."

"There's a scary thought. You can't promote people."

"I hired you, didn't I?"

"Yo, Trob. How's it going?"

"I'm thinking of moving a bed into my office. No sleep."

"I told you, get a nanny."

"Allison's almost there."

"Good news. Jan and I think we may be zeroing in on your culprits. I do have one question though. Who exactly hired us? I mean, you hired me, but who hired you?"

"I was contacted by the project comptroller, Julio Vargas. Why?"

Well, crap. So much for figuring it all out. Why would Julio Vargas call the dogs on himself if he was involved in an embezzlement scheme with the Gang of Four?

"Oh, just wondering."

"So, you think you are close to unraveling this puzzle?"

"Uh, well, maybe not so much. Get some sleep."

Jan and I were dejected.

Here we thought had, brilliantly of course, unearthed the dastardly culprits and now we were almost back to square one.

I have a lifelong habit for dealing with dejection: I leave town. I first ran away from home at three. Mother helped pack my bag.

"Po Thang, how would you like to go for a boat ride this weekend?"

He thumped his tail, probably thinking I said, "Po Thang how would you like to eat the entire state of Baja California Sud this weekend?"

Jan, however, didn't do anything near a tail thump. "Hetta, you promised Jenks you wouldn't leave the dock until he returned."

"So? I lied. He's used to it."

"I'm not going."

"Fine, I'll be back Sunday afternoon so you can get a room in town while I'm gone, or take my pickup and head for Camp Chino."

Silence.

"I have to get back in time to spiff up the boat and have Topaz's room all ready for Monday morning."

Silence.

"Earth to Jan?"

"Where are you going?"

"Just out to San Marcos island. You can see it from the flying bridge."

"What if Jenks calls?"

"Cell phones work fine out there. It's not like the middle of nowhere, you know. There's that big phosphate mining operation on the south end of the island and the village of San Bruno on shore."

The frown on her face smoothed some.

"Look, it's only an overnighter. An escape from WiFi, a chance to exercise the engines, watch some movies, chill. Jenks and I met *pangueros* from the Sweet Pea cove fish camp before he left and I'm sure they'll sell me fresh fish and maybe a lobster or two. I found a couple of good bottles of white wine at the liquor store to go with the lobster. So, I'll see you Sunday afternoon when I get back?"

"Lobster?"

"You know, those spiny little things you love?"

"What's Geary say the weather 'sposed to be?"

"Dead flat calm, light variable breezes. Nada. Sweet Pea cove is only a hop skip and a jump from the marina, so if the wind comes up from the wrong direction I can be back in less than an hour, so you don't have to worry about me."

"I won't then."

"Good then."

"Fine then."

I busied myself on the computer and counted to ten before Jan growled, "Oh, okay. I don't want you out there by yourself."

Friends, sometimes you gotta know what it takes to reel 'em in.

Saturday dawned Charlie Charlie, as Geary had predicted: clear and calm.

Po Thang, when I started the engines, paced the decks in worry. He stood on the bow and watched and whined as we backed away from the dock, made the turn and motored out the harbor entrance. Once we cleared the harbor, however, he joined Jan and me on the bridge and settled down for a nap.

Jan made us an underway Bloody Mary, light on the vodka. I'd long ago learned that no matter how good the weather, or how well the boat was running, keeping a clear head when away from the dock is a smart idea.

Po Thang suddenly levitated, rushed to the bow and began barking wildly, somehow alerted before we were that dolphins were about. The first one we saw was a big guy executing a double flip right off the bow, his splash spraying Po Thang and backing him up a bit. He quickly shook off the water and spent the next hour communing with the dolphins, both bottlenose and their little buddies, called common dolphins.

The dolphins wove in and out of our bow wave and frolicked in our wake, performing twists, turns and other acrobatics and occasionally turning sideways, looking at Po Thang and chattering, or maybe chiding.

Jan and I took great delight at Po Thang's antics as he ricocheted between being intrigued, annoyed, confused, and downright manic. Dogs are better than television.

"Ya know, Hetta, you were right. It is good to get away from it all. Nice thing about boats is that you can."

"When I bought her everyone, and I mean everyone, including you, thought I'd finally lost my last loose screw, but as it turned out, it was a life-changing move. If it weren't for *Raymond Johnson*, I'd probably have never met Jenks."

"And God knows you need someone like him, what with your track record."

"Yeah, there's a lesson there."

She sighed. "I know, I know. I should appreciate Chino more. If he takes up with Doc Di, it'll be all my fault."

"He won't. Wanna call him and make nice?"

"I better not. What if he wants to drive over for a visit? I'd have to tell him what we're doing and then he'll rat us out to Jenks. I'll call him when we get back."

"I'll call Jenks then, as well. What they don't know won't hurt us."

Chapter 34

We made too many wrong mistakes.—Yogi
Berra

Sweet Pea cove is named for a hapless sailboat that was caught on the lee shore when a hurricane passed and the wind suddenly changed direction. The gale was so fierce their small engine couldn't power into it enough to raise the anchor, and when they cut the anchor line to escape it wrapped the prop, sealing their fate. Fortunately for the people on board they jumped to safety when the boat hit the beach. Two other boats that did manage to move to the relative safety of the other side of an outcropping took in the wet, frightened sailors. Pieces of *Sweet Pea* can still be found on the beach.

Matter of fact, the shores of the Sea of Cortez are littered with wrecks, each one with its own sad story. In 2003 over a hundred boats and two marinas were destroyed by Hurricane Marty and many vessels can still be seen either in pieces or semi-submerged. Over the centuries hundreds, maybe thousands, of boats of all sizes have met a nasty end due to the freakish nature of the Sea's weather, but wrecks that pose a hazard are, for the most part, marked on charts. Once in awhile, though, a cruiser gets a nasty surprise when they hook a wreck and lose an anchor. It is for this reason that every time I anchor I mark the location in my GPS, so I can avoid snagging something the next time, but also so I can return to that anchorage in the dark.

And, as Jan and I had already learned the year before at a nearby anchorage, just because the weather is benign when you go to bed, it isn't guaranteed to stay that way. It was that harrowing middle of the night anchor drill that had Jan spooked about leaving a nice safe marina, but lobster always trumps worry.

We were the only cruising boat in the cove. Once anchored we took my panga, *Se Vende*, to shore and let Po Thang run wild while I scored a couple of sea bass, three lobsters and a half-kilo of illegal shrimp (the best kind) at the fish camp. I worried when Po Thang charged in and out of the water near the camp, afraid he'd pick up a fish hook or go after a stingray, but he was so happy I didn't have the heart to curb his joy.

Back at the boat I made him stay in *Se Vende* until we hosed him down with fresh water and then once we let him on deck, Jan gave him a shampoo. He took it all in stride, probably thinking this boat thing at anchor was a blast. I was thinking what a pain in the ass a large, hairy boat dog can be. Maybe I should convert *Se Vende* into a dog house?

We ate our dinner of broiled sea bass and lobster and were finishing the one glass of wine—albeit a large one—allowed while at anchor, when Po Thang's tail went into overdrive. Sure enough, rounding the point came *Lucifer*, bristling with fishing poles. The Gang of Four pulled alongside.

"Ahoy there," Safety hollered above the whaler's engine noise. "I wondered where you went. Looks like you two had the same idea as we did to get away for a night."

"Ya gonna sleep four guys on that little boat?" Jan asked.

"That an offer?"

"Nope."

"Shoot. In that case we'll stick to our original plan and head for the hotel at Café Olé in Conception Bay. Maybe hit that bar at Santispac for some beer and dancing on the way. Want to go?"

"No thanks, we'll hang here. You can speed down there in no time, but it would take us way too long," I told him. As if I'd even consider taking off with our four major suspects.

"Yeah, we gotta get on down the road if we want to make if before dark. Have fun."

"You too," I said with a wave. Then with a wink at Jan, I added, "Hey, you might want to try out that hot spring at Posada while you're there."

"Great idea. Thanks."

They sped south, their huge engines throwing a four-foot rooster tail in their wake.

Jan turned to me with an evil grin. "I cannot tell you what a pleasure it is to be your friend."

We finished off our wine and moved into the galley to do the dishes that Po Thang had so kindly pre-cleaned.

In the middle of that chore, I had an epiphany.

"Jan, let's go back to the dock. We can still make it before dark if I put the pedal to the metal."

"Why, what's wrong?"

"Nothing that a couple of turtlenecks, leggings and knit caps, all in black, of course, and a credit card won't fix."

Since it was Saturday night and Mexicans are notorious late nighters, we waited until three AM to make our foray up the hill and park a block away from Bert's house. At that hour Po Thang wasn't really miffed at being left on the boat.

We sat in the car with the windows down, listening and watching for anyone who may have noticed our arrival, but the neighborhood was as quiet as a cemetery. Even the hospital was dimly lit and the parking lot empty. Without street lights and only a few lit porches—thankfully not on our targets' houses—the going was slow as we crept up the street. When we were almost there, several dogs set up barking, freezing us in our tracks, but I've noticed that in Mexico dogs are always barking and no one pays any attention. For some reason Mexicans seem to have an enviable ability to tune them out. No lights came on so we continued on our mission.

Three company pickups were lined up in front of the darkened houses. We'd seen Safety's dually where he left it, in the marina parking lot.

I pointed out Bert's large Victorian for Jan, and the two smaller ones on either side that housed the other three men. "Which one should we hit first?" I whispered.

Jan didn't hesitate. "The big kahuna's. Bert has to be the gang leader."

We went right through the front door, using a credit card to open the simple lock. Once in, I exhaled loudly, letting go a breath I hadn't realized I was holding and asked, "So, what are we looking for?"

"You're asking me? This was your bright idea."

Now that I thought about it, what exactly did I expect to find? Surely he wouldn't leave incriminating evidence laying around in plain sight. "I dunno. Maybe get a feel for his contacts outside of work. I mean, if he's making off with money, it must be going somewhere."

"So, ya wanna check under the mattress?"

"Sarcasm has it's place, and this is not it."

"I wasn't being sarcastic. I mean it."

We headed for the bedroom.

I put my penlight in my mouth, like in the movies, and felt on one side of the bed while Jan did likewise on the other.

"I've got something," Jan said, so I joined her. She fished out a handful of envelopes and laid them on the bed. One was from a Canadian bank showing deposits of paychecks. "Jeez, this guy is pulling in the dough. Maybe I should try to get his job when he gets the boot."

"Yeah, Hetta, you're certainly qualified. You said project managers should be ass-kicking meanies."

I hit her on the head with the envelope. There were a few pieces of personal correspondence: a birthday card to the best uncle ever, a nasty letter from the soon-to-be ex and an equally devastating letter from her lawyer.

As I was sorting through them, Jan spit out her penlight and said, "Paydirt."

"Whatcha got?"

"Exactly what everyone tells you not to have: a list of his passwords and PINs. Uh, did we bring anything to write on?"

"Crap."

While Jan replaced everything except her big find back under the mattress, I made my way into the kitchen and found a drawer containing ballpoints and note pads. There was also a phone number list. We sat at the kitchen table and while Jan copied one list, I did the other. We carefully replaced everything and were almost to the exit door when we heard a noise and hit the floor.

Turning off the penlights, we lay still, ears pricked. Nothing. After what seemed an eternity but was probably five minutes, Jan said, "Let's go."

I agreed, and was pushing myself onto my knees when something hit me in the head and let out a horrifying screech. Or maybe that was me.

The emergency room reception area was dark, but since the front door was unlocked, we figured someone must be around. While I cradled my swelling hand and neck, Jan went in search of anyone who could help.

She returned dragging a sleepy looking guy by his white coat sleeve.

Luckily for me epinephrine is *epinefrina* in Spanish.

Did I mention that I am highly allergic to cats?

It was almost dawn when we dragged ourselves back onto the boat. I was jazzed by the shot that jangled my nerves and sent my blood pressure soaring but thankfully opened my bronchial tubes.

Po Thang sniffed me suspiciously, probably thinking I'd been unfaithful. Jan, in an ill-timed attempt at humor, said I indeed looked like something the cat dragged in.

"Not at all funny. Who the hell ever heard of an attack cat? And how come he didn't savage you instead of me?"

"Gee thanks."

"Sorry, what I mean is, you aren't allergic. Boy, I could really use a glass of wine before we turn in."

"I'm sure gonna have one, but I don't know if you should, Hetta, what with that shot and all."

"You get the wine, I'll Google it."

WARNING: Using chlorpheniramine (epinephrine) together with ethanol (booze) can increase nervous system side effects such as dizziness, drowsiness and difficulty concentrating.

Some people may also experience impairment in thinking and judgment.

Jan returned with two glasses and bottle of chilled white wine. "What'd you find out."

"Wine shouldn't have any effect at all on my normal state of being."

Chapter 35

Where there's smoke, there's fire.

I didn't wake until noon, and even then it was a struggle to pull myself from what was probably a self-induced near epinedrine/wine coma.

Jan sat on the edge of the bed and Po Thang stood over me, licking my face.

"Phuhh, dawg! Get off me."

"He's just concerned. I was gonna get a mirror to see if you had enough breath to fog it up."

"Speaking of breath, what in the hell did you feed this dog this morning?"

"Raccoon shit."

"What?"

"Well, I'm not certain, but I caught him chewing something that looked like it."

I shoved Po Thang off the bed and was reaching to throttle Jan when she deftly avoided my intended choke hold and sashayed to the door. "Your breakfast is ready," she cooed over her shoulder. "Po Thang left you some."

"Why are you being so crappy?" I asked Jan when I managed to get out of bed and haul myself up to the main saloon.

"I saw that Google search you did last night. Are you trying to kill yourself?"

Busted. "I really wanted a glass of wine and figured it wouldn't hurt anything."

"In spite of what you read."

"Oh, come on Jan. Everyone knows you can't believe anything you see on the Internet."

Coffee and eggs helped my recovery. Jan dosed the cat scratches on my neck and hands with peroxide and antibiotic cream as instructed. Luckily there were no bite wounds, but just in case the intern gave me a prescription for antibiotics. Jan had gone into town, found an open *farmacia* and filled it for me. A good thing, too. Heaven knows what bacteria lurk in raccoon scat.

She called Chino and I called Jenks.

"Hetta, you don't look so hot," Jenks said. "Are you okay?"

"Rough night. Po Thang ate raccoon poop and then licked my face."

"Oh, sure, blame it on the poor dog. How's your investigation going?"

I brought him up to date, naturally leaving out the boat trip, breaking and entering, and cat attack. "So, to summarize, our friend Rosario isn't what he seems. We had six suspects, but now we're down to five after talking with the Trob. That comptroller we figured was dirty turns out to be the one who hired us. It's all giving me a giant headache."

"It sounds to me like you two may be in over your head. Have you called Nacho yet?"

Jan had sauntered up and was listening in. Skype calls do have privacy issues when you have nosy friends. But then again, she learned from me.

"Hi, Jenks," she said with a wave.

I glared at Jan and shooed her away. "Jenks, I'll call you back when we can talk *privately*. But to answer your question, the Luján thing is over. He's still alive, dang it, but has relocated after Nacho evidently strongly suggested he do so. And the guy in the hot spring died of natural causes, so no one is looking for me anymore."

That was a simplified explanation of a complicated plot, but so far as Jenks is concerned, all he really need know.

Jan returned as soon as I hung up. "I still cannot believe Jenks told you to contact Nacho. I mean, what with you lusting after his criminally gorgeous bod and all. How come you didn't tell me you'd called him?"

"Because, Miss Meddles, not all of my bidness is your bidness. And I do not lust, I simply...admire. Anyhow, when I saw him—"

"You saw Nacho? Like in person? And you didn't tell me? Spit it out."

"Only if you'll make an apple pie. And get Topaz's cabin ready."

"No prob, Chica. Matter of fact, I've already cleaned the guest cabin. All I have to do tomorrow morning is change the linens."

"And give me a pedicure."

"It's apple pie or nothing."

"Po Thang, your Auntie Jan drives a hard bargain."

"Woof."

Jan made two apple pies, saying that was the only way there was a snowball's chance in hell there would be any left for Topaz, what with the likes of me and Po Thang onboard. While the pies baked I told Jan about Nacho materializing and what he said about the boiled dude. I skipped his sexy cheek-stroke farewell.

"Did you discuss the Gang of Four?"

"No, but I emailed him a list of characters and what we suspect, just in case he has any input, but haven't heard back yet. I don't think white collar crime is his thing."

"Doncha just wish we knew what his thing *is*?"

We sighed a collective sigh and then got back to work.

While I was comatose she'd started tapping into Bert's information we'd lifted the night before, and we hit the computers so she could show me her findings. The Gang of Four still hadn't returned, but we still worked behind closed blinds and locked doors.

We did take our hot pie and iced tea out on the sundeck later. The fresh air felt wonderful, but a north wind was piping up. *Lucifer* was still not back in her slip and I commented on how they were going to take a pounding on the way home.

"Couldn't happen to a nicer group of guys."

Po Thang sprang alive from an apple pie coma of his own, and started to howl. I'd never heard him do that and it was eerie and chilling, like he was in mourning. Jan and I surrounded him and stroked his ears and back, risking major hearing loss in the process.

"What the hell?" Jan asked, and then we heard the sirens.

From my flying bridge we saw a huge plume of black smoke on the hill. Right by the hospital.

We couldn't get up the hill, as the police blocked our way. Turning around, I took the back road to Cha Cha's house and managed to get within three blocks. Putting Po Thang on a leash, we walked the rest of the way. It looked as though the smoke had diminished some, but was still significant.

I knew the town of Santa Rosalia had fallen victim to a few devastating fires over the years, but nothing had changed in the way of fire prevention except for the trucks. Water is the biggest problem, as there is no reservoir backing up the few fire hydrants in existence. The city water system is simply not sufficient to put down a serious fire, so they have a water truck. I'd heard that during one outbreak the truck ran dry and rushed to a large tank where people could wash cars and fill water jugs. Unfortunately there was a long line where they were forced to wait their turn.

Po Thang had stopped his howling, but still quivered. ChaCha, despite her concerns for her carpet, welcomed Po Thang into the house. I think when he lifted his leg on her faulty dirt hauler, he made a friend forever.

Since the wind had switched and now blew toward their house ChaCha and her neighbors were frantically throwing everything that would fit in their pickup, and other cars her husband was working on, so Jan and I pitched in. Jan drove an ancient Ford packed to the hilt with ChaCha's belongings, then hiked back up the hill. I continued to pack the next vehicle until it was full, then drove it to safety.

Dark fell as we were shuttling cars and belongings. We had just finished when we learned the fire was out. Not fond of the idea of hauling everything back up the hill, Jan and I said we had important business to attend to—not a total lie—and skedaddled.

I left Po Thang in my pickup and went to survey the fire damage. Bert's home was in ashes, as were the adjoining houses, and three company pickups. Safety was lucky his was at the marina.

Across the street, a bewildered little girl stood leaning against her mother. Her arms were wrapped around a singed cat.

He hissed at me.

Chapter 36

> Bad news isn't wine. It doesn't improve with
> age.— Colin Powell

We waited for *Lucifer's* return, dreading giving them the bad news despite the fact that we thought they were a den of thieves.

Neither of us could keep our eyes open past ten. The past twenty-four hours had been extremely exhausting, even for Po Thang. I gave him and Jan my bed and crashed on the couch so I'd be sure to hear *Lucifer* when it returned, but when I awoke at dawn the slip was still empty, and Safety's truck remained in the marina parking lot.

Topaz's plane was due in early, so I decided to go get her instead of making her take the shuttle, and I wanted to keep an eye out for *Lucifer* as I drove along the coast.

My pickup isn't meant for but two people, so Jan and Po Thang stayed on the boat. She planned to finish the search we were doing on Bert's information, using the PIN and passwords we'd lifted from the house before I was rudely attacked, and then the house went up in flames.

Topaz was surprised to find me waiting for her on the tarmac. The guys unloading cargo knew me from the marina, so we exchanged a friendly greeting, greasing the wheels on the already perfunctory luggage searches by the group of young marines bivouacked at the airport. There is no airport building and the teenaged soldiers were camped in a dilapidated building with few conveniences. A litter of pups seemed to be their only entertainment.

Until Topaz arrived. She was definitely the star attraction for the bored teens.

The diminutive deputy has an unruly head of hair closely resembling that of a shaggy German shepherd, and a show-stopper body that somehow manages to look athletic and softly sexy at the same time. I know she works out hard at least an hour a day, but all that exercise hasn't flattened any curves. Had she been in uniform and sporting that large gun on her hip, the marines would have gone bonkers.

"You tired from the trip?" I asked her after we'd loaded her suitcase into my pickup and buckled up.

"Nah. After the drive down yesterday I was pooped and went to bed at nine. Last of the big time party animals here."

"Good, let's take a little drive south. I'm not going to work today for a lot of reasons which I'll catch you up on, so I'll give you the Grey Line tour before we go back to the boat."

"There's more since we last talked?"

"Lots more." I filled her in while we made the thirty mile trip south to Mulege, one of the prettiest towns in the Baja. The village claims a population of about four thousand people and is nestled between two hills hugging a fresh water river that runs into the sea. The contrast between the parched desert we'd driven through and this lush oasis delivered the surprise I had in store for Topaz.

"Wow! Sure didn't expect this."

"Let's get breakfast in town. I know a great little fish taco stand by the river."

As we ate our tacos I pointed up at the bridge over the main highway, way above our heads. "During one of the hurricanes this charming little river was two feet over that bridge. You can still see the devastation on both sides."

She looked up at least fifty feet to the bottom of the bridge. "Hard to imagine."

"It is. Okay, onward to Saul's groceries. There is Velveeta to be had."

While at Saul's (pronounced Sa-ool) store he pointed out for Topaz a spot six feet up the wall. "The mud was to here."

On that cheerful note, we moved on to Conception Bay, where I introduced her to Geary, then gave her the tour, stopping in at Café Olé to see how things were there. Their ordeal at the hands of thugs, and the death of one of those thugs, was shrugged off as part of doing business in Mexico. After nine years in a property dispute, little surprised them anymore.

We backtracked to Posada where I showed Topaz the hot springs. One would never know it was the scene of a grisly death.

All along our drive I asked Topaz to scan the sea, looking for boats. When she spotted one, she handed me the binoculars I'd brought from the boat. Only pangas and one fishing boat rippled the calm water. Not a roostertail in sight.

We were abreast of San Bruno, the village across from Sweet Pea cove, when Topaz spotted a boat making its way north in the channel between San Marcos Island and shore. I took a quick turn into San Bruno and down to the beach.

As we neared shore, I saw a telltale plume of black smoke spewing from the ship's stack. "Just a Mexican navy patrol boat."

Topaz handed me the binoculars. "Take a look at his tow."

I adjusted the eyecups and center access. "Good eye, Topaz. That's *Lucifer*, all right."

Jan made lobster Louis for lunch and we were eating when a smaller navy skiff maneuvered *Lucifer* into her slip. The Gang of Four was not aboard.

I walked over and asked the young marine where the men were, but received only a shrug in response. He didn't stop me, though, when I continued down the finger to take a look inside. I was standing there with my mouth agape when Topaz and Jan joined me.

"Holy crap!" Jan said.

"Ditto," Topaz added. "I don't know much about boats, but I know a fire scene when I see one."

The interior was fire gutted. The black streaks on the fiberglass hull and house, which I'd attributed to soot from the navy ship, were actually evidence of an interior fire.

"Looks like either an explosion or a really intense fire. Or both," Topaz told us. She sniffed the air. "Good thing she has diesels. Otherwise there wouldn't be much left."

"These whalers are built not to sink," I told her. "Lots of flotation chambers. The big question is, where are the guys? Safety's truck is still in the parking lot. Call me silly, but I smell more than smoke here."

I called the jobsite and reached a very distraught Laura. She hadn't heard from any of the men, but the Port Captain had called with disturbing news of the boat fire. That, coupled with the home fires did not bode well for the fate of Ozzie, Bert, Safety and John.

"It is *terrible, no*?" Laura sounded on the verge of tears. "We are receiving calls from Mexico City and Canada, and I do not know what to say. Can you please come?"

"It is terrible, *sí*. Look, close down the office and send everyone home. Leave a recording for anyone who calls to phone me here on the boat. I will be in tomorrow morning, for sure. Okay?"

I hung up and told Topaz and Jan about Laura's distress and that I'd sent her home for the rest of the day rather than trying to field calls.

"Poor woman," Jan said. "She's right, though, something terrible is going down here."

"And you know the worse part? That cat from hell survived."

"What cat?" Topaz put her hands on her hips and glared at me.

"I guess Hetta left out the breaking and entering part?" Jan asked.

"Jeez, Jan, she's a cop. You don't tell cops incriminating stuff like that."

"I am not anything here in Mexico, you dork. I'm here to help you, although that's beginning to sound like an impossible task, since it looks like I'll have to protect you from yourselves. Now you two sit down," she stabbed her finger at the floor, "and—

We all cracked up as Po Thang promptly sat and raised his paw for a high five.

"Is there anything else you've conveniently overlooked? Craig was right, you two are *way* in over your heads. I've been here, what, five hours? And you've already come up with a burned out boat, three burned houses and four missing men? What the hell kind of vacation is this? And what's a cat got to do with anything."

Chapter 37

The confession of evil works is the first
beginning of good works.— Saint Augustine

We began at the beginning, but were
constantly interrupted by my cell phone blasting "La
Cucaracha." I fielded all sorts of calls from Mexico
City and Canada and was glad when three o'clock—
official quitting time at the mine—rolled around and
I turned the cell off. Anyone I cared about had my
Skype number.

We sat out on the sundeck while Topaz tried
to get up to speed on what we'd learned. Or not
learned.

"So let me get this straight. Hetta was hired
to investigate cost overruns at the project, and she
hired you, Jan, to help."

We both nodded.

"And a guy breaks into your boat and is
stealing food, so Jan hogties him. He turns out to be
a reportedly dead guy, who also worked at the mine
and claims he'd discovered information about fellow

employees that got him killed...or rather, almost killed?"

"Uh-huh," I said, "he ate my Velveeta. We should have killed him ourselves."

"Doesn't something about this part of the story not add up to you two?"

"Well, duh. He doesn't even *like* Velveeta," Jan huffed.

"I'm serious here."

Although Jan's answer brought a giggle I had to tamp down, I went to her defense. "Yes, of course, now that we know more about our Rosario, we've already surmised his arrival was no happenstance. He targeted us. Or rather me. I don't think he was counting on being trussed up by a tall blonde."

"Which means that, before he allegedly disappeared, he knew who you were and why you were hired."

"Everyone did," Jan said. "If they had a newspaper in this berg Hetta probably would have made the front page. There are no secrets in Mexico."

"So this Rosario, who also turns out to be some kind of computer hacker whiz, sought you out, gave you the sad tale of his life, wormed his way under your protection, and then threw hints that certain people might be dirty? If you ask me he was *sent* to the Lucifer mine. Who would, or could, do that? And why?"

"The why is easy. Money." We told her about the upcoming payoff to some outfit in Monterrey for almost seven million dollars, and our suspicion that the merchandise—five large dirt haulers—was never delivered.

"Do you have a copy of the purchase order?"

Jan stood. "In the computer." She brought it up and printed out a copy.

Topaz unpacked her laptop, we connected her to the marina WiFi and she accessed her address book. "Can I use your cell phone? Mine won't work down here."

After punching a few numbers, she said, "Hey, MaGee, sorry to bother you at home. I need a favor. I'm visiting with Hetta Coffey down here in Mexico and—"

I could hear his outburst from three feet away. Not the words exactly, but the tone was unmistakable. Topaz held the phone away from her ear until Investigator MaGee quit his barking.

"Yeah, yeah. I know, MaGee, but she doesn't even *have* a gun on her boat." She hugged the phone against her chest to muffle the sound and looked at me. "You don't do you?"

I shook my head.

"Look, we'll talk about it when I get back. Right now I need your buddy, Jorge's, home phone number in Monterrey. I'll explain later."

While Topaz waited on the phone, I made a pitcher of iced tea and Jan ran out with Po Thang for a quick walk. By the time she returned, Topaz was already greeting someone in fluid Spanish, and then read off the name and address of the company in Monterrey. Another delay as she was evidently put on hold, then she grabbed a pen and made a few notes as the person on the other end talked.

"Okay, tell," I said as I handed her a tea when she hung up. "Who was that?"

"Guy we've worked with on occasion when they, or we, were looking for someone. I can't tell you more than that. Anyhow, unless your mine has need of a seven million dollar mani and pedi, that address sucks."

"Let me guess," I said. "A nail salon."

"See, you aren't half the imbecile Investigator MaGee said you are."

Jan piped up. "Yeah, Hetta's only half an imbecile. Isn't MaGee that blonde cop we think looks like a wheaten terrier?"

Topaz laughed. "And I have hair like a German shepherd. Gosh, maybe we should hook up and have very hairy pups."

The fake address wasn't much of a surprise, as we were already fairly certain the purchase order was suspect. "And the phony address isn't all that important because the invoice is paid by wire transfer, which Bert had already approved last...oh, hell."

I called Laura at home, who confirmed she'd couriered the paperwork to Mexico City on Friday afternoon, so by now the whole package was probably in the hands of Julio Vargas, the final person whose signature was required in order to transfer the payment.

I sighed. "So our Gang of Four each did what they were supposed to. Ozzie cut the purchase order, which was signed by Bert and Vargas and never mailed anywhere. Then John made out a fake

Material Receiving Report for four brand new Caterpillar 777Gs which never arrived, Safety wrote a bogus inspection report, then Bert approved the invoice. All the above mentioned paperwork was then sent to Julio Vargas for final payment."

"Double crap," I said. "Then the four conspirators take off fishing and vanish on the same night their houses and boat are torched."

Topaz nodded. "*Entre putas and cabrones, no hay fijones.*"

"What's that mean?"

"It's the Mexican version, a very rude one, of the proverb, 'There is no honor among thieves.' Looks like your Gang of Four may have been out-thieved."

I nodded. "Maybe in a classic case of what I call Get the Gringo."

I decided to go in early Tuesday morning and retrieve my bugs. With Bert, Safety, John and Ozzie still missing, they would have no new info on them, and there was no sense leaving them around to get found.

Jan and Topaz planned to spend the day delving deeper into the comptroller's background. We already knew Julio Vargas was a Facebook chum of Baja Gamer, a.k.a. Rosario. What was Rosario's role in all of this? I hated to think he had a hand in the disappearance of the Gang of Four, even if they had tried to off him. Somehow I wanted Rosario to be more honorable than I would be in the same situation.

While I was listening to what little was left on the bugs, I remembered something and called the boat. "Jan, do you recall when I sent Rosario a conversation between Ozzie and someone in Spanish? He never got back to us."

"I'll find it and have Topaz give a listen. Anything new out there?"

"Nah, too early. No one here yet."

"Plenty of folks here. Lucifer is crawling with official looking guys. Turns out the EPIRB went off on *Lucifer* and the U.S. Coastguard became involved."

An EPIRB is an emergency position-indicating radio beacon, a device carried by most boats, including mine, and is activated in several ways. If it hits the water, it goes off automatically, or it can be set off manually. My guess is someone activated it when the fire broke out aboard *Lucifer*.

"Get Topaz to talk with them. Maybe with her Spanish she can get more info. Short of sending you off to Mexico City so you can hogtie or sleep with Vargas, I don't know what to do next. If the money's already been transferred to God only knows where, it's certainly above my paygrade. I'll update the Trob later today, but for now I'll keep us on the payroll."

"You mean I'm gonna get laid off? Already? Do I get a severence package?"

"Jan, I'm hanging up now, before I fire you myself."

Laura arrived at the office early and by six thirty others, even those who normally rushed their desks at seven, began drifting in. The mood was gloomy and they were probably all wondering what came next, and how it would affect their jobs. When five people disappear off one jobsite in a short period of time, it's bound to cause feelings of uncertainty. Laura's puffy eyes were proof of that.

"Oh, Miss Coffey, do you think they are drowned?"

"I don't know. We are just finding out some details, like their emergency beacon went off. But guess what? The whole United States Coast Guard is looking for them."

This gross exaggeration fetched a small smile as she crossed herself and whispered, "*¡Gracias a Dios!*"

As things stood, I had little to smile about myself. In my mind one of two things had happened. Either my Gang of Four was feeding the fishes, or they were headed for banks on obscure islands to retrieve their booty.

I wasn't sure which one I hoped for at this point, but when the Mexico City office opened for the day, I planned to make the call that would answer at least the seven million dollar question: where is the money right now?

Chapter 38

HIGH AND DRY (Nautical term): Beached
or caught on rocks and standing out of the water as
the tide recedes (stranded or without resources or
support)

The minutes ticked by excruciatingly slow
until time for the Mexico City office to open. Unlike
the mine, they were on Mexican office hours, with
the switchboard coming to life at nine. I had decided
to take the bull by the horns, go straight to the
source, and gently stir the pot.

I could have gotten a home number for
Vargas through the Trob, but I wanted to feel the
comptroller out before sounding an alarm. The last
thing I wanted to do, if he was a part of the
embezzlement scheme, was to panic him so he could
rabbit with the dough.

At nine, Mexico City time, I called out,
"Laura, can you please put a call through for me to
Julio Vargas?"

"Of course. But he has probably left the hotel by now."

"What hotel?"

"Las Casitas, in Santa Rosalia. I will try to call."

"No!"

She looked startled by my outburst. "Uh, I mean, I'll talk to him later. Thanks." Vargas is here? That didn't sound good for anyone.

"Miss Coffey, Mr. Vargas should be arriving here at the office soon. I have set up a conference call for eleven with Canada and Mexico City. I am sure they will be discussing the...uh, accident."

"No doubt. Okay, I need to run down to the Equipment Yard, so call me on the radio if you hear anything new, all right? Or Vargas shows up."

"Of course."

Once in the pickup I made a beeline for John's office and that bug I planted. I had a feeling this place, the entire jobsite in fact, would soon be swarming with cops of all kinds and I didn't want bugs with my fingerprints on them found. Some sleuth I am, I didn't even wear gloves.

I had just arrived and was making my way to his door, hoping it would not be locked, when my cell phone rang and caller ID told me it was Jan.

"Look, I don't have time to worry about your future employment right now, okay?"

"Uh, sure Hetta. No problem. Uh, can you like ix-nay down to the boat?"

Ix-nay? Uh-oh. "Sure. What's for lunch?"

"How about fried ad-bay fish?"

Okay, so there's a bad fish, or bad guy, involved somehow.

"Great. What kind?"

"Those amera-cay we bought at Sweet Pea on Saturday."

"My favorite. See you—" The phone went dead.

I didn't waste time going back to my office. I booted up John's desktop, went online and activated my boat cameras.

Jan, Topaz, Po Thang and Rosario were crowded together on the settee, and no one looked happy. I turned on the sound and heard a male voice, but he was out of camera view. I could manipulate the camera, but was afraid it would make a noise or he'd see the movement.

"Nice work, Blondie. Let's see, it should take her about forty-five minutes to an hour to get here...what was that?"

At the same time I heard that question, the building rocked so wildly my office chair rolled across the room. I pushed it back to the computer, and just before the screen went blank, I caught a glimpse of a man rushing out onto the boat's deck. I recognized him from the photo ID Jan pulled up on the computer: Julio Vargas.

I fled the still swaying trailer and was met with a chaotic scene of workers running helter-skelter with no idea where or why. I joined them, but made a beeline for my pickup, feeling for some reason it might be safer. Safer than what I had no idea. I'd almost reached my truck when a second shock wave hit, and this one knocked me to my knees. I crawled the rest of the way and climbed in.

The truck's radio was useless, as everyone was trying to talk at the same time, and our two-ways were not full-duplex, as are telephones. On a simplex radio, only one person can talk at a time, thus the need for saying *over*, especially in an emergency situation. No one was getting through to anyone, so I checked my cell, saw I still had a signal, and called Laura. "Are you all right?" I asked her when she finally answered.

"Yes, I was under my desk. You said that is what to do."

"Well, never listen to me. Get out of the building, right now. Go sit in the biggest pickup you can find outside."

"Yes, Miss Coffey. Are you coming?" She sounded terrified, and for some reason she had the ridiculous idea I could help.

"Yes, but the radios are *no bueno* so I cannot call you. Do you have a cell phone?"

"No."

I'd read somewhere that over eighty percent of the people in Mexico have a cell phone. How did I end up with a secretary who didn't?

"Okay, get to a pickup and tell everyone else to do the same. I'll be there as soon as I can."

The roads, nothing to write home about in the first place, were littered with large boulders, some of them still on the move. Looking up at a nearby bluff, I rethought the safety of my pickup and took off for the equipment yard, and the biggest machine in it, the 777G.

I hunkered down in the driver's seat, feeling much more secure from whatever the earthquake brought next. Cocooned within almost two hundred tons of steel, I was thinking of yelling something like, "Bring it on!" when somehow, through all the chatter I heard Laura, who was frantically calling my name. I grabbed the mic and held down the transmit button, effectively cutting all communication. After a very long three minutes I let the button up and was gratified with nothing but static.

"Laura, are you hurt? O-ver."

A couple of people tried to transmit, but once again, I held down the button, this time for about two minutes. When I let up, I heard Laura transmitting, repeatedly, "Not hurt, not hurt. Building gone, over."

All hell broke loose again, so I threw the useless mic down. I was trying to figure out what to do next when my phone rang. Laura had commandeered a cell phone. A woman to my own heart. "Miss Coffey, did you hear me? The building is gone."

"It collapsed?"

"No, there is a large...*hoyo*."

Hoyo? You mean a pit? The office is in a hole?"

"Y-es. Miss Coffey, you have saved my life."

"Laura?"

"Yes?"

"Don't you think since I saved your life you can call me Hetta?"

"Yes, Mi—Hetta."

Someone on the two-way fired off a string of machine gun Spanish. The only thing I caught was *Cuesta del Infierno*.

"What was that, Laura? What did they say on the radio?"

"They say there is a *derrumbe*. On the *Cuesta*. And there is smoke from *La Vírgen!*"

Derrumbe. I had seen signs along the roads and looked it up in my Spanish/English dictionary: landslide! And that volcano I didn't trust? It was spewing smoke?

A few minutes, and two aftershocks, later what I had feared most was confirmed by someone on the radio; Hell Hill was blocked by a large landslide. Mex 1, the only highway to Santa Rosalia, and my boat, was impassable.

"Laura, stay right there. I'm coming."

I called the boat and by some miracle Jan answered.

"Is everyone all right? We had a huge earthquake up here."

"Here, too. Yes, for now we are."

"Sorry I won't be there for the amera-cay lunch, but Hell Hill is blocked by a landslide."

"Oh, no."

"So, looks like it will be a long, long time before I get there, Ot-nay."

"Sure. We'll wait."

The big Cat started right up after I went through the steps taught me by John Warren. I was worried there was some kind of locking system, but if there was, no one had bothered to activate it. Man, if I were running this jobsite I'd instigate some seriously stringent safety measures to keep the likes of me out.

I patted the steering wheel and sang, "Here I come to save the dayyyy. Mighty Mouse is on her wayyyy!" Unfortunately I'd left my cape back on the boat.

No one seemed interested in a big Cat on the move. I had on a hard hat and dark glasses, so I guess they figured I knew what I was doing. Silly twits.

I knew, from what John told me, that these machines could do up to sixty miles an hour, but the first twenty felt like a hundred, so I slowed to five. It took me almost an hour to reach Laura because of boulders and debris in the road.

Only one corner of the office building roof was visible, the rest swallowed up by what could have been a collapsed mine shaft from yesteryear. As a civil engineer I was dumbfounded that they hadn't at least performed an ultrasound test on the site before they built in an area as full of holes as Swiss cheese.

The look on Laura's face when I stepped out on the walkway of the big Cat and motioned for her to come up was priceless. She hesitated, probably weighing the odds between staying and maybe dying, or joining me and dying for sure.

Another ground wave made up her mind for her and she dashed for the Cat.

Others tried to follow, but I took off before they could catch us. I felt badly about leaving them, but the only place for more passengers was in the body, or dump bed, and even though there was a rubber liner, with what I figured lay ahead there was too much risk of serious bodily injury.

I was right.

Chapter 39

CUT AND RUN (Nautical term): Sever the anchor line in an emergency (leave abruptly and abandoning others).

Just as Safety told me, the back road out of the mine site was marked by whitewashed rocks. And as he'd also said, the road was little more than a goat path. I knew the brine truck was almost as wide as the big Cat, though, so I was certain we could get through, if, and that was a big if, the road hadn't suffered too much damage from the earthquake.

The white rocks Safety and the old brine man had placed were a godsend, for like Google Earth showed, the desert was a maze of roads and paths. If it weren't for the markers, we could be out there for days trying to find the way. And even knowing which way to go didn't make the trip easy. We rarely hit more than ten miles per hour, and even that was pushing our luck.

Several times we ended up in a precarious tilt that, had we not been strapped in, would have sent us slamming into the cab's steel interior. As it was, we were still going to show some nasty bruises from our seat belts.

After we bounced over a rise and did a three-tired side-slip—all three tires being on the same side of the rig—into a narrow ravine, we stalled in a cloud of dust and laughed to tears. Nothing like surviving a near death experience during something akin to a disaster film to send you into hysterics. It took some agonizingly slow maneuvering, but we were eventually underway once again, but now at a prudent five miles per hour.

Time ticked away, and constantly in the back of my mind was what was happening on the boat. We lost cell service about what I hoped was halfway into our trip to meet up with Mex 1, sending my tension level even further into the ozone layer.

Another worry was the fuel gauge. I had no idea what the big Cat burned, and certainly no clue how far a quarter tank would get us, even at such low speeds. After an intense two hours of jockeying us around slides, crashing into ditches and plowing through desert growth, I realized we had somehow gone wrong when I made a turn and was forced to halt. A high chainlink fence with a PELIGRO! NO TRASPASAR! PROPRIEDAD PRIVADA! blocked our way.

"Gosh, Laura, you think they want us to stay out?"

She looked dejected. I hadn't told her about the hostage situation on my boat, but she clearly wanted to get home and check on her family. No one at her house had answered her cell phone calls before we ran out of service.

"We must find another way, Mis...Hetta."

"Whose property do you think this is?"

"It must be the Boleo Mine. No one else has money for such a grand fence."

"Oh, goody! A shortcut!"

"What is a short...Hetta!"

That fence, well built or not, was no match for my two hundred ton dumpster of doom.

After we crashed through the fence, it was only another mile before we entered a working section of El Boleo, and a blessedly smooth road. They had evidently suspended all operations due to the earthquake, for vehicles of all kinds were stopped on the road, making me go around them. Several workers, at their peril, tried waving us to a halt.

Once I spotted the Sea of Cortez, shining like a turquoise beacon in the distance, I knew exactly where I was from a previous tour of the mine. That wrong turn had saved us hours. Elated, I sped up to forty miles an hour, racing past large yellow signs warning of dire consequences if one exceeded twenty *kilometers* an hour and I was doing about sixty. Let them dock my pay. Better yet, maybe they'd take my birthday away? But first they had to catch us.

Making a beeline for the entrance to the mine, I was spotted by the gate guards, who rushed out and began waving wildly for me to slow down and stop. Lucky for us they were unarmed, and the gate was obviously made of inferior materials.

Mex 1 was jammed with parked cars, most empty as their drivers lounged around on the fenders, waiting to hear when the road north was cleared. One unfortunate vehicle had been abandoned in my lane, so I plowed into it and shoved it to the side of the road, much to the amusement of the crowd and even my passenger, who was by now egging me on.

I knew we couldn't get all the way into town with the Cat, but was determined to get as far as possible before blocked by buildings. I didn't think even the big rig could take out a house on the first run.

The decision to abandon ship was made when I spotted a military truck loaded with marines weaving in and out of traffic, headed north. Before they could react to the threat of a large yellow monster speeding toward them, I skidded to a stop, and ended up sideways across both lanes. We scrambled down the side facing away from the marines and fled, leaving the engine running. Hitting the streets on foot, we ran to where Laura said a cousin of hers lived, only two blocks away.

We couldn't resist climbing to the second floor of Laura's cousin's house and looking back down at Mex 1, where Big Yeller was surrounded by marines. It looked as though they thought someone was still inside, and no witnesses seemed at all inclined to report that one of their own and a redhaired Gringa had hared off up the hill. You gotta love Mexicans for such wonderful passive aggression: their way of dealing with any kind of authority.

I called the boat and once again Jan answered. I guess the little turd Julio Vargas didn't want to alert me that anything was amiss, and it was working in my favor. "Everything still okay in Santa Rosalia?"

"Yes. Everything is exactly the same here." There was a shuffling sound, and I pictured Jan with the phone in hand, Julio listening in and covering the mouthpiece, then Jan asked, "Where are you?"

"Still stuck at the ix-nay mine. I guess the road will be blocked for hours."

"Okay. I'll save some amera-cay for you."

"Great. Listen, my cell batteries are getting low, so can't recharge because they've cut the generator power on the job. I'll call when I can."

I hung up and asked Laura if her cousin had Internet service. Nope. They had a quick discussion and Laura told me there was an Internet café on the main street, but she didn't think I should be seen hiking around the streets of Santa Rosalia, in case someone finally ratted us out for leaving a large yellow behemoth blocking Mex 1.

Her cousin gave me a baggy dress befitting almost every old Mexican woman's Sunday go-to-church attire and a large hat festooned with flowers. I pulled the dress on over my clothes and jammed on the hat, and with my scuffed tennis shoes peaking out below the dress's uneven hem, I accomplished a fashion statement like that of the famed Minnie Pearl. The cousin, dressed in similar garb—even including sneakers—insisted on going with me so I wouldn't stand out quite so much as I would alone. I made a note to reward her hugely if I lived through this day.

Laura wanted to go to her own house, so we said our goodbyes. I considered telling her what was happening on my boat so there would be a witness later down the road, but figured she had enough to worry about at the moment.

As we walked through town, it was obvious there had been little damage. Shop clerks were placing some merchandise back on shelves, but other than that the town had emerged unscathed. The same cannot be said for people's nerves.

The Internet café was jammed.

Unlike the States or large cities in Mexico there were no television helicopter crews feeding live shots to a waiting public. It would probably be hours before any coverage of the earthquake and landslide showed up, so everyone was using the Internet to tweet and email family members. Needless to say, with the slide blocking Mex 1 and a volcano thought dormant spewing smoke, people were frantic for word of the men and women stuck at the Lucifer Mine and other outlying areas.

I felt a twinge of guilt at my selfish escape, but if I'd let those people ride in my dumpster bed they would probably be badly injured, or worse, by now. Besides, I had my own big fish to fry, namely why Jan wanted me to turn on the boat cameras again. Something new was afoot and I needed to see what it was.

Chapter 40

An insincere and evil friend is more to be
feared than a wild beast; a wild beast may wound
your body, but an evil friend will wound your
mind.—Buddha

There were only three public computers at
the Internet café and they were occupied. Rather
than yank the youngsters playing games on them out
of their chairs by their scrawny little necks, I waved
a five-hundred peso note under their noses. The first
to grab it, a twelve-year-old by the looks of him,
quickly abandoned his computer, politely ushered
me into the seat and stayed around to see if he could
help show the old Gringa granny how to use it.

He was clearly dumbfounded when my
adrenaline infused fingers flew over the keys and
quickly brought up my security site. He made a
comment I didn't understand and others gathered
around behind me, so there was no question of
privacy, but I knew no one would have any idea
what they saw on my screen was live and local.

Jan and Topaz were being tied up, Po Thang was no where to be seen, and that little rat Rosario was doing the tying. I vowed to unfriend him.

I activated the sound, hoping the soft click involved would alert Jan's sharp hearing that I was once again watching and listening. It evidently worked, for she looked straight past Rosario at the camera. "Rosario, listen to me. You can't trust that creep, you know."

"Julio has promised no one will be harmed. He only wants to talk with Hetta in person. To reason with her."

"Like he *reasoned* with Bert, Ozzie, John Warren and Safety?"

A gruff voice came from off camera, "Shut up, Blondie."

Rosario turned and looked toward the voice. "What is she talking about?"

"We think he killed them all," Jan blurted, but it was her last blurt. Julio Vargas rushed forward and stuffed a napkin in her mouth. One of my embroidered linens, I might add. At least he has good taste.

The people behind me in the Internet café moved in for a better look. I think they thought I'd tuned in to an American *telenovella*.

"Jan, Julio won't hurt you. He promised me."

Jan, although tied and gagged, managed a rude grunt and shot Rosario the finger.

Being so small in stature, Topaz looked as though she posed no threat to anyone, but I knew better. I didn't remember telling Rosario she was a cop, so maybe she'd have the advantage of surprise.

Especially since it was obvious Rosario couldn't successfully secure a shoelace; he'd tied Jan's wrists in front of her and finished off the job with a bow, for crying out loud.

Rosario moved toward Topaz with a ball of what looked like string. I began to wonder if Rosario wasn't playing Julio himself. After all, he knew there were probably three or four hundred feet of line and a bag of at least two-hundred tie wraps on the spare bunk in the guest cabin. And he knew about the cameras, but evidently hadn't mentioned them to Vargas, as they were still running. I began to have hope.

I heard a whine off-camera. Rosario turned and said, "You know, Julio, we must take this dog out for his walk."

"Let the mongrel go."

Po Thang growled. I mean, *mongrel*?

"We cannot do that. If he is loose the marina personnel will bring him back."

"Then take the *pinche* dog out, but be quick about it. I'll keep an eye on these two. Damned earthquake. We should be half-way to Belize by now. On second thought, while you're out with the dog see what you can learn about the road. I...uh, we, can't stay around here forever."

"Why do we not just leave? What are we waiting for?"

"I need to know how much Coffey knows, and who she told."

"She won't tell you anything. Hetta is...well, scary. And very stubborn."

I'm scary? Good.

"Oh, yes she will. If she values her friends here."

"You said—"

"You know, Rosario, you were always a wimp, even in high school. I should have known better than to hire you for a job that takes a *real* man. Look, I know what I said, but if Coffey won't talk I'll make her, you understand? You had no trouble taking the money, did you, *hermano*? Man up. We will do whatever it takes to get out of here and we don't want a bunch of loose ends."

Chapter 41

Texas women have an amazing sense of
purpose when they lose it. They're the best girls in
the world—they're loyal and fun, but when they get
mad, they'll try to kill you.—John Cusack

Don't Mess With Texas—Hetta Coffey

Now me and my friends are just loose ends
to be tidied up? I knew what that meant.

Anger fueled my feet. I didn't realize I could
run so fast.

The minute I heard Julio Vargas tell Rosario
to go ahead and take Po Thang for a walk, I knew
what to do. I covered the three blocks to the marina
in what seemed both seconds and hours. I had to
catch Rosario and Po Thang before they went back
into the boat. Po Thang is a creature of habit and I
knew he'd stretch that walk as far as possible, and as
long, sniffing everything and doing at least one or
two false squats. This ritual I normally found
annoying was suddenly his best trait.

Good dog.

I had to take my chances with Rosario. I didn't dare contact the cops, as they were most likely looking for some Gringa who abandoned a huge yellow monster on Mex 1 by now. I had shot a quick email to Nacho, but had no idea where *he* was, and anyone else I knew who would help me was definitely too far away.

I had to act now, and alone if I couldn't count on Rosario. And if Rosario interfered in any way, he'd end up badly. I wasn't sure how I would accomplish such a feat, but I can be one very determined, scary, stubborn woman when I have to be.

Man, oh, man, where are my guns when I need them?

When I reached the marina grounds, I entered through a back gate they left open most of the day for delivery and garbage trucks. From there I took the stairs to the second level, where the swimming pool and marina offices were. Luckily, the offices were on the opposite side of the building, and accessed via a different set of steps. Maintenance staff had left for the day and I thanked my lucky stars that I was pretty much the only occupied boat at the marina, meaning no nosy cruisers around.

Hugging the wall, I made my way to where I had an unhampered line of sight of the docks and the grounds. I didn't see Po Thang and Rosario at first, but had a clear view of the Port Captain's office next door. It occurred to me that they could see me, as well, but I knew they wouldn't think twice about a cruiser wandering around the pool area.

I spotted Rosario and Po Thang coming into the parking lot and hoped the dog didn't give me up. Scooting back down the stairs, I hugged the building near the ramp down to the docks. I knew for a fact that there was no way Po Thang was going down that ramp without one last shot at an oleander bush next to the building. I moved behind the bush, taking that dress off as I did so.

Now hidden from prying eyes at the Port Captain's office as well as anyone on the docks, I waited and sure enough, I heard Rosario say, "Oh, okay. One more stop, but that's it, you hear?"

About that time Po Thang either sensed, saw or smelled me. That smelled part was a serious possibility, as it had been a pretty stinky day for me. Anyway, he whined, barked and surged forward, dragging Rosario into range before he could put the brake on the twenty-five foot retractable leash. When he did, he sealed his fate.

Throwing the dress over his head, I grabbed the leash and wound it around his neck and torso. Po Thang, still attached to the leash, was pulled into the mess and ended up bound to Rosario. Both dog and man were struggling, making matters worse. I managed to get Po Thang's collar released before he strangled, but Rosario wasn't so lucky. He stopped fighting, dropped to his knees and began gasping for air.

I kicked him onto his back and rolled him on the ground, unwinding the leash like a top, but not as fast. By the time I freed Rosario and pulled the tattered dress from his head, his lips were slightly blue. Po Thang bravely dashed in to administer his version of CPR, taking full advantage of an inert figure that couldn't reject his overactive tongue.

I was trying to recall my CPR training when Po Thang took matters into his own paws. He jumped into the middle of Rosario's chest, his front paws landing in the right spot to make Rosario cough and gasp.

There was a water hose nearby, so I turned it on and gave the still gasping Rosario a drink. Po Thang took this as a sign it was water toy time, lunged in and took the hose from me, happily spraying us all in the process.

Rosario, resuscitated and sprayed, focused on me with somewhat crossed eyes. "Hetta? How did you get here? I was told the road is still blocked."

"Later for that. Look, I know Julio Vargas hired you and that you're up to your scrawny neck in this embezzlement thing, but right now I have to trust you to help me get Jan and Topaz away from that boat."

"But—"

"No buts. If you help me I might, and that's a big might, let you live."

"He won't harm them."

"Really? And why not? Do you know Bert's and the others' houses burned to the ground Saturday night? And that their boat was found torched on Sunday? Your good friend Julio has most likely murdered four of your coconspirators. Why should he let you, me, Jan, Topaz, or anyone else involved, live? What's to keep him from taking the entire seven million and disappearing?"

"How did you know about the seven million?"

"Jan downloaded the contents of your laptop, that's how. You aren't the only one hacking into people's stuff."

"She did? You knew I was involved?"

"Yes, we finally figured it out. Tell me this, though, did you fake your own death and then throw suspicion on Bert, Ozzie, John and Safety?"

"Yes, Julio said that once we left the country, they would not be looking for me, and the other four would take the fall, but the mining company would rather take a loss than make such inept management known to the investors. Julio would stay for a time in Mexico City, indignant that these foreigners would steal from them, then he'd resign. No one would be hurt."

"Except it didn't quite work out that way, did it? "

Tears sprang into his eyes. "I was friends with those men. I never would have taken part had I know they would be harmed."

"We can talk morality later. Right now I need you to do something for me. We have to access the Internet, pronto."

Chapter 42

Beware of false knowledge; it is more
dangerous than ignorance.—George Bernard Shaw

When Rosario, Po Thang and I rushed into
the Internet café, the kid I'd given five hundred pesos
to less than an hour before jumped up from his
computer with his hand out. I greased his greedy
little palm once again, thinking we had a young
Rosario in the making here.

It cost me another two hundred so Po Thang
could stay inside, but at least this time Rosario sent
the onlookers packing, so we had some privacy.

I'd told Rosario what I needed done as we
left via the back gate and made our way the few
short blocks to the Internet café, so he went to work
as soon as we arrived.

I bribed yet another kid away from his
computer and accessed the security system on the
boat. It's a good thing I'd hit the ATM in Mulege on
Monday as the six thousand pesos I'd withdrawn was

dwindling as fast as the financial status of the Mexican tween population improved.

The cameras showed Vargas pacing, clearly upset that Rosario was taking so long to return. He took his cell from his pocket and said, in English, "Vargas here. We are delayed due to the earthquake. It could be a few more hours."

He listened, a deep V forming between his eyes. "I don't care about the friggin' runway lights. We take off when I say so, lights or no."

He clearly didn't like what the other party said next. "Those marines can be bought. Or if necessary, take them by surprise when I call. There are only five or six of them. I will anchor off the runway, and come in to the beach by panga. You can taxi down the runway to meet me. We'll be well out of the country by the time the marines are found."

I had reached over and punched Rosario on the arm so he could hear what his ex-BFF had to say. Just as he leaned in to listen, Julio said to what was surely his pilot, "Yes, there will only be me. The others have been permanently delayed."

"You heard it, Rosario," I said. "We are the 'others' the bastard is talking about. Vargas plans to take us out on *my* boat, and feed us to the fish."

Rosario turned his fury at such rotten betrayal onto his keyboard, determined to make his hacking job pay off. And pay *back*.

As I watched, things quieted down on the boat. Jan had been un-gagged, at least, and Topaz sat there looking totally innocent, while I knew she was focused on ripping out Vargas's throat the minute she had a chance. Both still had their hands tied.

There was a knock on the boat's door. Vargas growled, "Finally," slid it open and stepped back in surprise at what he saw. He recovered quickly though, whipped what looked like a .45 from his waistband and yanked Doctor Diane Powell roughly into the main saloon. He shoved her down next to Jan. Lucky for her, Jan was still tied up.

"Oh, no," I moaned.

Rosario leaned over. "It's Diane! What is she doing there?"

And why do only the bad guys in Mexico seem to have guns?

Vargas, his frustration boiling over, yelled, "Who in the hell are you?"

"She's a boyfriend stealer, that's who," Jan said. "If you'll untie me I'll scratch her eyes out."

Diane moved away as far as she could from Jan without falling off the couch.

Vargas grinned. "Normally I would enjoy a good cat fight, but right now I simply don't have the luxury. Okay, who are you and what are you doing here?"

Diane's emerald eyes were wide with surprise and fear, but she said, "I was in Loreto when I heard of the earthquake and came here to see if Hetta, Jan, Po Thang and Rosario were all right."

"How sweet of you," Jan meowed. "Rosario is out walking the dog and Hetta's still stuck at the mine because of a big landslide at *Cuesta*."

"I know about the slide, the marines at the roadblock south of Conception Bay told me. They weren't going to let me through, but having doctor in front of your name opens many doors in Mexico."

"You're a doctor?" Vargas asked.

"So what?" Jan spat. "Wait a minute, how did you know Rosario was here? He is, but he's supposed to be at Camp Chino. And speaking of, where is Chino?"

"As far as I know Doctor Yee is still at the camp. Rosario left two days ago and said he was coming here to meet a friend."

Jan tossed her head. "Well, *that* was clearly a lie; Julio Vargas is no one's *friend*."

Vargas's eyes narrowed dangerously. "How is it you know my name, Blondie?"

Oh, crap! Jan, shut up! I willed. I grabbed my cell phone and called the boat.

This time I could see what happened when the phone rang. Vargas looked at the caller ID and handed the phone to Jan. "It's your buddy Hetta again. Go ahead and answer, but be very careful what you say."

Jan looked squarely at the camera as she spoke. Vargas leaned over so he could hear, getting dangerously near Topaz in the process. "Hetta, everything still okay at the mine?" Jan asked.

"Yes, but still no word on the road opening, although the mine has sent heavy equipment to help clear it. You know those babies can go offroad. Sure wish I could be there for our five o'clock cocktail hour. You know I *never* miss it."

"Five o'clock is your favorite time. And it's almost that now."

Vargas made a cut sign with his hand and Jan ended the call with a goodbye.

I leaned over to Rosario. "Set it up for four thirty."

He hit some keys. "It is done."

There was sudden movement on my screen and the sounds of a scuffle. As Jan was handing the cell phone back to Vargas, Topaz lashed out like a cobra, using both fists on Vargas's nose. He reeled back and almost lost the hold on his gun. Blood spouted from his crushed nose, all over my couch and rug. I'd make him pay for that mess.

Jan, at first frozen with surprise, hip-bumped Diane onto the floor and began scooting off the settee, while Topaz did the same on the other side. Unfortunately Vargas recovered too soon and trained the gun on Jan. "Hold it right there. You, doc, get me a towel. What do I do for this nose?"

"Take at least four aspirin, blow your nose repeatedly, and lie down with your head back. Whatever you do, do not pinch your nostrils. And if you can, apply hot compresses, as hot as you can stand them."

Jan gave Diane a look meant to kill. "Traitor."

"I'm a doctor, remember?"

Vargas nodded gingerly, which let lose another gush of blood. He glared at Topaz. "I have clearly underestimated you women, so I'm going to lock you up so I can tend to my nose. When Rosario gets back, I will deal with you personally, and you will not like it."

Waving the gun, he herded everyone into my master cabin and jammed a chair against the lock. More blood leaked onto my stuff and I looked forward to breaking that nose even better for him.

I watched in dismay as Julio disappeared into the guest cabin where Topaz told him she had a bottle of aspirin and reappeared with a stack of my brand new guest towels.

"You know, Rosario, your friend Julio isn't as smart as he thinks he is. Don't you suppose he'd wonder why a woman he was holding hostage would be so free with helpful medical advice?"

Rosario shrugged. "Diane is a very special woman."

"So you say, and I tend to believe you. At least they're all away from him for now. And knowing at least two of them quite well, they are already untied and making plans. Let's take a look." I activated my bedroom camera and sure enough, Diane was untying Topaz. Jan, her hands still bound, was scrounging for weapons.

"Thanks, Diane," Topaz said, exercising her freed wrists.

Jan two-handed a can of hair spray she'd found in the head to Topaz and held out her arms. "How about undoing me, Diane?"

"I don't know. Are you going to scratch my eyes out?"

"Are you kidding? With that medical advice you gave Vargas, he'll be lucky not to bleed out or choke to death. And Topaz, way to go with that sucker punch. You two are my new best heroes.

Well except for Hetta, of course. Hetta, have you been watching all this?"

Both Diane and Topaz looked puzzled, and I nodded, even though I knew they couldn't see me. I maneuvered the camera slightly, knowing Jan would catch the movement.

"Hetta can see and hear us?" Diane asked.

"Yep, she's somewhere nearby and planning something. What, I have no idea, but knowing her it's gonna be good, huh, Hetta?"

I waggled the camera.

"Five o'clock, right?"

Waggle.

"We'll be ready."

Waggle.

Chapter 43

BAIL OUT (Nautical term): Remove water
from (assist or rescue)...but how?

We had almost an hour until all hell broke
loose, but we had work to do.

On the way back I locked Po Thang in a
marina shower room, much to his dismay. I couldn't
risk him on the loose for the time being. Since I was
the only one in the marina who used that bathroom,
and there was never any hot water anyway, I figured
the chances of someone letting him out were nil to
none.

Now that I had no way to see what was going
on inside the boat, I opted to return to the swimming
pool area and at least keep an eye out on the docks. I
was rewarded with the satisfying view of Vargas flat
out on the sundeck, his head back, trying to staunch
an ever-increasing flow of blood.

I needed a way to get to the boat unseen by
Vargas, but couldn't figure it out without swimming
and there was no way in hell I was going into *that*

harbor. Raw sewage had flowed in for centuries, along with God only knows what in the way of mining chemicals.

While Rosario and I were at the Internet café, the ferry had arrived and was unloading. Armed marines milled about as people and cars disembarked. I looked longingly at the soldier's weapons. Vargas's gun was the only thing that worried me. If he were not armed, I'd gather a posse and storm the boat. Oh, for just a little grenade or two.

Rosario showed up with the binoculars I'd sent him to buy, and a large sack. "I bought them all, Hetta. The vendor was very happy."

"I'm glad someone is." I glanced at my watch. "You're certain you set it up for 4:30?"

He looked indignant. "It was slightly harder to get into the Mexican government system, but certainly not impossible. What is the saying, the impossible only takes a little longer?"

"Do you have your cell phone? Mine is showing low batteries and my charger is back at the office. Or what's left of it."

"It looks fine to me."

"Not my phone, the office." I told him about the building disappearing into an old mine shaft, and my wild drive down the back roads to Mex 1.

"Oh, that was you? I heard people talking about this large yellow machine on the highway while I was buying the binoculars."

"I doubt I'll be up for woman of the year."

"Actually, they are all laughing. Anything that annoys the *federales* is good for us."

"Right now we could use a few *federales*."

He looked suddenly sad and gazed out to sea. "Do you really think my friends died out there?"

"I don't know. Probably."

"I will never forgive myself. I set them up."

"You were set up, as well, don't forget. What will you do when this whole thing is over?

"I have been sending money to San Francisco and plan to go there."

"To your dad? Huh, Baja Gamer?"

Rosario's jaw dropped, then he gave me a wide smile. "Oh, you women are so good. Julio is in big trouble."

"Yes, he is. Tell me, what was the plan? For the money?"

"We were, all six, to fly to Belize. Julio had set up accounts for all of us, but he had to sign them over. Once that was done, he would return, as we said, then resign in a reasonable amount of time."

"But he double-crossed you. How is it you trusted him?"

"He was the only one in my senior year at the American School who was my friend. He is not from a rich family, but a diplomatic one. We kept in touch through gaming, and when he was hired as comptroller, he called."

"So he actually recruited Bert into his scheme early on, and Bert hired the right men, those in need of money, as his accomplices. Then Vargas sent you here to set them up as suspects so you two could take the money and run. To put the icing on the cake, he hires me so I can further incriminate the four men with evidence fed me by you. Pretty slick.

Except it's not, because if that Julio harms my friends, I am going to do him in. And you, as well, and this time you're going to stay dead."

"I do not blame you. I will kill myself and save you the trouble."

"All hell is about to break loose in a little while, but before it does, I've been meaning to ask you where you hid for so long after your so-called death."

"A mine shaft way up in the hills behind San Bruno."

"How did you find it?"

"Julio. Oh, Hetta! I think I know where Bert, Safety, John and Ozzie may be!"

Every siren in town went off at four-thirty-five, minutes after the Port Captain was notified by Mexico City of the tsunami coming our way.

We watched as the ferry hastily left port, and fishermen on the beaches began dragging their pangas to higher ground. Several boats left the old marina, headed for the safety of open sea.

Marines boiled out of the navy installation on the hill above my marina, and the nuns constantly tolled the bell at the old folks home they ran. Curiosity seekers began lining the hills and bluffs, waiting to see what happened.

Then the sound trucks began their patrol, their loud speakers echoing through the town, repeating the now terrifying international word, tsunami. No one had forgotten Phuket and Japan, or the horrifying images we witnessed for days after those disasters.

The guy running the Pemex station at the marina locked up and started running toward the main street, but stopped short and turned toward the docks. He made a beeline for my boat. Crap, I'd have to remember not to tip him so well.

He knocked on *Raymond Johnson's* hull, yelling, "Tsunami!" but when no one answered, he took off, evidently satisfied we were not on board.

I handed Rosario the bag of stuff he bought in town, and yelled, "Okay, you're on. Go!"

Rosario raced down the dock, only stopping momentarily to light the paper bag and launch it over onto *Lucifer*. Then he jumped onto *Raymond Johnson's* deck, and above the sirens and several pounds of fireworks going off, which sounded very much like automatic weapons fire, I heard him shouting dire warnings to Vargas. He disappeared inside the boat and my heart arrested a couple of minutes later when Julio emerged, alone.

White faced and probably nearly in shock from blood loss, Vargas slammed the door behind him and made his way, painstakingly, onto the dock.

I lost sight of Vargas as I scrambled down the stairway to the Ladies' room and grabbed Po Thang's leash, but knew I could cut the bastard off since he was having trouble keeping his balance.

As he passed by the building, I let Po Thang go and yelled, "Kill!"

Po Thang looked puzzled, but then gave me a dog style shrug and ran out to jump on Julio, his new best friend. All Julio heard was, "Kill," before the dog blindsided him and knocked him down, face-first, on that nose. As he howled in pain, I grabbed the gun from his waistband and yelled, "Freeze!"

Man, did it feel good to have a gun in my hand again. Until I realized the damned thing was plastic, which pissed me off so bad I kicked Julio in the balls. Now *that* felt really good. I looked around and spotted a wrought iron chair. Unlucky for Vargas, I didn't have anything to tie him with, so instead I hit him over the head with the chair.

Satisfied that the jerk was good and out, I raced to the boat, praying Rosario wasn't hurt. At least I knew he wasn't shot with anything worse than a pellet.

I rushed to my bedroom door, removed the chair jamming the lock and flung it open. Everyone was there, safe and sound.

"Jeez, Hetta, what the hell took you so long?" Jan yelled. "We gotta get out of here, there's a tsunami coming!"

Rosario and I burst into gales of laughter.

EPILOGUE

When Nacho rushed into the marina parking lot to find Topaz straddling Vargas, and bopping the slimeball in the schnoz every time he moved, he was so smitten he made certain the rest of her vacation was very rewarding, in a shadowy, criminal sort of way.

Julio was overwhelmingly grateful when the police arrested him and hauled him off to jail for possession of drugs and weapons. Somehow his plastic gun had morphed into a real .45, and paperwork found on his person suggested he was the head of a drug cartel. He offered to give up a huge amount of cash for immunity, but when authorities tracked down the Belize account, the money had vanished. He's being held in a Mexico City prison and knowing the system down here, he'll probably walk eventually. He protested long and loud when they charged him with the death of his friend, Rosario Hidalgo Pardo, but this being Mexico, he's guilty until proven innocent. Unfortunately for him there are no plastic surgeons available to prisoners.

Fortunately for him there is no death penalty in Mexico, but it didn't matter anyway, because Rosario reappeared at the job site and told the acting project manager, me, that he had left suddenly to claim a big inheritance from a long lost grandmother, and he was surprised he was considered missing. Hadn't Ozzie gotten his email with his resignation and request to hold his personal belongings until he returned? And no, he knew nothing of someone taking the company boat out the night he fixed the radio.

By the time the cops and marines showed up at the marina, Rosario was long gone in Safety's pickup. He'd found the keys in Julio's briefcase when he lifted Vargas's passport. Certain now that his friends were imprisoned in that mine shaft, he planned to liberate them and beat feet to the airport where a perfectly good plane waited to take *someone* to Belize. I sincerely hoped there would be five passengers in total.

Two weeks later, Safety, Bert, Ozzie and John were rescued, in amazingly good condition, on an island a hundred miles south of where the burned out *Lucifer* was found abandoned. All of them claimed being traumatized by Mexico and resigned their positions.

I am still on the payroll at the mine, at least until they find a new project manager to replace Bert. As a dubious reward for all of my good work the Trob has stuck me with that job, and Ozzie's as well, until replacements can be found. I immediately implemented measures to beef up security to prevent the likes of me and Rosario from playing loose with the equipment and computers, and ordered ten brand new 777G's from a bona fide Caterpillar agency in Monterrey. Turns out the first five were shoddily refurbished models from some outfit in Nigeria, no less, and bought for less than twenty percent of new list price. The repairs and spares on these money pits accounted for most of the cost overruns on the job, which had cleverly been spread about into other departments by persons unknown, but Vargas took the rap.

Having Laura now in what was Rosario's job helps me put up with the scores of bean counters, investigators and the like who showed up the first week after the earthquake. It is a half-hearted attempt, at best, since whatever money was lost, it was well balanced out by the vast amount of gold and Boleite found in the old mine shaft the office building ended up in. Besides, letting anyone know that at least seven million bucks had walked off the job was not something the company wanted to share with the stock-buying public.

The Mexican Tourist Bureau issued a statement to the world press to the effect that while there had been a slight earthquake in the Baja resulting in the closing of one measly highway for a few hours, the rumors of volcanic activity and tsunamis were unfounded. They also said there was an investigation underway to find the source of the false tsunami report.

I gave myself a few days off for my birthday so Jan and I could take *Raymond Johnson* to Conception Bay for the much dreaded event.

As Jan, Po Thang and I lounged on the sundeck at anchor in front of Café Olé, we discussed the events of the past few weeks. We planned on going to shore for a hamburger later, but for now I was content to spend the worst day of my life with my best friend and a dog.

I had received all sorts of calls and emails before we left the dock, and I appreciated them, but this birthday was better spent in private mourning. However, one of those presents was really good news. Craig had hired a private detective to check out the scuzz who wanted to sue me for a hate crime and, due to his findings the suit never made it off the ground. Turns out bacon rind boy is still part owner in a *carnitas* stand in Hermosillo and when that information somehow leaked out, his Muslim jailhouse buddies dropped him like a hot porker.

We'd wasted away the uncommonly warm afternoon hanging out in the water in the shade of the boat's hull, beers in hand. Po Thang happily dog paddled around us, occasionally swimming off to chase a gull or a fish. Even with the water hovering at eighty, we ultimately were chilled and pruned up, so moved onto the boat and upgraded to champagne.

"Nacho and Topaz, who'd a thunk it? An odd combo if there ever was one," I commented. I had to admit I was slightly jealous of that relationship. "I mean, we suspect he's a hardened criminal of some sort. Maybe she's uncovered his soft side."

"More like she's discovered his *really* hard side."

"You are sooo bad!"

Po Thang's ears drooped. "Not you, Furface, your Auntie Jan."

"Hetta, I wasn't talking about *that.*"

"Well then, neither was I."

We shared a giggle and took sips of champagne.

"Think we should call the guys?" I asked. "I have the WiFi password from the café. Cell doesn't work down here, but we might get through on Skype."

"Nah, maybe after dinner. Wanna dress up for your birthday?"

"What for? We look fine. Or rather as fine as two women can look after swimming around with a dog all day. I kinda like this look." I grabbed a handful of stiff salt-encrusted hair and pulled it straight up, where it stayed. "Very punk."

"Your birthday, your call."

"I'm gonna declare Happy Hour a little early."

"What have we been having for the past two hours?"

"Pre-Happy Hour?"

Jan opened another split of champagne. "We're breaking the rules, you know. We're at anchor and getting drunk."

"It's my boat, my birthday. I take full responsibility."

"That'll make me feel sooo much better if the wind comes up and puts us on the beach."

"Geary said if there is any wind, it'll be from the south. We can handle that. You gettin' hungry?"

"What time is it?"

"Does it matter?"

"Not any more."

I should have picked up on that comment.

We pulled the dinghy up onto the beach. Po Thang had already launched himself into the water and was now tearing up the sand, playing with the café's collection of adopted strays.

Jimmy Buffett's "Tequila Sunrise" wafted from the outdoor speakers, and I heard some chatter inside the bar. "Well, Jan, at least you won't have to spend my birthday with only mopey old me."

"That's a relief."

"Some friend you are."

"Hey, I'm here for you in your darkest hour, ain't I? Go on in, I gotta hit the head. Order me a Tequila sunrise."

The first person I saw inside was Geary.

The second was Rosario, who had an arm possessively draped over Doctor Diane Powell's lovely shoulders.

Chino and Granny Yee held signs declaring:

LORDY, LORDY, LOOK WHO'S FORTY!

CHAOS, PANIC & DISORDER
HETTA'S WORK HERE IS DONE

HETTA'S IMMORTAL.
WAIT, IS THAT MISSPELLED?

Craig and his cowboy, Roger, were there, as well as ChaCha, my newly appointed trainer for heavy equipment, and her husband, the new Mechanic Shop manager.

All wore tee shirts reading, WE SURVIVED HETTA'S TSUNAMI!

My hand flew to my hair and I rued not taking that shower. I smelled of Coppertone and salt, and the sarong wrapping my bathing suit had seen better days.

But none of that mattered when I spotted the next person: JENKS!

He was wearing a tee shirt that declared: HETTA NEVER GETS OLD TO ME.

It was the bestest birthday ever!

NOT THE END...YET!

Books by Jinx Schwartz

The Hetta Coffey series

Just Add Water, Book 1
Just Add Salt, Book 2
Just Add Trouble, Book 3
Just Deserts, Book 4
Just the Pits, Book 5
Just Needs Killin', Book 6

Troubled Sea
The Texicans
Land Of Mountains

All available at http://amzn.to/o0gXOy
Jinx on Facebook: http://on.fb.me/OegHma
Jinx's Twitter handle @jinxschwartz
Jinx's Twitter page: http://bit.ly/peOlj6
Jinx's website: http://jinxschwartz.com

Books by Jinx Schwartz

The Hetta Coffey series

Just Add Water, Book 1
Just Add Salt, Book 2
Just Add Trouble, Book 3
Just Deserts, Book 4
Just the Pits, Book 5
Just Needs Killin' Book 6

Troubled Sea
The Texicans
Land Of Mountains

About the Author

Raised in the jungles of Haiti and Thailand, with returns to Texas in-between, Jinx followed her father's steel-toed footsteps into the Construction and Engineering industry in hopes of building dams. Finding all the good rivers taken, she traveled the world defacing other landscapes with mega-projects in Alaska, Japan, New Zealand, Puerto Rico and Mexico.

Like the protagonist in her mystery series, Hetta Coffey, Jinx was a woman with a yacht—and she's not afraid to use it—when she met her husband, Robert "Mad Dog" Schwartz. They opted to become cash-poor cruisers rather than continue chasing the rat, sailed under the Golden Gate Bridge, turned left, and headed for Mexico. They now divide their time between Arizona and Mexico's Sea of Cortez.

Her other books include a YA fictography of her childhood in Haiti (**Land of Mountains**), an adventure in the Sea of Cortez (**Troubled Sea**) and an epic novel of the thirty years leading to the fall of the Alamo (**The Texicans**).

Just Needs Killin' (Book 6)

After several months of cruising Mexico's hauntingly beautiful Sea of Cortez, Hetta's in Puerto Escondido, a place once described by author John Steinbeck as "a magic harbor." Anchored out, swaying on the hook at the whim of breeze and tide, surrounded by magnificent views and turquoise water *can* be magical. Stuck at anchor alone? Not so much.

So when her best friend, Jan, gets them an invite to a party at a nearby luxury resort hosted by a Japanese businessman—all expenses paid—Hetta figures, why not? Why turn down an evening of free food and booze? And besides, what could possibly go wrong?

With Hetta involved? Plenty.

Not only are she and Jan soon up to their necks in hot sake, a succession of unsavory intruders sends Hetta scurrying for a safe harbor, but not before she reaches the conclusion that some folks just need killin'.

Amazon link: http://amzn.to/1qBNndD

From the author

Thank you for taking time to read my book. If you enjoyed it, consider telling your friends about Hetta, or posting a short review on Amazon. Word of mouth is an author's best friend, and is much appreciated.

I have editors, but boo-boos do manage to creep into a book, no matter how many people look at it before publication, and if there are errors, they are all on me. Should you come upon one of these culprits, please let me know and I shall smite it with my mighty keyboard!

You can email me at jinxschwartz@yahoo.com

And if you want to be alerted when I have a free, discounted, or new book, you can go to http://jinxschwartz.com and sign up for my newsletter. I promised not to deluge you with pictures of puppies and kittens.

Also, you can find me on Facebook at https://www.facebook.com/jinxschwartz That puppy and kitten thing? No promises on FB posts :-)